THE CHARA TALISMAN

a novel of T-Space tm

Alastair Mayer

Mabash Books

THE CHARA TALISMAN

This is a work of fiction. Names, characters, places, and incidents are either the product of the author's imagination or are used fictitiously, and any resemblance to real people or incidents is purely coincidental.

Chapters 1, 4 and part of 6 originally appeared in slightly different form as the short story "Stone Age" in *Analog Science Fiction and Fact*, June 2011, Dell Publications.

A Mabash Books original.

Mabash Books, Centennial, Colorado

Second edition, July 2019

Hardcover: ISBN-13: 978-1-948188-081
Trade Paper ISBN-13: 978-1-948188-098

For Douglas W. F. Mayer, 1919-1976.

Dad, I'm sorry you missed it. I think you would have enjoyed it.

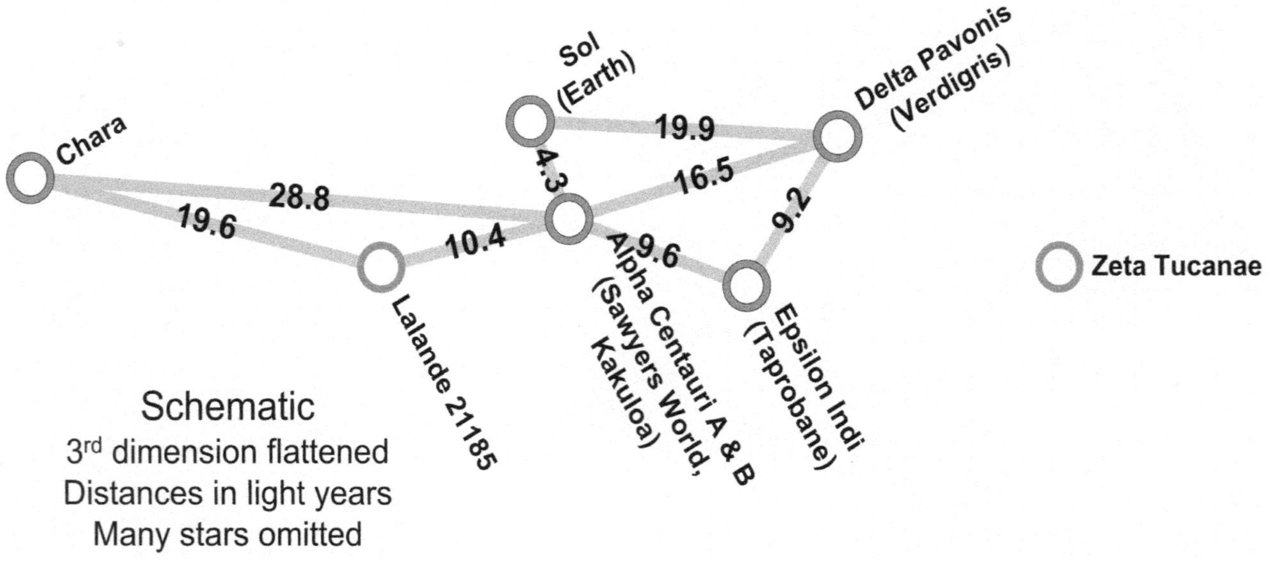
Sol
(Earth)
Delta Pavonis
(Verdigris)
Chara
19.9
4.3
16.5
28.8
9.2
19.6
10.4
9.6
Zeta Tucanae
Lalande 21185
Alpha Centauri A & B
(Sawyers World,
Kakuloa)
Epsilon Indi
(Taprobane)
Schematic
3rd dimension flattened
Distances in light years
Many stars omitted

Contents

THE CHARA TALISMAN

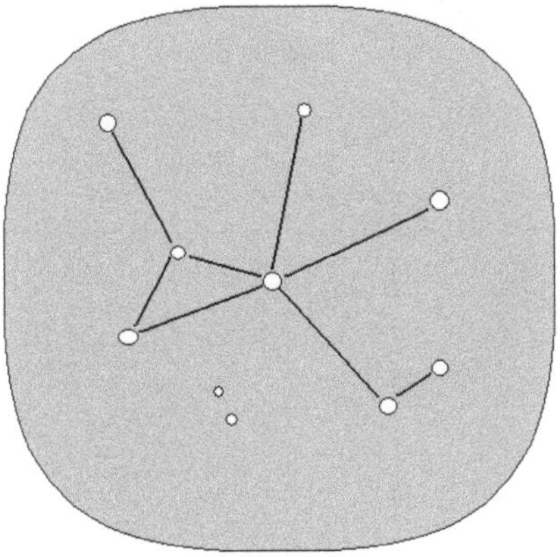

Chapter I: Verdigris

The jungle, Delta Pavonis III

"WE'VE FOUND something!"

Dr. Hannibal Carson looked up over the heads of his men to see a ridge, or perhaps a wall, extending into the jungle on either side of the trail they had hacked through the thick vegetation. It stood four meters high and overgrown with moss and vines. A scattering of pale blue starbursts of tiny flowers punctuated the green. Carson pushed his way to the front. "Let's clear a wider space here, let's get a good look." Together the four men cut away at the tree branches until they had made a small clearing.

"Is this it?" asked Brian, one of the two workers Carson had hired back in Verdigris City. The eager note in his voice reflected Carson's own hope.

Carson's gaze took in the wall curving away on either side, the upper surface arching over into a dome. *Damn.* His shoulders slumped. "This has curved sides. There's nothing unusual about it." He slipped his omni off his wrist and unfolded it into a slate, then accessed the radar map. He checked it, then looked up and around. The dense greenery made it impossible to see more than a few meters. "We're a bit off track." He faded the slate and held it up at arm's length, looking through it at the virtual track projecting through the jungle. "All right, the one we want is forty-two meters that way." He gestured at an angle from the path they had come from. "Sorry gentlemen, not much farther now."

He closed the omni and wrapped it back around his wrist as Brian and Gregor, the other hired hand, powered up their machetes again. Rajesh Gupta, his ship's pilot, came over and fell in beside him to talk.

"So it *is* the shape, isn't it?" Gupta said. "The square tomb. That is why we are out here 200 klicks from the city when there are plenty of ruins closer."

"That's part of it. Close to the city the structures have already been explored. Most have been picked over and looted."

"And the shape?"

Carson paused, debating how much to tell. "I think it's a pyramid. Pyramids have been found on nearly every planet that ever showed signs of intelligent natives, but most of the burial structures here are round."

"But surely the pyramid is a basic shape. Is it not just coincidence?"

"No, I don't think it is. I don't believe in coincidence. Tetrahedral pyramids, with a triangular base, would be a more basic shape, and no planet has them. Nobody constructs cubes or cones. And the dating; all the pyramids we've found on other planets are ten to twenty thousand years old." As he spoke, Carson noticed a slim green ribbon ripple out of the jungle canopy ahead. It glided toward them and settled on Gupta's shoulder. A jade ribbon snake.

Carson reached over and flicked it to the ground, then stomped on its head, hard.

Gupta flinched, then looked down. "A flying snake is only mildly toxic to humans, there was no need to do that."

"Flying snakes on Earth, perhaps," said Carson. "This is a jade, its venom compares to that of a krait or a taipan."

Gupta paled. "That deadly?"

"Only if you let them bite you. Come on."

Gupta looked up at the branches above them, then down at the body of the snake. He brought his heel down hard on its already flattened head.

Carson looked at him, an eyebrow raised.

"Just making sure," Gupta said. "Thank you, Hannibal."

"Nothing," Carson said.

"You were talking about pyramids," Gupta reminded him a few moments later.

"Only that we've seen their like on many different planets, with not a lot of difference in age. There must be a connection."

"Spacefarers?" Gupta shook his head. "Come on, I like a good story as much as the next person, but there is no evidence for them."

"Says the man walking on a planet that was terraformed long before humans got here," Carson said, and grinned.

"The Terraformers have been gone for over sixty million years. It is unlikely that they have anything to do with ten-thousand year old pyramids."

'No, of course not." Carson took a moment to wave away a tiny flying insect that whined around his head, then cursed and swatted one that was biting his neck. He brought his hand around to examine the smear of blood and crushed insect on his fingers. "Speaking of Terraformers, what possessed them to import *mosquitoes* to this planet?" He wiped his fingers on the side of his pants leg.

Gupta just shrugged.

"Anyway," Carson continued, "I have a theory, but I'm looking for more evidence. My dean will have me back cataloging arrowheads if I don't turn up something concrete." The dean, Matthews, had been emphatic about that at their last meeting, calling Carson's theory of a recent, non-human spacefaring species "crackpot" and even "von Dänikenism," threatening dire consequences if word of it tarnished the university's reputation.

"So what do you think was the reason for making this tomb a pyramid?" Gupta said. "If that is what it turns out to be." The jungle's canopy blocked any direct view from the air, on the mapping radar image their target showed as little more than a blurred square.

"I don't know. There may have been something special about the person it was built for." Carson hoped that would turn out to be the case.

"Ah. I just wondered . . ." Gupta's voice trailed off.

"Wondered what?"

"Oh, nothing. When pilots get together they swap many tall stories, some of them quite strange."

"Like what?"

"Nonsense stories, old spacer tales. Seeing ghosts out the window in warp, signs of a spaceship landing too big for any possible ship, flying pyramids. Most of it bullshit."

"Flying *pyramids*?" Carson wasn't sure he had heard that right.

"As I said, bullshit stories," said Gupta, straight-faced.

Carson was trying to figure out if Gupta was serious or just pulling his leg when Gregor, now in the lead, called out.

"I think this is it!"

Carson came forward to the wall Gregor had reached. This too was covered with a growth of vine and moss, but it had straighter, flatter sides. Could it be?

"Let's take a look." Carson eased a patch of moss away from the sloping surface to reveal mottled stone beneath. "So far so good." He peeled away another strip of moss, then another and another. His heart beat faster when one of the patches lifted to reveal that the chiseled edge of one stone abutted the next perfectly. *Constructed, not natural.*

Carson moved quickly but precisely, pulling back the loose vines and stripping the moss away from the rock in a grid. By the time he had uncovered half a square meter of the underlying stone, it was obvious that this was part of a larger stonework wall. The individual blocks had been carefully shaped and fitted together. "Yes, this is it."

The others surged forward and began to rip vegetation from the wall, their earlier fatigue gone.

"Wait, stop!" Carson waved them back. "Take it easy, we don't want to damage anything. Spread out. Remove it in strips, just enough to see what's underneath."

They did so, every man moving a meter or so from his neighbor, removing a handful of vegetation, enough to see the smooth rock beneath, then moving farther along the wall. After several minutes of this, there was a shout from Gregor.

"Dr. Carson, here! I've found a carving."

The group scrambled over. Carson examined the sculpted surface of the bared patch of stone.

"Gupta, would you set up the recorder? The rest of you, when Captain Gupta is set up, we will *carefully* peel back the moss." He gestured to outline an area roughly two meters square. "Let's say this area here."

With the recorder running, they set to it with such enthusiasm that several times Carson had to remind them to slow down. He was as eager as they were, but training and experience forced him to be methodical. When they had cleared the section, they all paused and stepped back to look at what they had unveiled.

"Wow!" someone said in a hushed tone.

"Excellent!" said Carson, as he gazed at the relief carving of a face. The face was humanoid in that it had two eyes, a nose, and a mouth, but then so did any vertebrate. The eyes were too far apart, and wide open, showing slit pupils like a cat's. The nose was a pair of thin vertical ovals. The effect would have been reptilian if it were not for the mouth, which opened in a big O nearly a meter across.

Carson pulled out his omni and panned its camera across the face, speaking his observations into it as he did so. As he closed the omni and stuck it back in his belt again, he looked around at his team and saw that Brian had his own omni out.

"Hey, Dr. C," Brian called, "stand beside it and I'll take your picture."

"You don't need to . . ." Carson began, then yielded. "All right, make it quick though." He was impatient to get to work.

When Brian was done, Carson called to get the others' attention. "All right!" He pointed to the tangled vines and moss that still adorned the wall, and said "let's get more of this stuff cleared away and see what we've got."

∞ ∞ ∞

An hour later, they had begun to stack carefully documented artifacts outside the tomb entrance. Carson was alone inside the pyramid. The other two workers—there was barely room in the tomb for three people, four if you counted the original occupant—had stepped out for fresh air, taking more of the artifacts with them. Carson was examining the slab that the body lay on when he heard a shout.

"Dr. Carson! Dr. Carson, come out here please!" one of the men called from outside.

"All right, all right, just a moment." Carson went back to the entrance hole and knelt down to crawl through. "What is it?" he said as he poked his head out, but the answer was obvious.

In the cleared area around the tomb there were a half-dozen men: his three, and three others he'd never seen before. What fixed his attention, though, was the very lethal-looking assault rifle pointed at him. Glancing about, he noticed the other automatic weapons the newcomers were holding, aimed at him and his men. Worse, one of his own, Brian, was standing with them. "Bloody hell," he muttered, "tomb raiders."

∞ ∞ ∞

A half hour later, they had removed enough of the vegetation to completely clear the face and the adjacent gray stone wall, recording it all as they went. Carson waved the workers back and bent to examine the face more closely. Its expression was, if human ideas of facial expression applied, one of somebody shouting or screaming. A thick stone rim outlined the wide circle of its mouth. *Perhaps it was just laughing.*

He got down on his knees and examined the mouth more closely, probing the dirt still left in the recesses. He had studied the construction of Verdigris tombs. If this was like others, there should be . . . there. He felt a projection beneath the damp grit on his fingers. As he pressed in, he heard a muffled "clunk" and the round slab that formed the inner circle of the mouth settled backward, just enough to clear the inner rim. Cool air wafted out of the gap.

"Got it!" said Carson, triumph in his voice. "Here, help me roll it out of the way."

Brian and Gregor knelt down beside him and they all worked their fingers into the gap. It was awkward with the three of them together in the close space, but they managed to persuade the heavy stone to roll back behind the wall, leaving a clear opening. Carson took off his omni and waved it in the entrance to check for toxic gases; it was clear. He put the omni in a pocket and pulled out a flashlight. Shining it into the hole, he stuck his head in and looked around. In the middle of the small chamber was an oblong, roughly coffin-shaped bundle atop a raised platform. Small piles of artifacts—trinkets, primitive though artistic weapons, jewelry and the like—surrounded it. It was a body, possibly the tomb's sole occupant, except for a few bugs and spiders, but if Carson was lucky the raised platform itself might hold another. This was fantastic.

"Wonderful! It hasn't been touched!" Carson called back. He crawled in a little farther, then paused at an insistent warble from his omni.

"What is it?" he heard Gregor ask from behind him.

"Radiation warning, hang on." Carson pulled out his omni and checked the reading. The radiation was at very low level. "It's probably just radon build-up, or maybe it's the rocks this thing is made from," he said. Radon gas often accumulated in poorly ventilated structures, and rocks on this planet had a slightly higher concentration of natural radioactive elements than Earth. "A bit odd for this kind of rock, but it's a low reading, nothing to worry about," he called back to his men. He turned off the omni's rad sensor to silence the warning.

He backed out of the entrance and turned to the others. "All right, get the recorders in, I want it recorded from here first, then we'll go in and image everything in detail."

Chapter 2: Roberts

Starship Sophie, *near Epsilon Eridani*

JACQUELINE ROBERTS heard the shrill of the radiation alarm and swore. She grabbed for a handhold but the ship's gravity quit before she reached it. They had dropped out of warp. Her momentum carried her forward into the cockpit, over the back of the control chair. She pushed herself down from the overhead and shut off the alarm, wishing she could do the same with the wail from her passengers.

"Captain, what's happening?"

"Sorry Mr. Geary, we hit an unexpected dust cloud. Are you all right? What about Mrs. Geary?"

"We'll be all right. You could have warned us."

Then it wouldn't be unexpected, would it? Jackie bit back her response. "It's unusual to encounter thick dust this far out, even near this system."

"Look, I know the Epsilon Eridani system has a lot of dust, but what if that had been a rock, or a chunk of ice?"

"Then we wouldn't be having this conversation, would we?" *No, we'd be a cloud of plasma.* "Sorry, that was inappropriate." It didn't help Jackie's temper that they'd been cooped up together in a living area the size of a trailer for the past week.

No starship was very large, and the *Sophie* was only a medium sized ship to begin with. Her design sacrificed comfort for range. As if the close quarters weren't enough, the Gearys had been acting like, well, like the newlyweds they were. Only a pair of geologists would go to Epsilon Eridani, with its two asteroid belts and a barely habitable planet, for a honeymoon.

"There's no harm done." She eyed the radiation display to check. No, not enough to bother breaking out the antirad drugs. "We'd be out of warp anyway in another half-hour, we're almost in-system. I'm sorry you didn't get more warning."

Roger Geary grumbled but acknowledged her apology.

"Okay, I need to check our position. If there's an easy way around this dust cloud I may be able to return to warp and restore gravity for a while longer." She hoped so. If they couldn't do another thirty minutes in warp it would add *weeks* to the trip, travelling in normal space. It *had* to be an anomaly; Eridani's dust ring didn't extend out this far. She strapped herself into the control seat and began to check the displays.

Fifteen minutes later she had worked out the new course. "Folks, we're going to have a day of microgravity as we get out of this dust cloud, then a half hour in warp to bring us into the inner system. Sorry for the delay."

Laura Geary floated forward and gripped her husband's shoulder. "A day in zero gee? That could be fun." She giggled and tugged her husband back toward the aft cabin. "Come on, Roger, let's try it in freefall."

Jackie shook her head. There really shouldn't be dust thick enough to worry about this far out-system. She hated flying into the Epsilon Eridani system, and she hated flying married couples, especially rambunctious newlyweds. She turned back to the controls.

When the dust had hit the Alcubierre-Broek warp bubble the resulting radiation burst had tripped the safety relays in time, but some components were more sensitive than others, and all should be checked. She began to set up series of diagnostics.

Chapter 3: The Diagram

Sawyer City, Alpha Centauri A II

JAMES SMITH—not his real name, he'd had almost too many to remember that—examined the image he had captured. It depicted a talisman or amulet, square with rounded corners. Stones, perhaps jewels, were inset on its face at random. Lines connected some of the stones. A constellation? From what Smith knew, it somehow connected to alien technology, possibly weapons.

If Maynard catches me with this, he will kill me.

He closed the file and touched the SEND key on his omniphone again. Nothing. They must have a jammer. He would have to leave the building or get to an exterior wall where the signal might penetrate. This had gone far beyond just keeping tabs on a religious cult. He had to report it to Ducayne.

He slipped out of his room and down the short hallway to the stairs, then paused. The foyer at the foot of the stairway was empty. He descended with quick, quiet movements. As he reached the bottom he heard voices from behind one of the closed office doors.

". . .find the key." That was Maynard's voice. Smith stopped to listen.

"We can check the archeology databases, but something like that might be in the hands of a private collector." A different male voice.

"So you follow up on black market connections." Maynard sounded dismissive. Smith darted toward the exit.

The office door opened just before he got there. "Brother Smith! Are you going somewhere?"

"Ah, Brother Maynard." Smith stopped and turned, palming his omni. "Just for a short walk, a bit of exercise."

Two other men had stepped out of the office behind Maynard, and they moved to block the exit. Smith turned his head toward them, raising his right hand to his chin in a nervous gesture. His left arm hung by his side, holding the omni in his cupped hand while he slid his thumb over its slick surface. He pressed hard, once, twice, and felt the surface change beneath his fingers, extruding pushbuttons. He probed with his thumb, seeking the right one.

"Exercise is good for the mind as well as the body, of course, but you seem troubled by something. Perhaps you are not fully Clear? I'm sure one of the Brothers," he gestured at the two large figures now blocking the exit, "would be happy to Audit a session with you."

Crap, they're on to me. "Uh, that's very kind." His thumb scrabbled over the surface of his omni, pushing a sequence by feel. Sweat slickened his palm; he was losing his grip. "Perhaps when I return from my walk?" The omni slipped and fell to the floor with a clatter.

There was a split second of hesitation, then:

"Grab that!"

The two by the door dove for it.

Smith, already reaching for it, grabbed it first and straightened up.

One of the two clutched his hand, trying to pull the omni from his fingers. The other reached around him from behind and pinned his arms, trying to keep him from struggling.

Smith clutched the omni. If he could just work his thumb loose . . . but the big man's hand wrapped around his. He wriggled his hand and his thumb felt a button. Was it the right one? He squirmed again, trying to free up his right arm. No good. Smith swung his head back savagely, catching one of his attackers a blow to the face. The impact stunned Smith, but it also shook the attacker. He kicked out at his other attacker, connected, and the hand holding his loosened for a moment. Smith hit what he hoped was the SEND pad with his thumb. The omni beeped. It was!

"*No!*"

The man who had pinned him threw him to the floor, but Smith still had hold of the omni. A foot came down, hard, on the outstretched hand, breaking the omni and the bones in his hand. He screamed. Something slammed the back of his head, and his vision dazzled.

Then it went black.

Chapter 4: Tomb Raiders

Delta Pavonis III

"DOCTOR CARSON, I presume." The tallest of the newcomers took a step forward. He was better dressed than the others, something Carson wouldn't have thought possible in bush wear. "Tomb raiders? You're the one who opened it. Myself, I prefer the term 'art collectors'."

"Collectors? Dealers, more likely," said Carson. "You know my name, who are you?"

The man paused, then grinned. "Just call me John Stephens."

Carson scoffed at the name. "The real Stephens is better than you in two ways. Even though he was an amateur, he was a fine archeologist." John Lloyd Stephens had been pivotal in uncovering Mayan ruins in Mesoamerica three centuries earlier.

The tall man, Stephens, raised an eyebrow. "And the other?"

"He's dead."

Stephens frowned, angry. "That's enough. Come on, first slowly hand over your weapon, and then get up."

Carson reluctantly surrendered his pistol. The odds were not in his favor, but perhaps they'd leave his group unharmed if he cooperated. His group. He looked over at Brian, the turncoat. That's why he'd had his omni out. He must have sent a signal when they'd found it, and probably sent the picture too.

Brian caught his glare. "Sorry, Dr. C," he said with forced cheeriness, "they outbid you."

"I didn't realize you were up for bid," growled Carson.

"All right, cut out the chit-chat." Stephens turned to his men. "Rico, Smith, keep them covered. Brian, search them. No weapons, no omnis. Come on, make it snappy."

Carson and his two loyal men grudgingly stood to, hands on their heads, while Brian patted them down. Carson had already turned over his gun; Brian relieved him of his omniphone. He patted down the others, taking their omnis, and from Gregor a rather wicked-looking sheath knife. He brought the goods over to Stephens.

Carson sneaked a glance at a laser machete leaning against a nearby tree. If he could reach it and power it up while the others were occupied . . .

One of Stephens' men must have seen him look. The man strode over to the machete and yanked its cable from the power pack, then looked around and did the same with the other one.

"Good catch, Rico," said Stephens, who had been watching. "Okay, dispose of the weapons, smash the omnis and recorders." He was taking no chances on communications.

Carson started at this. "Hey, wait a minute, you can't—"

"Carson." Stephens waved his gun. "Of course we can." He smiled, looking amused. "What's the matter, don't you make backups?"

Of course Carson did. Every hour his omni backed itself up to the net. That wasn't the point. "I don't care about the omnis, they're low bandwidth. The recorders are high-resolution multi-spectral, and they're *not* backed up. The data is irreplaceable."

"Why should I care?"

Good question. Carson thought fast. "You're joking, right? Those artifacts are worth far more to a collector if their provenance is established."

"True enough. So?"

"Leave me the data and I can publish a report on the findings. Not the same quality or level of detail as if I had the artifacts to examine more closely. Can you at least leave me some?" It was worth a try. "If I publish on them, any collector will know they're the real thing and not something fabbed in a workshop."

"I can fake my own provenances. It wouldn't be the first time."

Fake? The thought disgusted Carson. "Professional journal articles? I don't think so. Think how much more you could get." *And you'll need me alive to write them, and if you need me alive, you'll leave my men alive.*

"You have a point." Stephens didn't say anything else for a few moments, evidently weighing the options.

"It's not like we have anything on the recordings to identify you." Carson added.

"Why would you publish, why do me that favor?"

"You know academia, 'publish or perish'. I'll get *some* credit for it."

"Okay." Stephens turned to his men. "Go ahead and smash the omnis but don't damage the recorders, we'll take them with us."

"What?"

"Don't worry, Carson, if you behave yourselves we'll leave them at your ship. I just don't want anyone to get funny ideas about recording us before we're gone, or making calls until we're well away."

"What about leaving me some artifacts?" Carson said, somewhat encouraged.

"Don't push your luck. We'll leave you the tomb, we can't carry that."

∞ ∞ ∞

Stephens organized the gathering and packaging of the artifacts, then had Carson accompany him back into the tomb.

Carson watched in silent rage as Stephens looked around the interior, noting a few more items to take.

"Okay, last item. Rico, go cut a couple of branches and make a stretcher, we're taking the body."

"Got it, Boss."

Carson's gut wrenched. "Leave that at least! What good will it do you?" That body was his main hope. If this tomb was unique, perhaps so was the occupant.

"Are you kidding? Some collectors love this kind of stuff. Bit weird if you ask me, but you didn't."

"Collectors!" Carson's anger overcame his caution. "That's all you care about? A few credits for what could be priceless scientific information? Dammit, we don't know much about this species, or why this tomb is different. Let me—"

"I'm not going to 'let you' anything, Carson. Your scientific information isn't priceless, it's worthless. Maybe you haven't noticed, stuck in your ivory tower—"

"I don't—" Carson tried to interrupt.

"Shut up!" Stephens gestured with his pistol. "You have no concept of the real world, you with your university benefactors paying your way. You think living out here on the frontier is easy? There's damn little to trade that Earth wants and is worth the effort to ship, and—"

"But, what about biologicals?" Carson said, thinking of the main local industry.

"They have a trading lifetime of a couple of years before some bright boy in a lab figures out how to synthesize them or genetically modify them to grow on Earth. Look at what happened to Kakuloa: two years of a thriving trade in squidberry extract and then the bottom falls out when General Pharmaceuticals learns to synthesize it.

"No, don't be stupid, Doctor. You know that the trade in alien antiquities is about the only thing that brings hard currency out to the colonies. I'm doing my bit to support human expansion into T-space. You'd be more useful if you figured out where the Terraformers went, and if they're coming back. Where do a few scholarly reports on long-dead stone age aliens get us?"

Carson was taken aback. He knew the economic situation wasn't as bleak as Stephens, or whatever his real name was, painted it, but Carson recognized Stephens' point. His anger ebbed. It was then he noticed that Stephens' pistol still pointed at him. Was there an edge of xenophobia in Stephens' voice? What would he do if he thought there'd been spacefarers back when humans were barely into their own neolithic civilizations? "All right, damn it. Let me at least take a sample, do a DNA check."

Stephens looked at him, an eyebrow raised. "A bit out of your line, isn't that? But okay." He lowered the pistol and turned to the body, looked it over, then broke off its equivalent of a little toe. He tossed it to Carson. "Here."

Carson's hands shook with another surge of anger, and he fumbled the catch. He swore. "I hope the bloody tomb is cursed, you bastard."

Stephens grinned. "None of them have been yet," he said.

Carson carefully bagged and pocketed the toe.

Just then Rico came back with a makeshift stretcher, and they carefully transferred the body to it and maneuvered it out of the tomb.

Carson looked around at the tomb, now empty save for the raised stone platform in the center. "There's nothing left," he said, although he knew that perhaps there might be.

"We'll see," said Stephens. "Brian, help me move the lid off of this." He started to push on the slab that formed the top of the sarcophagus.

Damn, this Stephens knew the tricks. Knew that sometimes the body on top is a guardian or decoy for the important one inside.

Stephens and Brian had shoved the lid a half meter to the side, and Stephens shone his light in. "Damn, it's empty. What's the point of an empty crypt?"

"What?" Carson looked in and saw by the light of Stephens' torch that it was indeed empty, nothing but dirt and a few loose stones. *Now that's interesting. Perhaps the body* is *special.* His pulse quickened but he kept silent.

"We're done here. Everybody out," Stephens said.

Outside Stephens turned to his gang, who had finished packaging the artifacts for travel. "Gather up the recorders."

"You promised to leave those!" Carson protested, wanting to keep Stephens distracted.

"Oh, don't worry Doctor. I told you, if you're good and give us a head start, I'll leave them at your ship. Now, you three," he pointed to Carson, Gupta and Gregor, "you're going into the tomb."

"What? We're not going back in there." None of them wanted to just disappear in this jungle.

"Don't worry, I'm not sealing you in. But you won't be getting out quickly either." He turned and shouted, "Rico!"

"Yes, Boss?"

"You stay here and give us the usual head start. If anyone pokes his nose out of that hole before that, shoot it off."

"Got it, Boss," Rico said, and grinned. He picked up his rifle and found a tree to lean on. It was about twenty meters from the tomb; too far to rush, but close enough to make shooting easy.

Carson was convinced he'd do it, too. *He knows his stuff,* Carson thought, *that's a pity.*

It took a few more minutes as the thugs gathered up packs, double checked for anything left behind, and herded the prisoners into the tomb, then they were ready to go.

"Hey!" Carson called from the entrance of the crypt. "You will leave the recorders, right?"

"Don't worry," Stephens called back, amused. "You will write a report, won't you Dr. Carson?"

Carson just cursed.

"Back inside, Doctor!" Rico raised his weapon to the ready position for emphasis.

∞ ∞ ∞

Carson waited ten minutes, then tried hailing. "Rico? You out there?"

There was no answer, so Carson took off his hat and extended it out of the entrance. He heard the *crack* of a gunshot and felt a tug on his hat. He quickly snatched it back inside. There was bullet hole through it.

∞ ∞ ∞

Rico chuckled to himself at the sight of the hat disappearing back into the tomb. He'd wondered if Carson would try something like that, after trying to call him.

Carson was a wiley one. Rico smiled, remembering the look of disappointment he'd seen on Carson's face when he'd ripped the power cords out of the machetes. They'd have made a formidable weapon with the beam stops removed. The boss—Hopkins, not "Stephens"—had taken quite a chance there, but it looked like it had paid off. Rico didn't get all the fuss about ancient relics; they didn't seem to have much practical application. Still, the job paid okay, and he sometimes got to play with weapons and gadgets that most people didn't.

He glanced at the clock face on his omni. The others should be almost back to the ship by now. He'd wait a little longer. He shifted the rifle to a more comfortable position and leaned back against the tree.

Three minutes later Rico checked his omni again and then began to slip back along the trail. Where the path angled away, he turned. The tomb was just visible around the trees. He raised the rifle and fired another shot at the entrance—to encourage them to stay put—then turned and jogged quickly to get back to the ship.

∞ ∞ ∞

Carson heard footsteps fading back along the trail. He edged toward the tomb entrance, and there came another shot. This one sounded more distant, probably a last warning shot, but Carson waited five more minutes before he stuck his hat out again. It drew no response this time.

Sure that they'd gone now, Carson led the others out of the crypt. "Gregor, get back to the ship, bring back a spare omni and a recorder. We should see if there's anything left in there."

"I'll go," said Gupta, "I want to check my ship." At Carson's nod, he took off at a quick jog.

"Something left? With us crowded in there?" asked Gregor.

"It was dark. Maybe in the sarcophagus."

"That was empty. If somebody took a body, why leave everything else looking untouched?"

"There may never have been another body." Carson hoped there had not. It would increase the odds that the body Stephens had stolen was special, and Carson had a sample of that. "But who knows what alien motives might be."

"Fair point." Gregor then changed the subject. "Are you really going to publish a paper on these findings?"

Carson's jaw clenched. He growled the words out. "Sure. In a year or two. Let Stephens stew about that." He picked up a small branch from the ground and worried it, twisting the bark off. "The first thing I'll do is hand a copy of the data over to law enforcement. If any of those artifacts ever show up, maybe they can be traced back to him. Bastard." He whipped the branch against a nearby tree trunk.

Gregor shook his head. "Remind me never to get on your bad side." He paused a moment, then: "You realize if you ever cross paths again he'll have it in for you."

"I hope we do cross paths again. As long as I see him first." With a jerk of his arms, Carson tore the branch in half and tossed the pieces aside.

∞ ∞ ∞

Gupta returned about thirty minutes later. "The ship is okay. Here's the gear." He handed the recorder and omni to Carson. "So, why are we still here?"

"I wanted to check it completely before we left. Stephens may have missed something."

He got down and crawled in through the opening. Once again as he got inside the omni sounded its warning. *Didn't I turn that off? Oh, right, this is the one Gupta brought back from the ship.* Stephens had destroyed the other.

"Are you getting radiation again, Dr. Carson?" Gregor called from outside. He must have heard the warning.

"Yes, which is odd. Radon should have dissipated by now." Carson checked the sensor setting. "Definitely some slight radiation inside, though." He held the omni near the roof of the chamber, then near the floor. "It's stronger on the floor, so it's not the rock that the pyramid is made of." He moved over to the sarcophagus. Near the edge of the lid the radiation reading jumped again. "More here. Very interesting."

He called back to the others. "It's safe enough, low level. Come on in, I'd like some help with this slab."

They moved the sarcophagus lid to one side and Carson examined the interior. He leaned in and swept the omni back and forth. Near one corner the radiation reading spiked. Looking closer he found a small, flat object, broken along one side, the edge looking crushed. Dirt covered it and it had looked just like a rock in the beam from Stephens' flashlight.

Carson double-checked that the radiation wasn't harmful and picked the object up. It was half of a rounded square, with markings and what might be inlaid gemstones on one side. Carson examined the broken edge. Was there something metallic in there? He was about to brush the dirt off then remembered the radiation and stopped.

"What is it, Doc?" asked Gupta.

"I'm not sure. Some kind of talisman perhaps. Looks like it got caught on the edge of the sarcophagus, then damaged when the lid was put down. There must be dust from it where it got crushed, and scattered around the floor."

"But radioactive?"

"Not that unusual in the rocks on this planet. It might be these gems. I'll know more when I have it analyzed." He bagged it and put it in a different pocket from the DNA sample. He checked the other pocket to be sure the toe was still there.

They inspected the sarcophagus and the rest of the chamber, but found nothing else. "Come on," Carson said as he took a last look around. "We're done here. That bastard Stephens cleaned it out. Let's take some final recordings and get back to Verdigris City. Stephens, or whoever he is, is probably off-planet by now, but we need to report it."

∞ ∞ ∞

The officer finished taking Carson's report and saved the file, then opened another. "From your description of him, he sounds like an artifact smuggler named Marrok Hopkins," he said. He turned the screen toward Carson. "This him?"

Carson nodded grimly. "That's him. Hopkins, you said?"

"Yes. Stephens is an alias he uses. He has others."

"For what good that does me. All right, thank you." Carson got up to leave.

"Where can we get hold of you if we need to? Not that that's likely, I'm afraid."

"I'll be heading back to Alpha Centauri. I'm at Drake University in Sawyer City." Carson didn't mention the specimens he was taking back with him. The lab at the university could do a better analysis than anything here, and for what he had the paperwork wasn't worth the trouble. He would file retroactively if they were significant. He still had his hopes on the DNA sample.

Chapter 5: Spitzer Spaceport

Spitzer Spaceport, Epsilon Eridani II

JACKIE LANDED her ship and took care of getting her passengers disembarked, then went back to analyze the diagnostics log. The radiation burst hadn't damaged anything. It shouldn't even have tripped the warp shut-off.

The aging sensors were getting too sensitive. That was better than the alternative, but she'd have to get them replaced or the *Sophie* would be continually dropping out of warp too soon. She didn't need that. She considered her options. Spitzer was very much an outpost world, popular with Eridani's belt miners and geologists but only marginally habitable. She couldn't get the work done here. She called the spaceport cargo office.

"This is Captain Roberts of the *Sophie*," she began, and touched a control on her omni to transmit her ship's information and her own captain's and courier's license data. "Do you have any small cargo going to either Tau Ceti or Alpha Centauri?"

"Hello Jackie, this is Pete. I heard the *Sophie* was in again. It's been a few weeks."

"Hey, Pete, I was hoping you'd be there." Which was why she hadn't queried the port database directly.

"Centauri? Aren't you still based out of Tau Ceti?"

"I am, but *Sophie* needs some work. Nothing critical but if you've got cargo to make it worth my while . . ."

"Sure, then you might as well get the work done at Kakuloa. Let me check." There was a pause as Pete checked the inventory of outbound cargo and mail. "Nothing for Kakuloa but I have a couple of packages for Sawyers World."

"Close enough." The Alpha Centauri system had two stars with terraformed planets around each, Kakuloa orbiting Alpha Centauri B, and Sawyers World around Alpha Centauri A. They were twenty seconds apart in warp, and Jackie knew the crew at the shipyard orbiting Kakuloa; they were familiar with the *Sophie.*

"Are you in a rush, Jackie, or can I persuade you to join me for dinner when I get off shift?"

Jackie considered. She knew Pete would be interested in more than just dinner, and after four days with a honeymooning couple aboard—maybe she should improve the soundproofing—she knew she would be tempted. However . . . "Just dinner, Pete, you know I don't date passengers or port crew."

"And just when do you ever see anybody else?" Pete asked, in a lighthearted tone. Jackie didn't take offense.

She thought about it as she clicked off. That was a good question. *Had* there been anyone since that damn archeologist?

Chapter 6: Unexpected Results

Sawyer City, Alpha Centauri A II

"I HAVE THE preliminary results, Dr. Carson."

Carson had taken his specimens to the lab as soon as he got back to the university. Fortunately, Dean Matthews had been away so Carson had gained a few days reprieve.

"Great. What can you tell me about the sample?" This was it.

"The bone is mammalian. The structure looks the same as the indigenous Verdigrans, which isn't surprising considering where you found it. Preliminary DNA tests confirm that."

Carson slumped. "You're sure?"

The technician nodded. "Yep."

Damn. He'd been so certain that there was something special about that pyramid. He'd been hoping against hope that the body had been a spacefarer. Even if Stephens had made off with most of it, this sample should have been enough for Dean Matthews to give him another chance, to keep on looking. But now . . .

"Oh, okay, thanks," Carson said. As an afterthought he added, "What about the stone fragment, the talisman?"

"Sorry, we must have messed up the analysis on that."

"What do you mean? It was radioactive, was that a problem?"

"Oh, no. Well, no and yes." The technician looked a bit sheepish. "We get radioactive specimens in all the time, so that wasn't a problem. It's the source that's messed up."

"I thought it might be the gems. What do you mean, 'messed up'?"

"Not the gems. The thing contains several grams of isotope technetium-99."

"What?" Carson said, straightening.

"A beta-emitter. If the talisman weren't broken you'd never have noticed the radiation; it wouldn't get through the case. Technetium-99 betas are low energy."

"What's the half-life?" Carson wasn't sure what the significance of the technetium was, but it was something that could be dated.

"About 211 thousand years. It's artificial, of course, technetium isn't part of any natural decay sequence, and geologically speaking all its isotopes are short-lived."

Carson felt his heart pound. This meant a technological origin. With the provenance corrupted it wasn't scientific proof, but he was sure the origin was alien, not human. Had there been another body in the sarcophagus after all? Retrieved by comrades, perhaps? They might well have left the other artifacts alone.

"So, not a product of a primitive civilization, then?" Carson wanted to be sure.

"What? You're joking. You need a reactor to make technetium. In this it's part of a betavoltaic battery. I've never seen this specific design, and the whole thing looks like carved rock except where it's smashed, but there's some kind of circuitry inside. That battery will put out a couple of milliamps for a hundred thousand years."

"How old is it?"

"That's the weird thing, sir. I wasn't going to bother running isotope ratios to determine the age—"

"What? Why not?" *To be this close . . .*

"Well, I mean, how old could it be? Twenty, thirty years tops? I ran them anyway. I'm sorry, but the original sample must have been contaminated, I don't trust the results."

"Just tell me." Carson felt a knot growing in the pit of his stomach.

"About fifteen thousand years. Like I said, it makes no sense."

"Oh." There was a ringing in Carson's ears, and the room seemed to sway a bit. It wasn't proof enough to publish, not yet, but it should be enough to persuade Dean Matthews. He'd get his second chance.

He realized the tech was waiting for something more from him. "Right. Well, thank you. Just email me the reports."

As he walked back to his office, Carson thought about what the technician had said. If the case hadn't been broken he wouldn't have noticed the radiation—and it would look just like a primitive talisman. If there was one, there might be another, possibly intact. He'd have to search the artifact databases, run an image comparison. Carson chuckled to himself. Dean Matthews was going to be amazed at Carson's sudden interest in cataloging, well not arrowheads, but talismans.

∞ ∞ ∞

Two days later, Carson stood in Matthews' office, looking around while waiting for Matthews to finish a call. The case against the wall held several actual books—Croft & Jones's classic on *Archeological Field Techniques*, Jackson's *Combat Archeology*—and artifacts from different cultures and planets. The walls held, along with Matthews' various diplomas, framed prints depicting ancient stone ruins, overgrown by jungle. The ruins were being uncovered by a few men, some with antique machetes. Carson thought wryly about how familiar *those* scenes felt. He looked closer and recognized them as Frederick Catherwood's 300-year-old drawings of the first discoveries of Mayan ruins in the Yucatan, by the original John Stephens.

Carson's own omni signaled an incoming call. He silenced it and glanced at the caller information. *Office of Techno-Archeology*?. What the hell was that? It would have to wait.

Mathews said goodbye and clicked off his own omni. "Hannibal, welcome back, have a seat," said Matthews, gesturing to the chair in front of his desk.

"Thanks," said Carson, sitting. "You wanted to see me?"

"Yes. A couple of things. First, since I wasn't here when you got back, I wanted to ask how your little expedition to Delta Pavonis went. I heard you ran into some trouble?"

Carson scowled at the memory. "Yes. We got bushwhacked by tomb raiders."

"Nobody hurt, I hope?"

"Just my pride. They must have been on to me from the start. They bribed someone on my recon team to squawk when we found something."

"So you did find something."

"Yes, a pyramidal tomb. You should have seen the artifacts, a wonderful collection. Then Hopkins and his men jumped us." Carson leaned across Matthews' desk, his fists clenched. "Damn it, I should have checked my crew, or had them turn over their omnis to me, or something." He thumped his fist down on the desk in frustration and slumped back into his chair.

"The looters are getting more aggressive," said Matthews. "Did they get everything?"

Carson looked up, a smile coming to his face. "Oh, they did leave us our recorders, so we have the data. But even better . . ." Carson paused, waiting.

"Yes? Go on, what?"

"We found an advanced technology artifact."

"What? How? What did you find?"

"Hopkins missed it, it looked like a rock. But it was radioactive. It looks like a talisman, but there's a technetium betavoltaic battery and some circuitry inside. Damaged, unfortunately."

"And you can authenticate this?"

Carson knew that was a problem. "I've got recordings, but with Hopkins and his men in and out of the tomb before we found it, I can't prove it was there originally."

"So he could have left it."

"With the technetium showing fifteen thousand years of decay? Not likely." Carson saw the stony expression on Matthews face. "But no, I can't prove that he didn't."

"That's unfortunate. I—"

"But I might be able to find another."

"What?"

Carson outlined what the technician had told him and his own online searches for images of similar artifacts.

"Yes, I'd heard you were being rather industrious. What did you find?"

"That's the odd thing. I'm not getting any hits at all. I was expecting to have to weed out a lot of false positives."

"No hits at all?" Matthews looked skeptical.

"I'm sure it's just some glitch. I know I've seen something like it before, I just don't remember where."

"Well, speaking of memory, that brings us to the other topic I wanted to see you about. Apparently you also forgot to turn in your official grades for the semester before you left. That was over four weeks ago."

"Yes. Sorry about that. They were in my computer, but all the interim grades were on the system." Carson hated this sort of administrivia. The data was there, just not his officially blessed version of the same damn numbers.

"That's not the point. The official grades have to be available by certain deadlines. Make sure you get that taken care of if you haven't already. Remember, this is just as much a part of the job as the field work." Matthews looked thoughtful for a moment. "I think that was all. Was there anything else?"

"Ah, no. Thank you." Carson started to rise, then stopped and sat down again. "Actually yes. Do you know anything about an Office of Techno-Archeology? They called me just as I came in here."

"Office of what?"

Carson checked the call information again. "Techno-Archeology. Division of Astrocartography, Astronomical Survey Group," he read off. "That's quite a mouthful." He looked at the screen again. "Somebody named Ducayne."

Matthews shook his head. "Never heard of him, or them. It does sound like there's a government connection. One of your grant proposals?"

"I'd remember. With a name like that, it's probably two guys in an office the size of a closet, in a temporary government building that should have been condemned twenty years ago." Carson knew how these things went. They made up in length of title what they lacked in real size. "Techno-Archeology, that's interesting. I've certainly never heard of them. I can't imagine they have any real budget." The latter, of course, was the critical issue.

Matthews chuckled at the "office in a closet" remark. No doubt his years of academic bureaucracy convinced him of the probable truth in those words. "Well, that's as may be, but if it is about project funding, you'll want to get back to them quickly."

Carson knew when he'd been dismissed. "Right," he said, getting up from the seat. "If you'll excuse me then?"

Matthews had already shifted his focus to something else, and he gave a back-handed wave. "Oh, and do try to remember to keep your records updated, won't you?"

Carson thought about the call as he walked back to his office. What *was* this really? Some collector trying to scam him with a phony government agency? Unlikely, the penalties for impersonating a government agent were high. In any case, the artifacts recovered usually went to either or both of the investigator's academic institution or to the museum or museum-connected organization—Department of Antiquities, for example—that financed the expedition. And what was "Techno-Archeology"? He'd just have to ask this Ducayne character.

∞ ∞ ∞

Back at his desk, Carson returned the call.

"Office of Techno-Archeology, Ducayne speaking."

"Ah, Mr. Ducayne, this is Dr. Hannibal Carson, at the—"

"Yes, Dr. Carson. Thank you for calling. I understand you're looking at mounting an expedition to Gliese 68. Is that right?"

"Yes. But I was wonderi—"

Ducayne cut him off again. "Excellent, we're looking for somebody to do a little side investigation for us in that direction. Why don't you come in to our office and we can talk about it."

"Well, but I have a few questions—" This call wasn't going at all the way Carson had expected.

"Of course you do. You want to know who the Office of Techno-Archeology is, I'm sure—we're not widely known—and how funding will work, and so on."

Carson's ears pricked up a little at the word "funding." That was always the key to getting academic work done. "Well, yes, but —"

"I'll clear up any questions you have when you come to the office. Here, I'll beam you the address information." There was a soft "beep" in the background of the call, as Ducayne uploaded an address file to Carson's omni. "That will give you the details on how to find us, the office is a little out of the way in a corner of the spaceport."

"Um, thanks. When is a good—"

"Anytime tomorrow will work. Say, after lunch?"

"All right." Carson felt as if he were three moves behind in a chess game.

"Great. See you then. Bye." The omni clicked off.

Carson sat there a moment, staring at his omni. "What just happened?" he said to the empty office.

Chapter 7: Special Delivery

Sawyer City Spaceport

JACKIE ROBERTS flared the *Sophie*'s approach, killing her forward velocity, and gently dropped the remaining few meters on vertical thrusters. "Sawyer Ground, this is *Sophie*, request clearance to a parking area," she called over the radio.

"*Roger* Sophie. *Are you staying long?*"

"Just a couple of hours. Some packages to deliver and then I head out for Kakuloa." Kakuloa was almost a sister planet to Sawyers World, orbiting the second sun, B, of the double star comprising the Alpha Centauri system. They were about twenty seconds apart in warp at this stage of their mutual orbit, although with take-off, landing, and in-system maneuvering the trip would take several hours.

"*All right,* Sophie." Ground control assigned her a short-term spot and cleared her to taxi to it.

Her ship parked and the flight systems powered down, Jackie grabbed the packages and walked them over to the port building. She didn't recognize the female clerk on duty, which didn't surprise her. Sawyer was big and busy enough that it got a lot of turnover, and she didn't get here often.

"This package is a rush delivery, Captain Roberts," the clerk told her when she had logged in the packages. "I can authorize a delivery bonus if you want to walk it over. The address is a building here in the spaceport."

"Oh?" Normally Jackie might not have bothered, but now she was intrigued, and the bonus, however small, would help pay for the repairs she needed. "All right then, where?"

∞ ∞·∞

The destination turned out to be an office in an old hangar building. It must have been one of the first built at the spaceport. Jackie found the door, with the building number and a pushbutton beside it. A doorbell? She checked the package. Yes, this was it. She pushed the button. She didn't hear anything. A moment later she heard a male voice from an unseen source. "Yes, who is it?"

"Courier." Jackie wasn't going to give out any more information than she had to. "A rush package just came in on the *Sophie*, from Epsilon Eridani. It's for a Q. Ducayne. Is this the right place?"

"Yes, just a moment."

Jackie looked around, wondering what kind of person would have an office—or perhaps live?—in an old hangar like this. It had a disused look to it, with fading paint and grime accumulating on old oil stains on the main hangar doors.

The smaller door opened and Jackie saw an athletic-looking man, taller than Jackie and perhaps in his forties, holding it.

"Sorry for the delay." He looked her over, but not in the usual way a man might look at her. It was as though he was assessing her, taking in details of the ship coveralls she was wearing, the way she carried herself, rather than anything overtly sexual. He held out a hand to take the package. "Are you from the *Sophie*?"

"Yes, she's my ship. How did you know?"

"Ship coveralls. And they've got 'Sophie' on them, the name of a ship that just landed. I'm guessing that's not your name?" He smiled at her.

"Uh, no." The man was observant. And smooth. "I'm Jackie Roberts, captain of the *Sophie*."

"Quentin Ducayne, pleased to meet you. Now, my package?"

"You'll need to confirm delivery," she said as she handed it to him.

"Of course." He waved his arm, with his omni around the wrist, across the package's label. The label chirped a confirmation. Ducayne looked at Roberts. "If you have a few minutes, I'd like to ask you about this. Would you like coffee?"

Coffee sounded wonderful. Jackie accepted and followed Ducayne into the hangar. The interior space was devoid of aircraft or spacecraft. It felt like there hadn't been any vehicles in here for a long time, and smelled more of old dust than of fresh hydraulic fluid, ozone, or any of the other odors she associated with a spacecraft repair bay. She followed Ducayne up a metal stairway to the observation mezzanine and an office overlooking the hangar floor.

"What kind of work do you do here, Mr. Ducayne?"

"That's, ah, that's in a state of flux at the moment, Captain Roberts." He gestured at the chair across from his desk. "Have a seat, I'll just be a moment." He went to the small autochef in the corner and returned with two cups of coffee. He handed one to her.

Jackie raised the cup and smelled the rich aroma of the coffee. Could it be? She took a sip, and raised an eyebrow. It was smooth with no hint of bitterness. "Tau Cetan?" she asked. "This is great coffee."

Ducayne smiled. "Actually it's what Tau Cetan derives from, although the growing conditions are more important than the breeding stock. This is Jamaica Blue Mountain."

"From Earth? I am impressed." She took another sip of the coffee, closing her eyes and savoring it.

"All right, Captain, this rush package from Eridani, is there anything you can tell me about it?"

Jackie opened her eyes and sat up straighter. "Not really. I was coming here—well, to Kakuloa—from there and just made a routine check for any cargo to help make the trip worth it. And you can call me Jackie."

"Ah, I see. Kakuloa? Is that just a vacation or does your ship need work?"

The man was astute. Although when it came down to it, those were about the only things Kakuloa was known for: great beaches and the orbital shipyards. "A bit of both, really. My ship does need some minor work, but I could use some beach time. Right now I'm between charters."

"Charters? Tell you what, Jackie. If you don't hear from me before you're ready to leave the Centauri system, give me a call. I may have something for you."

"Thank you. I'll do that." She would, even if another job came up. One never knew when a casual contact would lead to a charter.

"Good." He glanced at his wrist omni and stood up. "Sorry to be so abrupt Captain . . . Jackie . . . but I have a meeting that I need to prepare for. I'm afraid I have to ask you to leave."

Jackie stood, drank down the last of her coffee, and handed the cup back to Ducayne. *If he gets Jamaica Blue Mountain flown in from Earth,* she thought, *he's definitely worth staying in touch with.* "Thank you for the coffee. I hope we can do business sometime."

"I'm sure we will."

∞ ∞ ∞

Carson had been right, the Office of Techno-Archeology *was* little bigger than a closet, in a building that should have been condemned twenty years ago, making it one of the older buildings on Sawyers World. It was a hangar in a corner of the spaceport, which surprised Carson.

He walked up to the building, an immense dirty-gray half-cylinder set sideways, its paint fading. To Carson it resembled a big Quonset hut, or a huge Iroquois longhouse. The large main doors, used for air- and space-craft, were closed, and it took Carson a minute to find the human-sized door nestled in one corner. He checked the address against his omni. Yes, this was the place, and noticed the small, faded "Astronomical Survey Group" nameplate near a large doorbell pushbutton. He reached over and pushed it.

A voice came from an unnoticed speaker grill. "Yes, who is it?"

"This is Dr. Hannibal Carson. I have an appointment with a Mr. Ducayne."

"Oh, yes, Dr. Carson. Please come in, follow the painted path to the stairs, my office is on the left at the top of the stairway." Carson recognized Ducayne's voice.

As he reached for the handle the door swung open on its own. Carson shrugged and entered. Inside, the hangar looked even bigger—an optical illusion with nothing in here to give a sense of scale. The hangar floor was empty, or nearly so. No ships or aircraft, just a few tool benches and a couple of service vehicles. A painted outline marked a path which followed the outside wall from the doorway where he was standing and around the back wall. To keep people out of the way of operations, no doubt, thought Carson.

At the rear of the hangar was a metal platform, a mezzanine, which looked to have several small offices on it. At least, there was a wall with several doors and windows, probably so the occupants could observe work on the hangar floor without being disturbed by noise, although Carson didn't understand why they didn't just use cameras. He scanned overhead, and yes, there were cameras mounted, although the whole place had a rather shabby and unused air about it. There didn't seem to be anyone working here, either. The hangar was quiet and dim. Most of the overhead lights were turned off. *Or burnt out?* wondered Carson. His initial doubts about this grew stronger.

He followed the path to the back of the hangar and found the stairs up to the office level. As he reached the top step a door on his left opened. A fit-looking man, of average height, perhaps in his forties, stepped out of the doorway and extended his hand.

"Dr. Carson! Thank you for coming. It's good to meet you," he said, taking Carson's hand in a firm grip. Not bone-crushing, but Carson got the impression that Ducayne could if he'd wanted. Odd for a paper pusher. Carson squeezed back, enough to let Ducayne know that he could do some crushing himself, but without making it an outright challenge. Carson looked Ducayne in the eye, and some indefinable sense of recognition passed between the two.

"Come in, sit down." said Ducayne. "Can I get you something, coffee perhaps?"

"Thank you, Mr. Ducayne. No, no coffee. You might answer some questions."

"Whatever I can, Dr. Carson. I imagine you're wondering about the Office of Techno-Archeology?"

"Frankly, yes. I've never heard of it, and, well, it doesn't look like you have much of a budget." Carson glanced meaningfully around the office, the cheap paneling, the level of general wear and tear, and by implication the rather shabby hangar the office was housed in.

"Understandable." Ducayne didn't seem in the least offended. "We prefer to spend our budget on what counts, not on keeping up appearances."

"How, uh, unbureaucratic of you."

"Oh, I'll think you'll find we operate a little differently from most bureaucracies. But tell me, Dr. Carson, have you ever done any government work before? Any military service?"

"What? Well yes, I've done projects on government grants before, Department of Antiquities, things like that."

"Not quite what I meant. What about military?"

"I was in the reserves when I was younger. I can take care of myself, if that's what you mean. How is that relevant?"

"Security clearance?"

"Look—" *This is getting ridiculous*, Carson thought. Why did this guy—whoever he really was, and Carson was wondering if his earlier thought about a clever scam by an artifact collector was right—why did he care about military experience, let alone a security clearance? He'd had one, of course, a fairly high one. He'd joined the reserves in college to help pay his tuition, and spent summers posted to a couple of rather interesting locations, which he probably still shouldn't talk about fifteen years later. He *certainly* wasn't about to tell this bozo anything more until he got some satisfactory answers.

"I don't see how that's relevant to my proposal," Carson continued. Unless . . . "Wait, was there another site you had in mind? A restricted area?"

Ducayne sat back in his chair. He looked thoughtfully at Carson, steepling his fingers. "Sorry, Doctor," he answered, still in thought.

Carson got to his feet. This was a waste of his time. "I'm sorry too, Ducayne. I've had a enough of this . . . silly game. I have work to do." He turned to leave just as Ducayne leaned hastily forward.

"Just a moment, Carson. Please."

Carson paused at something in Ducayne's tone. "You have something to say? Say it."

"All right, Dr. Carson." Ducayne looked at something on his computer screen, back at Carson, and appeared to come to a decision. "That last question was a bit of a test. I'm sorry it got your shorts in a shamble, but you passed." He moved forward on his chair, leaning on his desk toward Carson. "Are you sure you want answers?"

Carson sat back in the chair at this, the force of the question unexpected. "Damn right, Ducayne. You haven't told me anything yet. You drag me all the way out here with a vague promise about backing my next research dig . . . it better be good." Carson leaned forward himself.

"Very well. Dr. Hannibal Carson, under authority of Title 17, Section 201, Paragraph C, subsection 2, I hereby notify you that your obligations under the Official Secrets Act shall be in force from this point forward until you are notified otherwise. Do you understand and agree to be so obligated?"

"I, what?" Whatever Carson had been expecting, it wasn't this.

"Come on, Carson, I know you've held a Top Secret clearance and I also know you were cleared for SCI. If you want answers just say you understand and you agree. Otherwise turn around, leave, and forget you ever heard of this place."

Carson was tempted to do just that. This smelled too much like he was about to get drafted for something. On the other hand, he was *really* curious now, and other than teaching at the university, he had no other commitments. "All right, 'I understand and so agree'. Don't you need my fingerprint or something?"

"Oh, I got that already from the scanner in the doorbell. If you hadn't been you, you wouldn't have gotten in here in the first place."

"Bloody hell, what *have* I gotten myself into?"

Ducayne grinned and stood up, gesturing at Carson to do the same. "Come on, I'll show you."

Chapter 8: Shipyards

In orbit above Kakuloa, Alpha Centauri B

"KIAHUNA SHIPYARDS, this is the *Sophie*, Sapphire class, requesting docking instructions."

"*Roger* Sophie, *we have your reservation. Slave your controls to our docking computer, code one-five-seven-alpha.*"

"Any chance of letting me dock manually?"

"*Sorry, Jackie, company policy. Our facility costs a lot more than your ship. Nothing personal, we just trust our computers more than any pilot, even you.*"

"Roger that. One-five-seven-alpha," she punched in the code and activated slave mode. "You have control." She'd hadn't expected to be allowed to do it herself, for the very reasons the controller had mentioned, but it still galled her to be reduced to a passenger in her own ship. She stayed strapped in at her console, watching the viewscreens.

As she neared her assigned dock, she saw riggers working to attach large external tanks to a ship at a berth near hers. Roberts shook her head; she wouldn't want to try flying a ship with that kind of extra mass crowding close to the warp boundary.

The *Sophie* glided silently through the big airdock doors, then stopped with a burst of the forward thrusters. A long robotic arm extended from overhead to grapple a docking hardpoint on *Sophie*'s hull and eased the ship into position. A tunnel extruded itself from the wall of the airdock and pressed against *Sophie*'s hatch. The docking latches made a loud, rippling clack as they engaged, and Jackie saw a green light illuminate on her console.

"*Okay,* Sophie, *you're docked,*" a voice came over the radio. "*Secure your systems and come aboard.*"

"Thanks, Kiahuna, copy that," Jackie replied. On the rear viewscreen, the big outer doors of the airdock were already closing. It would take a half-hour to pressurize the dock so that the technicians could work on her hull without suits. In the meantime the pressurized tunnel connecting the *Sophie*'s hatch to the shipyard gave her direct access to the station.

Jackie unstrapped, collected a few items, and made her way to the spin gravity section of the station and the shipyard office to formally authorize the work.

∞ ∞ ∞

"A Sapphire," the desk agent said as he reviewed the file. "We don't see as many of those as we used to, they're more frontier ships. Is that the three engine configuration or four?" The data was in the file, of course, but apparently the agent wanted to make conversation.

"Just the three. You ever see any fours? That cuts into the range."

"Oh, a few. Some people prefer speed over range, if they're not exploring. Not that they were ever that much faster." He touched the screen and turned it to face her.

"Speaking of speed, will the repairs take long?" Jackie asked as she keyed in the credit transfer.

"Are you in a hurry?"

"Yes and no. I expect to be in the Centauri system for a few days, someone on Sawyers might have a job for me, but I'd rather spend the time down on Kakuloa than up here in space dock."

"So? Go soak up some sun on the beach. There's a shuttle, and we'll take good care of your ship."

Jackie grinned. "She wouldn't be here if I didn't think you'd take care of her. But these repairs are costing me enough. I don't want to pay for a shuttle and hotel on top of that. I figured I'd sleep aboard at the spaceport."

The agent looked Jackie up and down as though he were thinking about making some suggestion concerning where she could sleep. He apparently thought better of it and just said: "Fair enough. As it happens we're not super busy right now so I'll have them expedite the work."

She thanked him and headed to the observation area to wait.

Chapter 9: Secrets Revealed

Sawyer City Spaceport

DUCAYNE LED Carson along the catwalk outside the row of offices to the stairs, then down to the main level. Carson noticed a few doors in the wall across from the path he had walked in along, still rather shabby looking. They were headed for one. As they approached, Ducayne clicked a button on his omni and one of the doors opened inward, revealing as far as Carson could tell a rather dingy office. They entered, and the door closed behind them.

"What . . ." began Carson, and stopped when he realized that the floor was descending. This was starting to seem remarkably similar to a secret facility he had been posted to once as a reservist.

"Elevator," said Ducayne, in a tone that suggested he knew that he was stating the obvious. "The, ah, briefing rooms are downstairs."

Carson felt a mild jerk as the elevator/office stopped, and the door opened again. This time the door opened onto a brightly lit lobby area, quite clean, with corridors leading off. Glass doors isolated the corridors from the lobby, and a guard station faced the elevator door.

"Welcome to Homeworld Security," Ducayne said in a dry tone.

"Does the Sawyer government know you're here?" In theory Sawyers World, unlike most other settled planets, had been autonomous since the first landing. In practice the planet was dependent on trade with Earth, and the *Union des Terre* had a military base on Sawyers.

"Of course they do, Carson. Don't be naive." Ducayne walked over to the station, presented a card, and thumbed a print scanner. The guard checked his screen, pulled out a badge and handed it to Ducayne. "There you go sir, thank you. And who is this?" The guard gestured at Carson.

"Carson, Hannibal, Doctor. There's an entry for him."

"All right," the guard said. "Sir?" calling to Carson "Would you step over here and give me a thumb scan please?"

Carson did so. He had been through similar procedures, years ago, but was a bit bewildered by all this, here, now. What *was* this place?

"Okay, Doctor," said Ducayne after Carson had his badge. "This way, please." He held out an arm to indicate one of the corridor doors. The hall they walked down was unremarkable, except that none of the doors had the windows one might expect in a typical office setting, and they bore just numbers, not identifying names like "Conference Room" or "Research Lab" or even "Men".

Ducayne obviously knew where he was going, though. He stopped at room identified as 2-7 and palmed the scan panel beside the door. The door slid open, and they stepped through.

The small conference room held a table at which two men were already seated. The walls held several large screens along one wall, and there was a holodisplay installed across the room from the door they had entered. To Carson, the setup said *briefing room* more than anything else.

Ducayne made the introductions. "Gentlemen, this is Dr. Hannibal Carson. Dr. Carson, this is Mr. Brown and Mr. Black."

"Which is which?" asked Carson as he sat down.

The two men glanced at each other, and then to Ducayne, who smiled wryly. "It doesn't really matter, those aren't their real names."

It soon became obvious that whatever their names, they were highly knowledgeable about their fields—and his.

"Dr. Carson, your proposal mentioned some structures on Gliese 68 and a possible relation to other structures on Zeta Tucanae," Brown said.

"That's right. The Zeta Tucanae pyramids appear to date back about fifteen thousand years or so, well before the locals would have had the capability of building them. They've only had neolithic-level civilization for about five thousand years, at most. In fact, Zee Tee was probably in the middle of an ice age twenty thousand years ago."

"But those two systems are over thirty-six light-years apart," said Black.

"Yes. Troubling, isn't it."

"Very. But that's not really why you're here." Ducayne motioned the others to silence. "Dr. Carson, you found something on your recent trip to Verdigris, didn't you?"

"We found a pyramidal tomb, odd because the customary design there is a dome. Unfortunately we were robbed by an illegal antiquities dealer named Hopkins. He took all the artifacts, and the mummified body of a Verdigran." Carson decided to hold off on mentioning the radioactive talisman for now.

"You're sure it was Verdigran?" Brown asked.

"Yes. I convinced Hopkins to let me take a DNA sample. It checked out." Carson looked Brown in the eye. "Why, were you expecting something else?"

Brown looked down at his screen on the table.

Ducayne broke in. "Carson, you've been doing extensive image-matching searches on the net recently. Why? And where did you get the image you've been using as a target?"

Carson should have been shocked at this indication that someone had been eavesdropping on his computer searches, but he had already suspected something from the fact that none of them had returned any hits. "You've got a monitor program running, you've been waiting for somebody to look for that kind of image. Why?" Carson saw Ducayne's jaw muscle flex. He had guessed right.

"Answer my question first, Dr. Carson."

"All right. After Hopkins left the tomb I found something he'd missed, a piece of a broken talisman. It looked vaguely familiar, so I was trying to track down where I might have seen one like it before, or any others, and where they were found. What is your interest?"

"Do you do this kind of search for everything you find on a dig?"

"Ultimately, yes, to correlate with other collections, trace cultural influences, that sort of thing." That was true enough, but usually happened months or even years later, as part of a grad student's thesis work.

And apparently Black knew that. "That sounds like something you'd assign to a research assistant at a later date."

"Come on, Carson," added Ducayne. "Stop playing games, this is important. You show me yours and I'll show you mine."

What? His? "All right. It was slightly radioactive." That got their attention. The others at the table shifted in their seats and leaned toward him. "It turned out to contain technetium-99, and from the isotope ratios it was about fifteen thousand years old." Brown and Black began conferring with each other in low voices. Carson interrupted. "Now, why were you monitoring my searches?"

Ducayne digested that for a moment. "Not yours in particular, Carson, but anyone who was looking for something like this." He brought up an image on the main wallscreen. It wasn't a photograph, or rather, it was a photograph of a hand sketched, rough drawing. An object, flat and roughly square in shape, but with rounded corners and slightly curved sides. An indistinct pattern decorated the edge. From the sketched-in shading, there wasn't enough detail to tell if it was metallic, ceramic, or just what. On its face, there were several dots or small circles spaced irregularly around a central dot, with radial lines connecting to it. The handwritten dimensions showed it to be about ten centimeters across. If broken in half, it would resemble exactly what he had found on Verdigris.

"Where is this from?" Carson demanded.

"We'll get to that. You said you thought you had seen one before. Neither your searches nor ours have turned up anything like it. Where might you have seen it?"

"It must have been off-world. If it had been in the university's collection here my search would have found it, even in the private catalog. On the other hand, if it were in another university's or a museum's private catalog it wouldn't show up in my search."

Ducayne nodded. "And even if it were public, the data just might not be here yet." With ships the only fast way to transfer data between stars, the content of each systems' net was always a little out of sync with that of every other planetary system.

"Right," Carson said absently. He was staring at the image on the screen again. Seeing the whole piece, even in sketch form, it looked more familiar. There had been so many artifacts. He couldn't remember them all, that was what computers were for. If it were like the piece he'd found, those dots were colored gemstones. Then he had it. "I remember now, I have seen another one. Why? What's the significance?"

"And where is this artifact now? And the broken one?"

"Ducayne, if you want my help, you have to answer my questions once in a while. I'm getting tired of your constant evasion. You've cleared me, so *tell* me. Why do you want to know? What's so important about it?"

Ducayne's eyes narrowed and he gritted his teeth. He clearly wasn't used to being the one having to *answer* questions. He glared at Carson. Carson glared back, challenging. "Your life might be in danger," Ducayne said.

That took Carson aback. He didn't *think* Ducayne was threatening him, it hadn't sounded quite like a threat. But if not, then what? "My life's in bloody danger nearly every time I'm in the field, between blood-thirsty alien creatures"—all right, it had only been mosquitoes, that last time, not even truly alien—"and damned tomb-raiding bushwhacking artifact smugglers! What have you got that's different?"

"Ever hear of a group called the Velkaryans?"

"Valkyries?" Carson wasn't sure he'd heard it right.

"No, Velkaryans, although they may have chosen their name to sound similar."

"I'm not familiar with that name. Who are they?"

"What about Heaven's Gate, or the Raelians?"

Carson had heard of those. He had found references when researching possible evidence that Spacefarers had ever visited Earth. That was part of what had sparked Matthews' tirade about von Dänikenism.

"Yes," he answered, "late twentieth and early twenty-first century UFO cults. Pre-war. The Heaven's Gaters committed mass suicide when Comet Hale-Bopp approached Earth. Even stranger than most religions, they borrowed ideas from Christianity, other UFO cults, and some of the popular space-themed entertainment of the time. Is that what these Velkaryans are? A UFO cult in this day and age?"

Mr. Brown cut in. "There's nothing special about this age. There has been an extraterrestrial component in a lot of religions, from Ezekial's flying wheel in the Old Testament to the Scientologists' Xenu, from the Raelians to the Nazi's Vril Society. Even more cropped up after the first space flights. Some benign, some bizarre."

"That's right," Ducayne said. "We're not clear on the Velkaryans' roots, but it seems to be a fairly recent organization, or religion, that has drawn elements from both Christian tradition and from the teachings of Hubbard, Smith and even Applewhite."

"Applewhite? Heaven's Gate?" Carson let the implications sink in. These were some serious, and dangerous, whackos. "Yes, that did have a monastic element, but . . ."

"Yes, 'but'. Monasticism isn't what worries us."

"All right. And what does any of this have to do with this artifact?"

Ducayne took a breath, weighing what information to give out. "Very well. One of my agents infiltrated a Velkaryan cell. Routine surveillance, we like to keep on eye on the more extreme religious groups. Our civilization is too vulnerable to not watch anyone with ideas that odd." The Unholy War last century had proved that. "Anyway, my man began to suspect that they were planning something big. He sent a report indicating they were desperately looking for this object," he waved at the image of the talisman, "and that it was the key to something."

"Key to what?"

"We're not really sure." Ducayne expression was a mixture of worry and embarrassment. "We have some theories."

"Can your agent find out?" asked Carson.

"No. He was killed." Ducayne paused, a shadowed look crossed his face and he clenched his fists. "We think they found him out."

"I see," Carson said. If the Velkaryans had killed Ducayne's agent, then he wasn't kidding about them being dangerous.

"Which brings us back to my question. Where is this artifact now?"

"Off-planet. My dig partner took the artifacts back to his university to study and catalogue them there. They were providing a large piece of the funding." Carson paused, thoughtful. "Wait, you said I might be in danger. Do you have any reason to suspect they were on to me? Or my partner?"

"To you, yes, that's one of the reasons we called you in, that and the searches you were doing. To your partner, I don't think so. Our agent never mentioned anyone else."

"You mentioned some theories as to just what this was the key to locating. Care to explain them?" Carson leaned back in his chair, not really expecting an answer.

"From what we have been able to decipher—"

"Decipher? You have text? Glyphs? A bilingual?" Carson sat forward, eagerly.

"What? Oh, no, no, no. We don't. We think that the Velkaryans do. I meant decipher from encrypted Velkaryan documents that our agent was able to copy. The language apparently uses the phrase 'store house of powerful *something*', where the word *something* seems to mean knowledge, tools, and/or weapons. We don't know whether to translate that as archive, library, museum, tool shed, or arsenal. It's that last that concerns us."

"Wow. Understandably so. Any of those possibilities is awesome and a little frightening. So you think this artifact, this talisman, indicates its location?"

"Frankly, we don't know *what* to think, but it is fairly clear that the Velkaryans think so, and no, before you ask," Ducayne said, forestalling Carson's next question, "we have no idea *why* they might think so or where they got that knowledge. Or knowledge of the alien script, for that matter."

"Huh. Okay, tell me what you think might be in this arsenal, or archive, or whatever it is."

"Well," Black (or was it Brown?) picked up the explanation, "we strongly suspect that the Archive may contain an alien device of some kind, call it a Cosmic Maguffin, or perhaps directions to a location where the Cosmic Maguffin is stored. Needless to say we can't let the Velkaryans find it."

"Cosmic Maguffin? What's that?" Carson asked.

"We had to call it something. This has to be fairly advanced technology. Think about what they had to do to build those pyramids, move and shape that quantity of stone."

"Well, we can do that."

Brown—or perhaps it was Black—took up the argument. "Ah, but not with what can be carried in a starship. Limited volume, remember?" The power needed to create a starship's warp bubble increased faster than the size of the bubble; beyond a certain maximum size, no known source of sufficient energy was small enough to fit. "So, no heavy machinery, or at least not much, and the ship would have to be purpose-built to carry it. No, this had to be something small, vehicle portable at biggest, and with a very compact power supply."

"Fusion?"

"Well, we can't build a fusion unit into anything easily hand portable, at least not with the power output required. So whatever it was, it's new technology for us, and potentially dangerous in the wrong hands."

"The Velkaryans being the wrong hands. But why, exactly?"

"Right, you don't know who they are."

"You mentioned a UFO cult."

"Yes. As I understand their basic dogma, sixty-five million years ago God—and it's not clear if they mean the Judeo-Christian God or if they're referring to something alien like Xenu or the Flying Spaghetti Monster—anyway God wiped out the dinosaurs in a rain of fire and exploding volcanoes to make room for humans to evolve. At the same time God also terraformed planets in other solar systems so that we would have room to expand when Earth became overcrowded."

"All right, so far that's not much different than most other cults."

"Right. The problem is that they are highly xenophobic, and believe that the existence of any intelligent non-human species is contrary to God's Will, and that all the terraformed worlds are reserved for humans. They preach genocide, or rather xenocide, but they play it very close to their vests so that's hard to prove. You have to get deeply into their organization before some of this gets revealed to you. They also take very harsh measures against any of their members who stray."

"I can see why you would want to keep anything powerful out of their hands. They remind me of the Nazis or the Islamo-fascists."

"Fortunately they don't seem to have that kind of following, but economic disruptions in the colonies could add people to their numbers. But there's more to it than that, something you're in a position to appreciate."

"Oh?"

"You've been looking for evidence of advanced spacefarers in this region ten to twenty thousand years ago."

"And finding it."

"Exactly. Suppose they're still out there? What if these Velkaryans stumble across one of their ships, or worse, one of their planets? They could do something monumentally stupid and start an interstellar war. Look at how the Unholy War got started, or the First World War a century before that."

Carson scoffed. "You don't really think that a species that's had star travel for that long would get sucked into something like that, do you? Besides, interstellar war makes no sense, the communications and logistics are too difficult."

"Do you want to take that chance? More to the point, do you think Homeworld Security wants to take that chance? Of course not." Ducayne got up from his chair and paced the room. "I'll tell you a dirty little secret, Carson, although it's one you could figure out for yourself easily enough. The *Union des Terre* and the national governments that it comprises are very happy for people on Earth to remain ignorant of what's out here. Sure, everyone knows about terraformed planets, we even call this little bubble of stars we've explored T-space, but most people don't really think about it. Just like they don't really think about what wiped out the dinosaurs. It was millions of years ago, whoever—or whatever—did it is gone. They don't think about other civilizations, either—"

"But—"

Ducayne put up a hand. "Oh, I know, there's a big and mostly black market in artifacts from those primitive civilizations, but that's because they're dead. Human civilization is still around, alien civilizations were primitive at best and now they're gone. Therefore we have nothing to worry about." Ducayne leaned his fists on the table. "But most Terrans don't even think about aliens. Certainly not about the possibility that there might still be aliens twenty thousand years ahead of us that we could bump into any time.

"The idea understandably scares Homeworld Security, and it scares the *hell* out of the governments. It's not just the potential conflict with advanced aliens—and personally I'm inclined to agree that that's unlikely—but the reaction, the cultural shock if or when we make contact. The human race suffered two traumatic events last century; we're not ready for another one. At least, not Earth. People out in the colonies are more resilient, but they're not self-sufficient yet. They, *we*, still rely on too much high tech that there's not enough local infrastructure to replace.

"And that's another little secret I'll let you in on, although only the thinking behind it is really secret. We actively encourage, and even assist, the emigration of religious groups who shun high tech. If an Amish or Mennonite, or even Inuit or Yupik," Ducayne held up a hand, staying Carson's objection that the latter were peoples rather than religions, "or whatever community wants to set up on a frontier world, we'll help them out."

"But I thought official policy was to discourage emigration of organized religious groups," said Carson. "No exodus, no finding new homelands."

"That's the official policy, especially if they want to bring their twenty-second century technology with them. The last thing we need is a breeding ground for more religious wars fifty or a hundred years down the line. Of course we can't stop it totally, and we don't try to, just where it looks like it might lead to trouble.

"But the catch with the groups we do help is that then we leave them alone. If they can become self-sufficient, that's wonderful. If Earth goes through another convulsion and starships start failing because we can't get spare parts, then at least there will be places where that will have less impact."

Carson shook his head. He was having a hard time taking it all in. It all made sense, but . . . "Wow. When you said earlier that you operate a little differently from most bureaucracies, you weren't kidding."

Brown and Black both chuckled at that, and Ducayne grinned. "You have no idea," he said. "But you managed to get me quite off track, I'm not usually so garrulous. Back to my original point, there are too many risks to allow the Velkaryans to find whatever this cache is."

"The alien technology. You're afraid this 'Cosmic Maguffin' might be a weapon."

"I don't know. It may not be, but the potential negative consequences if it is are too great to ignore."

"So what do you want from me?"

"The location of any of these talismans that you're aware of. Keep an eye out for anything similar, let us know about any suspicious interested parties."

"Oh," said Carson as a wry grin came to his face, "there are always interested parties."

"I meant beyond the usual tomb raiders and artifact smugglers," Ducayne said. "We might ask for consultation on interpreting it the talisman."

"That's all?"

"Were you expecting something else?"

"When we first talked, you did hint at funding an expedition."

"Did I? Don't you have classes to teach or something?"

Teaching classes was the last thing Carson wanted to do if he could get a chance to track down this alien cache. "I'll be lucky to have a job the way Matthews goes on. But if there were a financed project I could make arrangements to cover all that."

"I've got my own people," Ducayne said, and nodded toward Black and Brown.

"Trained archeologists?" Carson caught the scowls which Brown and Black gave him. "With academic credentials?" The scowls slackened a little. "The other talisman is at the university on Taprobane."

"Your partner's a timoan?" Ducayne asked.

"Uh, yes," said Carson, surprised at how fast Ducayne made the connection. Taprobane was the home world of the only technological aliens humans had encountered, and at that only an iron-age level of technology. Away from the main timoan habitations, Taprobane held a human-timoan settlement centered around the university. "He'll let me have the talisman. I can get it faster and easier than your people."

Ducayne slumped back in his chair. "All right, Carson, just what will you need?"

"A ship and someone to fly it. The university's ships are booked on other projects."

Ducayne looked across the table at Brown and raised an eyebrow. "Well?"

Brown shifted in his chair. "That may take some time," he said after a moment. We don't have anything available right now, and charters are harder to find these days, all the charter operators are moving farther out."

Carson nodded. "Yes, the competition from scheduled runs. I could head out to Tau Ceti."

"That may not be necessary," said Ducayne. "There may be an available operator in-system now. A courier delivered a package to me today. I believe the ship needed minor repairs, she was going to be at Kakuloa for a few days." He looked at Carson. "If that gives you enough time, I can check them out."

"Who is it? Maybe I know them."

"*Sophie* Space Charters."

"Sophie? The owner is female?" Not that Carson had a problem with that, on the contrary, but it could complicate things. It had once before.

"Well, yes, but *Sophie* is the name of the ship."

"Ah." Carson had heard ship names ranging from the mundane to the weird. Gupta's ship—one of two that the university held a long-term lease on—was the *Subrahmanyan Chandrasekhar*, after both the twentieth-century astrophysicist and the first ship to land on an extrasolar planet, although everyone just called it the *Chandra.* But right now Gupta was off taking a geological expedition to a planet orbiting some obscure red dwarf star.

They worked out a few more details—advances for supplies, contacts on Kakuloa, that sort of thing—and Ducayne escorted Carson back out of the facility, checking him out with the guard, up the elevator, and finally the good bye handshake at the hangar door.

"All right, Carson. You got your expedition after all. Keep me posted."

∞ ∞ ∞

Ducayne watched as Carson walked across the field from the hangar to the main terminal. He keyed a number into his omni and waited for the reply. "He took the bait. I told you he would. And he knows where to find another one."

Chapter 10: Unwelcome Intrusion

Sawyer City

CARSON LEFT THE hangar, intrigued by the whole encounter and somewhat amused at both Ducayne's behavior and that of the characters Black and Brown. He dismissed it with a mental shrug and a shake of his head. "Spooks!" he muttered to himself.

He mulled it over as he walked from the older part of the spaceport to the terminal building. He didn't for a moment believe that the repository, the "store house", if it even existed, was an arsenal. An arsenal implied a large store of weapons, which implied war or the threat of war, and an interstellar war made no sense at all. Any civilization with interstellar technology had access to plenty of resources, and surely the size limit on a warp bubble and the impossibility of faster-than-light communication —short of hand-carrying a message—made the idea of fleets of interstellar battleships ludicrous. Didn't it? Carson remembered Rajesh Gupta's comment about signs of landing sites for impossibly large ships. And humans had fought some horribly destructive wars for illogical reasons. But no, it didn't make sense. Why contact primitive civilizations, in that case? And nowhere in T-space was there evidence of large-scale warfare. It couldn't be an arsenal.

An archive was also unlikely. Although, it occurred to him, off-planet—or out-system—storage was an excellent way to retain data even against such events as the primary star going nova. But a spacefaring civilization could predict something like that, surely.

No, as Carson thought about it more, it was probably a kind of monument commemorating the very existence of the race that built it. Or the gods thereof, if they had gone in for that sort of thing. The other possibility was perhaps as some sort of teaching museum, to give primitive cultures a boost. Maybe even a combination of the two. Raise the cultural level so the primitives can properly worship the spacefarers or their gods.

Or perhaps the talisman was just something pretty to look at. He planned to find out soon enough; he had travel plans to make.

He reached the main terminal building, where he had arrived earlier that day, and thumbed his omni for an autocab. It was just pulling up to the curb by the time he had crossed through the building and exited the other side. The cab door swung up and he climbed in. "Drake University, Archeology Building" he told the cab. It repeated the address back to him in confirmation and pulled smoothly away with a low hum. Carson sat back and considered his next actions. He would need to pack and make arrangements for his apartment. He had nothing scheduled at the office for the rest of the day, so it made sense to do that first.

"Cab, cancel Drake University, new destination 317 Armstrong Place"—his apartment building. Then he sat back and began to make calls.

∞ ∞ ∞

Hannibal finished arranging coverage for his classes just as the cab pulled up at his apartment building. He got out and walked into the lobby. Behind him, the cab lowered its door and pulled smoothly away. Carson sometimes wondered where the cabs went when there was nobody in them. Did they just cruise the streets at random, or did they link to the other cabs to provide a coordinated coverage pattern, minimizing how long a passenger would wait? He supposed that they had to report somewhere for periodic maintenance, but it had never really bothered him enough to find out where. This afternoon, though, Carson's mind was still on the talisman and whatever mysterious secret it was supposed to be the key to.

He walked up the hall and keyed his door code. As the door opened the lights came up on a scene of utter chaos. Drawers were pulled out, clothes and papers and data chips were scattered every which way. Books and disks had been pulled off shelves, furniture was pulled away from the walls. His bed had been stripped. Even the carpet, in the corner of the room where it had been loose, was pulled up and turned back. He had been ransacked.

Looking around, he saw his collected artifacts scattered about. Valuables had been tossed aside, but were still here. He couldn't be sure without an inventory, but Carson didn't think there was anything actually missing. Trashed yes, robbed no. But this didn't look like a college prank. Students might pull pranks like this—and worse—on each other, but he had never heard of it ever happening to a professor, not as a joke. Had somebody been looking for something?

Of course. Ducayne had warned him as much, although Carson hadn't taken that part of it very seriously. That cult, the Velkaryans, had tracked down his address and searched the place looking for the talisman. Of course they hadn't found it. They'd probably search his office next, he had better alert campus security.

He picked up his omni and started to call the university. What the heck was the number for security? Never mind. He called the main number. "Campus Security please." The comm system connected him.

"Campus Security, Rogers here."

"Rogers, this is Doctor Hannibal Carson, Department of Archeology—"

"Oh, yes Doctor, we were just going to call you."

"—I want you to . . . what? You were going to call me?"

"Yes, there was a break in at your office, looks a bit of a mess. One of our men happened to notice somebody in there and knew you were off campus this afternoon, so he got suspicious. Surprised somebody in there but he thumped our guy and got away. Empty handed as far as we know, but we'll need you to check."

Carson digested this for a moment. "Is your man all right?"

"Oh, he's fine, just a bump on the head and he's embarrassed as hell that they got the better of him. As he should be, I think." Rogers didn't sound too concerned. "Oh, but sir, you were calling us. How did you hear about it so quickly?"

"Actually, Rogers, I didn't. I was calling to ask you to send someone over to check my office. My apartment was just ransacked too."

"*What?* Really? Are you all right, Dr. Carson? Shall I get somebody over there?"

"No, no, I'm fine, I just came in and discovered the place like this." He panned his omni around to let Rogers see. "It's off campus, I'll let the police handle it."

"Whatever you want, sir. I'd be happy to send someone over. What's going on, though? Did you make an enemy of somebody?"

"I didn't think so, until just now." Carson hadn't, but with the memory of Ducayne's warning, he was rethinking that. He had a strong suspicion as to just who that enemy might be.

"Oh? Who, sir?" asked Rogers.

"Hmm? Oh, no idea really, just thinking that it is a bit too much of a coincidence. Never mind."

"If you say so. We do need you to come in to check if anything is missing from your office, and to sign the report."

"All right." Carson looked around his trashed apartment. he had better do something about that first, while he was here. "Let me get the police in here and do a bit of clean up first."

"Certainly, but as soon as you can, please. We don't want to touch much until you've seen it. Any time is fine, we're here twenty-six hours a day."

"All right, thank you, Rogers. I'll be there. Good bye."

"You welcome, good bye, sir."

Carson clicked off the connection, thoughtful now. The bad guys, whoever they were, seemed to be on to him. He had better get off planet quickly. But first, he had the mundane details to deal with. Still holding his omni, he thumbed the voice dial button and said: "Police, please."

∞ ∞ ∞

Rickon Maynard was in his office when his omni chimed. He checked the call info. Taggart. Maybe he'd had more success than Dominguez. He answered the call. "Yes?"

"Brother Maynard, the talisman was not in Carson's office, nor in the university storage. We checked the records, and we searched it physically. We were very thorough."

"Are you sure?"

"Yes, sir. Security came by just at the end, but we had finished searching."

"Damn. Dominguez said his apartment was clear, too. Double damn. It was in the list of artifacts from the expedition. Carson was the lead. Who else would have it?" Taggart was smart enough to say nothing. Maynard balled a fist and thumped his desk. "Do you suppose he has it with him?" That was a long shot.

"I wouldn't have thought so, but if he knows what it represents—"

"Exactly. We'd better cover that possibility too." Maynard said. If he *did* know, there had been a bad leak, but then they had already suspected that, and they had dealt with it.

"I'll have it taken care of, sir."

"Good. The sooner the better."

"Ah, sir. There was something else."

"Yes? What?"

"He's arranging another trip. His teaching schedule has been rearranged, he's ordering equipment, and he's booked on a shuttle to Kakuloa."

"Kakuloa? There's nothing on Kakuloa. It's only a few hours away, why rearrange his schedule?" Maynard considered this. A vacation perhaps? So soon after his last trip? That didn't make sense, and it wouldn't explain the equipment. "He must be going somewhere else from there." Damn, he *had to* know.

"I don't know why he's going, but it is sudden."

"Yes. Suspicious." Maynard mulled this over for a moment. "Okay, intercept him before that, see if he has it with him. If not, we'll need to keep an eye on him. Get to Kakuloa before he does. He hasn't left yet, right? Find out who he talks to, who he sees. Report back the moment you find out anything."

"Very well. I'll get on it."

"Good." Maynard clicked off.

∞ ∞ ∞

Two large men approached Carson as he crossed the campus that evening. They wore dark suits, clearly neither students nor faculty.

"Doctor Carson?"

Carson studied them before answering. They looked fit, tough in fact, with a vague air of officialdom. He wondered if they were Homeworld Security types.

"Yes? What can I do for you?"

"Come with us." The speaker grabbed Carson's arm in a strong grip.

Carson tried to shake it loose. "Where to? Who are you?" Government agents wouldn't be so abrupt, would they? And if they weren't government agents . . . He started to pay closer attention to detail.

"Never mind, just come along." The grip on his arm tightened. On his right, the other man pulled a hand from a pocket far enough so Carson could see the gun it was holding, then slipped it back into his pocket. Carson had little choice but to accompany them, at least for now.

Chapter 11: Repairs Complete

Kiahuna Shipyard, Kakuloa orbit

"THERE YOU GO, Jackie, she's all taken care of. Should be good for another five years or five hundred parsecs."

"Thanks. Are you putting a guarantee on that?"

"Sure, but the fine print voids it the first time you go to warp." Joe grinned as he said that, but Jackie knew that for all practical purposes it was true. If something went seriously wrong with ship systems in interstellar space, odds were you'd never get back to complain about it. She would run her own diagnostics before engaging the warp modules. "Anything else we can do for you or the *Sophie*?" he asked.

"No, that will do it for this trip."

"Where are you headed now?"

"Down to the surface for a day or two of R and R. I'm waiting to hear on a job. If that doesn't come through then I'll see what I can pick up for Tau Ceti and head back. But let me know if you hear anything, okay?"

"Sure Jackie, will do."

Back aboard the *Sophie*, Jackie did a systems check and prepared to debark. The airdock bay doors were open behind her, and the shipyard computers eased the *Sophie* back out and away from the station. On the planet below, the city of Kreschets Landing was visible to the west, and the blue expanse of ocean stretching beyond it faded into the blue glow of the atmosphere at the horizon. Pretty, but not the best angle for an approach. Jackie took control of the *Sophie* and swung her around. Kakuloa's sunset line was still a couple of hours east of the city. That gave her enough time to do a once-around orbit to reenter over the ocean and still land in daylight, rather than having to fly a retrograde approach with the sun in her eyes. Perfect. She dropped the *Sophie* away from the shipyards and began to set up the de-orbit burn. It would feel good to hit the beach.

Chapter 12: Mugged

Sawyer City

CARSON GLANCED around. No obvious sources of help, nor was there any refuge near enough that he could afford to ignore the gun, even if the gunman were slowed by pulling it from a pocket to aim. He went along with them, resisting enough to be a nuisance, but not so much they wanted to shoot him there in the open. His mind raced.

"So, are we going somewhere for a meal? I was thinking about dinner just now."

The thug holding his arm just squeezed tighter, muttered "shut up!" and dragged him to move a him little faster.

They rounded a corner, a little-used alleyway between two buildings. The big man to Carson's left—Carson tagged him Bad Guy One—abruptly turned and slammed him against the wall. "All right, Carson, where is it?"

"*Oof.*" Carson grunted at the impact. "Where is what?" He suspected he knew.

Bad Guy One punched Carson in the gut, knocking the wind out of him. "Don't get smart. You know what."

Carson gasped for breath. "No." Breathe. "No, really, it would help if I knew what you were talking abou—*Oof!*" He was cut off by a vicious backhand across the face, and he tasted blood.

"You found it on Ransom's Planet, at Zeta Tucanae. A talisman, about so big," Bad Guy One, the questioner, held thumb and forefinger about ten centimeters apart. "Stones and engravings on it. Where is it?" He gestured to his partner. "Pat him down, see if he's carrying it." His partner proceeded to do just that.

"Oh, that thing." This was his chance. The thug who was in the process of roughly frisking him had pocketed his gun, and his questioner wasn't holding one. Even if Questioner had a gun, the frisker was between them, it would interfere with the line of fire. Carson readied himself, waiting for the right moment. Rattling them a little would help. "It was bogus," he said, "totally wrong century. We threw it out."

The questioner's eyes bugged out and it looked like he might have a stroke right there on the spot. *That would improve the odds,* thought Carson.

Instead the man yelled. "Liar! No archeologist would do that!" He raised a hand to slap him again, just as Frisker had squatted to run his hands down Carson's pant legs. *Now!* Carson moved.

He grabbed Questioner's wrist, the arm that was swinging toward him, and at the same time he snapped his right knee up to slam into Frisker's face, connecting with a solid thump.

Frisker fell back on his butt, off balance and stunned by the knee to his face.

Carson pulled Questioner's arm in the direction it was going and ducked sideways out of the way, using his opponent's momentum against him. The man lost his balance and took a half-turning step away to recover.

Frisker was on his back, knees bent, scooting backward to get room. His hand scrabbled in his pocket, the gun pocket, trying to draw the weapon.

Carson saw the move. He saw the obvious best target and kicked Frisker hard in the crotch. The man spasmed, curling into a ball, everything clenched. There was a sharp *bang!* Frisker must have pulled the trigger.

Carson didn't have time to focus on that. The other thug had continued his turn and, his back toward Carson, jabbed his elbow into Carson's gut. He folded and staggered back.

The big man continued his turn and grabbed Carson's collar, punching him hard in the face with his other fist. Hannibal staggered again and his weight pulled them to the side, off balance.

They both tried to take a step to compensate, but Frisker was there. He writhed and groaned on the ground, blood pooling around him. It looked like he'd shot himself; in the leg, if he was lucky. Carson and the thug stumbled over Frisker's body and fell to the ground together.

Carson turned on the ground and, still on his side, brought his upper leg around and kicked Questioner solidly in the jaw. Carson heard the teeth slam together. He scrambled to his feet just as Questioner made a grab at him again.

Carson wasn't having any of it. He caught the wrist and twisted the thug's arm hard. With the wrist in his right hand, he grabbed the fingers in his left and brought the whole down sharply across his knee. He heard and felt a sickening crunch as bones cracked and joints popped.

Questioner screamed and cursed.

Carson dropped the arm, pushing Questioner to the ground again. The thug immediately started tugging with his good hand to get the gun out of Frisker's now blood-soaked pocket.

Carson shook his head, partly to clear it, partly in disbelief. This guy was persistent! He took a step and stomped hard on the gun hand, then for good measure kicked the man in the head to make sure he was out. Frisker had stopped twitching, he had probably passed out from blood loss.

Hannibal staggered back, leaning against the wall, breathing hard, trying to catch his breath. He was more angry than scared, still trembling from the adrenalin surge. "Nobody," he said to the unlistening bodies, "*nobody* fucking threatens me, and certainly not on my own fucking campus!"

He limped back around the corner of the building, gradually becoming aware of the ache in his guts, the lump on his head where it had slammed against the wall, the salty taste of blood in his mouth from the slaps and punches, and a sharp pain in his left shin. How had he gotten that? He didn't know.

The pain increased as the adrenaline wore off. The campus infirmary was a half block away, and he limped off in that direction.

It occurred to him to call Campus Security, to have them come pick up his assailants before they regained consciousness and got away. Or perhaps it would be to take the bodies to the morgue. He didn't think he had hit Questioner *that* hard, or that Frisker had bled to death just yet, but maybe he would get lucky. Hannibal was in a foul mood. *Bastards!*

∞ ∞ ∞

Two hours later Carson sat in the Security office, still a little sore from the fight. He had just finished making his report; earlier the medic at the infirmary had skin-glued his cut lip, sprayed on several bandages and given him a couple of painkillers. It occurred to him that these guys might try again.

Not Frisker, though. He had, as one of the Security guys bluntly put it, "just about shot his own balls off." The bullet had penetrated both that delicate portion of his anatomy and his left leg, narrowly missing the femoral artery. Carson didn't know whether to be sad that it missed—the man would have bled to death too quickly for anything to have saved him in that case—or happy that he had survived to enjoy the rearrangement of his anatomy. So, not Frisker, but there were no doubt more where he came from, and they'd be more careful next time.

He had better get off-planet, and the sooner the better. One thing about interstellar travel, with ships being the fastest means of communication available, there was no worry of your troubles waiting at your destination to meet you.

∞ ∞ ∞

Maynard's man Taggart hadn't heard about Frisker and Questioner. He was already on his way to Kakuloa.

Chapter 13: Old Friends

Kreschet Spaceport, Kakuloa

JACKIE ROBERTS lay sprawled on her bunk aboard the Sophie, still mostly asleep, when her omni bleated at her. She groaned, half opened one eye to glare at it, and thought about ignoring it. She had brought the *Sophie* down late yesterday, intending to hit the famous Kakuloa beach for some sun and surf, but her sleep schedule was out of sync with the planet's rotation, or at least with this part of the planet. The omni bleated again. That was the business ring tone, probably following up on the message she had got yesterday from Sawyers about a possible charter. She couldn't afford to frustrate potential customers by not answering.

She propped herself up on one elbow and grabbed the omni with her free hand, glancing at the call information. Hannibal Carson? She had never expected to hear from him again. Why was *he* calling her, and why was he on Kakuloa? Jackie blinked a few times and took a couple of deep breaths, oxygenating her brain and waking herself up. "*Sophie* Space Charters, Roberts speaking, how can I help you?" she said, more cheerfully than she felt.

There was silence. For a moment Jackie thought she had lost the connection. Then: "Jackie? Jackie Roberts? *You*'re *Sophie* Space Charters?"

Jackie felt a knot in her gut and groaned inwardly. "*Sophie* is the name of my ship. Please don't tell me that you're my charter." The last time she had flown with Carson—she had been the XO, not the captain—the trip had not ended well.

"It would seem so. I need to get to Taprobane and on from there."

Jackie was tempted to say something about already being booked, take a scheduled flight, sorry maybe next time, but she did need a job right now. "I may have schedule conflicts." It never hurt to leave an out. "What exactly did you have in mind?"

"I need to pick up something at Taprobane. Epsilon Indi."

"I know where Taprobane is."

"Of course you do. Anyway, that will give me the coordinates for the next leg of the trip."

"Why should I take you anywhere, Carson? You almost got me killed."

"I got you rescued," Carson protested.

"*Rescued!* If you'd just given them what they asked for I wouldn't have needed rescuing."

"Given them . . . Those were unique artifacts! I couldn't just turn them over to tomb raiders." Carson paused and shook his head. "Not that you were ever in real danger."

"*No real danger?* That's easy for you to say, Carson. You weren't the one locked up—" Jackie shuddered as the memory came unbidden. She had been bound and gagged, and locked in a dark windowless room. She shook it off. That was in the past.

"I—"

"No, I don't want to hear it," Jackie said, her tone becoming businesslike. "So how dangerous is this trip going to be? Or is it merely illegal?"

"Dangerous? No," Carson said, far too casually. "Just a routine investigation of a site I heard something interesting about. Pick up a few artifacts, you know."

"Then why do I get the feeling that you're lying through your teeth?"

"No, really. I'm not expecting any specific danger."

"'Specific', huh? That's what you said about Raven's Rift. And you didn't answer the part about 'not illegal'."

"I play it straighter these days, and there's no Department of Antiquities where we're going. I don't even think it's inhabited."

"I thought you didn't know the final destination?"

"Well, not exactly, but I have a strong hunch. Listen, let's meet somewhere and we can go over the details."

"Oh, all right." She could always say no later. *Like you've ever said no to Hannibal Carson*, the thought drifted up. *Shut up,* she told herself. "Anywhere," she said aloud, "as long as there's coffee involved; even better if there's breakfast."

"Fair enough, where are you now?"

"The spaceport." There was only one active spaceport on the planet, between the soured economy and the other continent off-limits because of the natives—although there was still debate as to whether the tree-squids deserved to be considered sentient natives or just intelligent animals. "It has a restaurant," Jackie said.

"All right, I just landed at the spaceport myself. The restaurant in the port building, then?"

"Sure."

They made their arrangements and Jackie clicked off her omni. She rolled back onto bed, staring up at the overhead, and wondered what she might be letting herself in for. *At least it's a job.* She forced herself out of bed and into the fresher. The hot shower revived her.

Out of the shower and feeling more human, she started to get dressed. *Casual or the dress uniform?* For a first meeting with a potential customer she would normally wear the dress uniform, it inspired confidence, but Jackie wasn't even sure if it was in a fit state to wear. The shipboard laundry system was fine for shipwear but did a lousy job on anything more formal. Screw it, it was only Carson, not someone she needed—or even wanted—to impress. The casual.

∞ ∞ ∞

To Jackie's enormous relief the waitress brought them coffee as soon as they sat down, its strong coffee aroma alone stimulating her brain cells like a beat to quarters. They quickly ordered breakfast—Jackie getting the scrambled eggs and sausage, and both of them asking for sweet rolls—and talked while waiting for the food to be delivered.

"So you have your own ship now?" said Carson.

"That's right." Jackie took a sip of her coffee, savoring the hot smoky taste. "It's an older model, but she's had some modifications."

"Oh? Tell me about her. Why *Sophie*, by the way?"

"*Sophie?* Two reasons. One, the ship was named *Surprise* when I bought her, but I didn't think that was the best name for a charter." Jackie paused, watching as Carson lifted his coffee mug to his lips. "In general, passengers don't like surprises."

Carson choked on the coffee he was sipping. He grabbed a napkin to wipe up what he had sprayed. Jackie hid her grin.

"There was a series of old time sailing ship adventures I read as a kid. My father had a leather bound set. It was a prized possession, printed on real paper. O'Brian, the author was. In the books, the captain's ship was the *Surprise*, but earlier in the series he'd commanded the *Sophie*. Hence the name."

Carson recovered from nearly inhaling his coffee, and, not without some wariness, asked: "And the second reason?"

"Oh, from the fact that it's a Mitsubishi Sapphire. Sophie, sapphire, they sound similar. They don't build them like that anymore."

"Strongly built?"

"Amazingly so."

"Here you go, gentles." The waitress appeared with their food. "Let's see, you had the eggs and sausage," she said, setting the plate down in front of Roberts, "and sweet rolls for both of you. More coffee?" She produced a coffee pot. Jackie wondered how she had managed to carry all that to the table. At their nods, the waitress topped up their cups then returned back to wherever she had come.

"Where were we?" Jackie asked, and took a bite of sausage, savoring the spicy, meaty flavor. "Mmm, these are wonderful!"

Carson looked at her plate, hesitated, then "They do look good. May I?" He picked up a fork.

"Sure, take one. They're a bit spicy though."

Carson speared a sausage on his fork and took a bite. His eyes widened, and his forehead glistened with a sheen of sweat. "I see what you mean." He gulped his coffee. "Good, though. What's the spice?"

Jackie grinned. She had thought he might know, with Kakuloa being so close to his home base on Sawyers World, but apparently not. "Oh, no spices at all. The animal's indigenous here and the meat is loaded with a kind of capsaicin variant, probably to discourage predators."

Carson shook his head and gulped down more coffee. "I should have known better than to ask about how sausage is made. And the eggs?"

"Just chicken eggs. The local birds don't take to domestication. I think some of them still have teeth."

Carson looked thoughtful for a moment, perhaps regretting he ever brought it up. "You were telling me about the *Sophie*."

"Oh, right," Jackie said around a mouthful of scrambled egg. "Well, an old Sapphire hull. I had the fusion unit upgraded with an electrolysis insert and converted the hydrogen tanks over to water. It gives me about another seven light-years range." She paused to take another bite.

"How is that? Wouldn't storing straight liquid hydrogen be more efficient?"

Jackie nodded and swallowed, then took a sip of coffee to wash it down. "Old fashioned thinking. It is, in terms of energy per kilogram. The thing is, a warp ship isn't weight limited, it's volume limited . . ."

"Sure, everyone knows that."

"So the neat thing about water—aside from it's being much more readily available and easier to handle—is that a liter of water holds more hydrogen than a liter of liquid hydrogen, so I actually get about fifty percent more hydrogen in the same size tank. It's standard these days, but most models reduce the fuel tankage and increase the living space. The power for the electrolysis is negligible."

"Ah. I see." Carson was staring into his coffee cup. She wondered if he was even listening.

Jackie wrapped it up. "Of course, the tanks will still hold hydrogen, so I can still refuel from a gas giant if I have to, but in most systems water or ice is easy to find." She quickly scooped up another forkful of scrambled eggs, to get another bite before Carson asked more questions.

"Well, good, the range might come in handy." Hannibal nursed his coffee and looked thoughtful, as if wondering how to broach the details of the charter.

Jackie took advantage of the opportunity to finish her breakfast. She wiped her mouth with a napkin and set it down on her plate. Almost instantly the waitress appeared at the table to clear the plate away, leaving the sweet roll on its small plate, and offering a refill on the coffee.

"How do you *do* that?" Jackie asked her.

"Do what, ma'm?"

"Appear and disappear like magic. Know when to refill the coffee."

The waitress grinned. "All part of the service," she said, not answering the question, and turned to remove the dirty dishes to wherever they got removed to.

Weird. Jackie shook her head, then looked across the table to Carson. It was time to find out what he really had in mind. "Okay, Carson, what's up?"

Carson set his cup down and leaned forward, clasping his hands together on the table in front of him. "Well, first of all we need to go to Epsilon Indi, to meet with Marten—"

"Who?" The name sounded familiar, but Jackie couldn't place it. Perhaps she'd heard it from Carson before.

"You remember, the timoan archeologist who worked with me on the Rift. Oh, wait, that was a different expedition."

"Nice, Carson. It's all just one big dig to you. Timoan, girlfriend," she cringed inwardly at the word, but it had been true enough then, "whoever, they're just someone in the background when you're on a site. Did tomb raiders kidnap him for ransom, too?" Carson had made some unique finds that trip. A band of black marketeers had hoped to trade her for the artifacts, and that bastard Carson had refused. Jackie picked up her fork and stabbed it down into her roll.

Carson blinked. "Uh, actually . . ." Jackie glared at him. "Um, no." He picked up his coffee cup, then put it down again without drinking. "Anyway, Marten is an archeologist I've partnered with before, on several different trips. I want to go to Taprobane and meet with him. I'm hoping to persuade him to come along, but in any case he has a talisman we picked up on a recent dig that I'd like to take another look at."

"Oh?" Jackie took a bite of the sweet roll and another sip of coffee. She didn't sugar her coffee, enjoying the interplay of flavors between the sticky sweetness of the roll and the slightly bitter taste of the coffee. She focused on that for the moment, shifting her attention back to the job at hand. "What's the significance of the talisman?"

"Well, let me give you some background. What do you know about this corner of the galaxy?" Carson began.

Roberts just gave him a look. "I'm a pilot and a damn good astrogator." She stabbed her fork into the sweetroll again. "I probably know more about it than you do."

"Sorry, I meant the history, or rather, prehistory."

"Same as everyone else. Most of the Earthlike planets we've found seem to have been deliberately terraformed and seeded with Earth life, about sixty-five million years ago. Nobody knows by whom. Since we haven't found any dinosaurs, it probably wasn't them. What's your point?"

"Okay, that's farther back than I meant. Actually some people would argue about the dinosaurs, but that's a side issue. I was referring to the ruins found on various planets."

Jackie started to feel like she was in school again and was thankful for the temporary reprieve when the waitress came by with a pot.

"More coffee, gentles?" she asked and, at their nods, refilled their cups. "Can I get you anything else?"

"Not just now, thank you," Carson said. He sipped the hot liquid and turned his attention back to Jackie. "So, what else?"

"Well, to date we haven't found any signs of prehistoric spacefarers on Earth or anywhere in the Solar system, or any indication of who or what did the terraforming." Jackie paused. "Does this have something to do with the Terraformers?"

Hannibal put his cup down slowly, a thoughtful expression on his face. "That's one theory, and it's one that has Homeworld Security nervous."

"I can understand that." Indeed, the Terraformers must have had fantastic technology. If any caches of that were still around, there would be serious implications if it fell into the wrong hands. But, Carson hadn't finished. "You don't think that's it, though," said Jackie.

"No, it doesn't make sense. The time scale is all wrong—sixty-five million years is geological ages, time enough for continents to drift and mountain ranges to rise or fall—at least on the more geologically active planets."

"Like Earth."

"Yes. And most of those terraformed planets *are* like Earth. There may well have been more of them, but some didn't stay terraformed."

"Okay, and?"

"My point is," said Carson, jabbing at the table with his index finger for emphasis, "that these artifacts are probably no more than a few tens of thousands of years old. I found the remains of a high-tech artifact on Delta Pavonis. It was fifteen thousand years old."

"Really? What was it?"

"I don't know yet. The point is, there was another spacefaring species that visited—or arose in—this area of space. They might even have visited Earth, we'd probably have been in the depths of an ice age, just as we were for most of the Pleistocene."

That was out of Jackie's field. Carson was the archeologist; she'd take his word for it. Still, there was a point he had glossed over. "But that's still a spacefaring race, wouldn't they have advanced and possibly dangerous technology too?"

"Of course. I'm not implying that Homeworld Security shouldn't be nervous, just that they should be nervous for the right reasons." Carson sat back and finished his coffee with a gulp.

Jackie pondered this. She was still missing some key information. "Okay, but you still haven't explained how this talisman ties in."

"Oh yes, that. What's left of the one I recently found is similar to one that we recovered at Zeta Tucanae. That one was in wonderful condition. The one from Verdigris is damaged and worn. This raises the intriguing question of how an apparently primitive artifact—except that it wasn't—has a twin on a planet light-years distant. Also, the faces of the objects have patterns or diagrams on them, dots marked by small colored stones connected with lines." Carson pulled out his omni, unfolded the screen and sketched a quick diagram on it. "Could be anything. An abstract design, a sort of Polynesian shell and stick map, a circuit diagram, or it might also represent a constellation or star chart."

"So you think it's a clue to the location of something more significant?"

"Exactly." Carson's eyes were bright.

"And you know how to interpret it?"

Carson's shoulders slumped. "Ah, no. I was hoping you could help with that. As you said, you're a damn good astrogator, you probably know T-space as well as anyone."

"So you want me to decipher it?" That could be challenging. Over thousands of years, stars would have drifted. A two-dimensional projection of objects scattered in three-dimensional space would also be a difficult match without knowing the point of view it was drawn from. "That may take some time."

"If it is a star map, then you're the one to do it."

"That will cost extra," Roberts said with a straight face.

Carson shook his head and chuckled. "I assume that means you'll take the charter?"

Jackie sighed, wondering what she was getting herself into. But the opportunity sounded too good to pass up. Damn it, she never could say no to Hannibal. "Yes it does. When do we leave?"

Chapter 14: Departure Preparations

Kreschet Spaceport, Kakuloa

THEY SCHEDULED departure for two days hence. Jackie still wanted some down time. She also needed to reorganize the ship, to lay in supplies and make sure there'd be enough room for Carson, his gear, and any other passengers they might pick up on the way. She might as well see if she could pick up any business on the side, too. She keyed her omni.

"Flight Information Office, Chang speaking, how can I help you?"

"This is Jackie Roberts of the *Sophie,* headed out to the Epsilon Indi system tomorrow. I'm putting the flight plan in now. I wanted to see if you had anything for me."

"Hey Jackie. Let me check." Jackie heard the tapping of fingers on a keyboard. "The *Celestial Princess* departed for there two days ago, so probably not much. Oh, wait, I'm seeing several exabytes of new data on the netcache. That's right, we got new Sol data traffic on the ship that came in to Sawyers World."

The netcache was a snapshot of a system's internet data, at least that which the owners wanted to make public or to transmit to out-system recipients. An intelligent versioning system tracked when the local copies of off-planet data were last updated, when local data was last sent off-planet, and where it was sent. Ships licensed to do so—it required the necessary secure computer gear and background checks for the crew—could earn fees by downloading the appropriate changes between what the netcache held now and what the versioning system thought was in the destination's netcache, then uploading it when it reached the destination.

Once there, that system's versioning AI would sort out what was actually new to it and make the appropriate updates.

"If you have the space I'll start the transfer now and you can do a final delta when you depart," Chang continued.

"Let me check." Jackie keyed a sequence on her control panel. "Okay, I'm good to go, it's ready to download."

"Connected and transferring. I see your flight plan in the system now too. Have a good one."

Jackie ended the call, then keyed the number for the Customs office. She was a bonded courier for small cargo, too—anything to help cover costs—and there might be something waiting to go.

"Sorry, Jackie," the outbound Customs agent told her. "We had a good couple of cubic meters of packages and a crate bound for Taprobane a few days ago, but that all left on the *Princess*. There's a small packet that came in yesterday, but that's all."

Damn. That story was getting more and more frequent; there was just too much traffic between the settled stars these days. "Okay, thanks, I'll swing by and pick it up just before departure tomorrow. There aren't any other couriers departing before then, are there?"

"Not that I'm aware of, not for Epsilon Indi. Epsilon Eridani, yes, and Sol, all kinds of traffic to there."

"Yeah, slightly different direction. All right, thanks. I'll check back again tomorrow, just in case."

∞ ∞ ∞

An athletic figure, Hopkins' man Rico, connected to the public flight control database and queried flight plans scheduled in the next forty-eight hours. He scanned the resulting list until he found the *Sophie*'s and began reading the details. "Passengers: Hannibal Carson." Yes, that was good. Skip over the usual equipment details, ship type, license details, etc. "Destination: Taprobane, Epsilon Indi." There, that was what he was looking for. He logged off, then keyed in a number.

"Hello?"

"Boss, this is Rico. Roberts filed a flight plan to Taprobane. Carson's on it. Departure time is tomorrow."

"Good work. Get back to the ship, we need to be ready for takeoff."

∞ ∞ ∞

Maynard listened to the tapped conversation and clicked off. In theory tapping the omniphone network was virtually impossible, but *something* had to route the message packets, even if only through the aether, and Maynard's group had associates in network operations. He thought about what he had overheard. So, Carson was going to Epsilon Indi. What or who is on Taprobane? he wondered. *Aside from too many filthy timoans.* And why is that antiquities black marketeer interested? Maynard considered this. It would make sense for a character like Hopkins to keep track of field archeologists. Maybe he could use that to his advantage.

He called his own ship. "Make ready for takeoff, we're heading for Epsilon Indi."

∞ ∞ ∞

Carson hurled his omni across his small hotel room, bouncing it off the wall. "Of all the pea-brained, small minded, bureaucratic, officious . . . dolts!" Just then the door buzzer sounded.

"Enter!" Carson shouted.

The door slid open. Jackie Roberts stood in the doorway. "Am I interrupting something? I heard shouting."

"Just me." Carson picked up his omni and looked it over, then at the small dent he'd left in the wall. "I swear they don't make these things like they used to."

Roberts entered the room and looked at what Carson had been examining. "What, they used to make bigger dents? So what was that all about?"

"Message from the supply department at the university. I requisitioned some gear, and they don't want to ship it here. Say I need to check it out in person or pre-authorize—again in person—the shipping."

"So? Sawyer's only a couple of hours away." Most of that was getting to and from space; the warp jump took about twenty seconds. "Take a shuttle and I'll come pick you up tomorrow on the way out-system. Or tell them what you need and we'll both head there tomorrow."

"Never mind, I'll just pull the gear together here. I'll find a local outfitter."

"Why here? I can take you back to Sawyers to pick up your gear from the university and you can get the rest of what you need from your usual supplier."

Carson said nothing for a moment. He looked down at the floor, then back up at Jackie. "Ah, I should probably stay away from Sawyer City for a while."

Jackie leaned against the wall and folded her arms. "So, does this have to do with the 'no specific danger' you didn't want to talk about? And the glued cut on your lip?"

Carson raised a hand to his face and turned to look in the mirror on the closet door. The cut was mostly healed, but still visible. "What?"

"I noticed it at breakfast. I didn't think it was worth mentioning then." She strode over to him and took his right hand, looking at the knuckles. "Spray-on bandage?"

Carson snatched his hand back. "A slight difference of opinion."

"What aren't you telling me, Carson?" Her eyes probed his.

"Noth—"

"The truth, Carson."

"All right." Carson looked away for a moment, then back to her. "My apartment and office were ransacked, and a couple of guys mugged me on campus."

"Ditched girlfriend's brothers, perhaps? I can sympathize. With them."

Carson shook his head. "You ditched me, Jackie." She started at that, but he kept talking. "No. They were probably looking for the artifact we're going to Taprobane to get."

Roberts swore. "I wish you'd told me that sooner. I filed a flight plan. Anyone can find out where we're going."

"Probably nobody knows I'm even here, let alone that I'm booking your charter. But can't you change or cancel it?"

"I could, but I also agreed to courier a package there. I could cancel that too with a good enough reason, but even a cancelled flight plan is a clue to where we planned to go." Jackie paced the room, then turned back to Carson. "Never mind, it's done. What are you going to do about your gear?"

"I'll just buy it here. I checked the local web while waiting for a response from Sawyers. There are some good deals available, especially on used gear."

"Yeah, the outfitters are moving closer to the frontier. Just be careful on the used stuff."

"I know. By the way, why are you here? Was there something you needed?"

"You promised to buy me dinner, remember?"

Had he? "Uh, of course. Let's go."

∞ ∞ ∞

Jackie added an entry to the manifest on the small wallscreen next to the aft compartment. She and Carson were stowing his newly acquired gear—an assortment of all-weather clothing, hiking and climbing gear, tents, excavation tools, recorders, medkits, ration bars, even snowshoes and diving gear—and the challenge was in imposing some kind of logical order to it all.

"I hope there isn't too much more," Jackie said.

"No, I—" Carson began, just as the chime of his omni interrupted. He looked at it, read what was apparently an incoming message, and then swore.

"More problems?"

"You could say that. Apparently the supply department heard about the mugging and the break-in at my office and took pity on me. The gear I asked them for just arrived on the shuttle. There are two crates waiting for me to pick them up."

Jackie rolled her eyes. "Good thing I reorganized the ships stores and lockers yesterday. Let's see what you've got." She turned to the computer screen. Carson touched his omni then waved it across the screen, which lit up with a list of equipment. Jackie tapped the screen, popping up the list of gear Carson had bought on Kakuloa, then tapped the two lists and merged them. Jackie scanned the result and let out a low whistle. Even if they eliminated the duplicates, that was a lot of gear. "Is there anything you're *not* ready for?" she asked, amused.

"I certainly hope not. I'm assuming you have suits for vacuum work?"

"Space suits? Of course, but why would you need space suits? There can't be any archeological sites on airless worlds."

"Hah. If we found one, that would prove my hypothesis. No, I don't expect to need them. Frankly I don't expect to need half this stuff, but I don't know which half."

"Okay." Jackie looked at the lists again, then at the aft compartment and around the *Sophie*'s cabin. It would be tighter than she liked, but with only a couple of passengers it would be manageable. "Let's go get those crates and finish loading."

∞ ∞ ∞

In the end Carson refilled one crate with duplicate and excess gear and arranged for that to be sent back on the shuttle. With some judicious rearranging, they managed to stow everything else aboard.

"Ah. Well, is that the last of it?"

"Just my personal bags. Where's my cabin?" said Carson, looking around.

"Cabin? You're in it. Your *berth* is that one," Jackie pointed to the lower of two horizontal, closet-sized cubicles. "This isn't a big ship, and you've taken up half of it with your gear." Okay, that was an exaggeration. "But you can get your privacy," she touched a button and a screen slid down, touched it again and it rolled up out of the way, "and there's room to read, or you can slave your omni into the ship's network. The galley is aft."

"Um, right. Thank you." Carson slung his bags onto the bunk. "And where's yours?"

What? Was he suggesting . . . ? "Not that it matters to you, *Doctor* Carson, but my *cabin*, the *captain's* cabin, is forward, just aft of the control deck. It's off-limits, as is the control deck unless I say otherwise. Clear?"

"Ah, abundantly so." Carson said, chagrined. "I don't know what you thought I meant," that was a lie, and they both knew it, "but I wanted to know in case of an emergency." That sounded truthful.

Had she misjudged? "Oh." She regained her composure. "Well, in that case, simply yelling 'Captain!' should get my attention. The ship's computer will wake me if I'm asleep." Jackie wondered if she were blushing, her face felt warm. She was also trying to decide which interpretation of his question she felt more insulted by.

∞ ∞ ∞

Departure time. Jackie stepped out of the ship and scanned the *Sophie* with a practiced eye. The area was clear of debris, and there were no tie downs, fuel lines or umbilical cables still connected. She went over to the hull then crouched down and peered up underneath it. Nope, no small animals had taken up residence in the landing gear wells or built nests in the lifting thrusters. She began her walk around the ship counter-clockwise. Whenever she passed a maintenance hatch or inspection port cover she gave it a tug to check that it was secure. The aerodynamic control surface clamps had been removed, the aft thrusters were clear, and no red REMOVE BEFORE FLIGHT ribbons fluttered in the gentle breeze. Every time Jackie did a walk around, even a quick one like this, she remembered the time in flight school when she had almost, *almost*, flown off in an aeroplane with its fuel cap still open. Her instructor had made sure that Jackie never forgot again. Finding nothing that would be embarrassing if it caused an aborted takeoff, Jackie re-entered the ship. She closed and secured the hatch behind her.

"All right then, Doctor," she said, moving up to sit in her pilot's chair, "take a seat." She gestured at the empty seats behind her. "Strap in, and let's get this show on the road."

As Carson strapped himself in, Jackie went through her preflight checklist, tapping out instructions on the console keyboard, checking the displays, and ensuring the controls were functional. Fuel tanks full, check ship mass—she glanced at the display, double checked that the weight-on-gear sensors were using *this* planet's gravity to do the calculations—circuits check, fusion generator on line. All go. She gently applied power to the thrusters and opened the intake scoops, mixing air into the exhaust to quiet and cool it. She eased the power up to take about half the weight off the landing gear, then called ground control.

"Kreschet Ground, this is *Sophie*, requesting clearance for hover taxi to the pad." You didn't just blast straight out of the parking area; that was hazardous to people and ships on the ground nearby and likely to get your licenses and permits suspended.

"Affirm *Sophie*, cleared to pad five, contact tower on 127.3"

"*Sophie*, pad five, contact 127.3, roger and thank you." Jackie increased thrust, lifting the ship gently until it hovered a meter above the ground then glided across the field to a circular paved area with a large and rather scorched numeral 5 painted on it.

She flipped the comm to the new frequency. "Kreschet Tower, *Sophie* requesting clearance to lift."

"Roger *Sophie*, cleared for lift at your discretion. Contact departure on 119.7 above ten thousand. Have a safe trip."

"Thank you, Tower. At my discretion, departure on 119.7 above ten K." Jackie glanced over to Carson. "Buckled in?" At Carson's nod, she smoothly increased power and the *Sophie* leapt into the air, powering skyward. Jackie tapped a control, causing the ship to vibrate and clunk briefly as the landing skids retracted, then she pitched the ship toward space and throttled up the aft thrusters. The acceleration pushed them down and back into their seats. As the altimeter neared 10,000 meters she flipped the comm to departure control, got clearance from them to orbit, and as the ship cleared the atmosphere she signed off with a "thank you, and please open the flight plan."

The flight plan was a formality. She would get to Epsilon Indi before it did . . . unless she didn't get there at all. In the latter case some records would be entered and some statistics updated, but the impracticality of an interstellar search meant that nobody would think much more about it. The exception would be if the ship showed up somewhere without a registered transfer of ownership, but anyone in the business of hijacking a starship probably knew enough to fix that.

"Roger *Sophie*, catch you on the return. Have a good one."

Jackie didn't exactly *enjoy* dealing with the bureaucracy of space traffic control, but at least they were always polite. She piloted the ship away from Kakuloa and began preparing for the transition to warp. It would take just over a week to reach Taprobane.

Chapter 15: Marten

Taprobane (Epsilon Indi III)

CLARKEVILLE ALWAYS reminded Carson of an Earth theme park. The human-timoan settlement, on the large island of Borealia, was built to resemble the native towns on the mainland. The stone buildings of Kangara University dominated the town. Not one of them was more than three stories high; timoans tended not to like heights. Most of the other buildings, the residences, shops and so forth of any small town, were one- or two-story structures with wood or thatched roofs. Behind that outward appearance, though, were systems for modern plumbing, electricity and communications, and much of the stone and thatch was simulated with concrete and synthetics. For all their apparent age, the oldest building in the town had been constructed less than twenty-five years ago. The cobblestone streets held only a few vehicles. The town was less than three kilometers square, so anything needed was within walking distance. Carson knew that the rumored tunnel with motorized carts running between the main university building and the spaceport was mythical, a joke played on naive freshmen.

Which was unfortunate, thought Carson, as he walked up to the *Pragarth Maga*, as the main pub on campus was called. The name translated to something like "albino deer." It had been a bit of a hike from the spaceport.

Carson entered the pub feeling only a little out of place. He tried to avoid student hangouts on campus, as a rule, but Kangara wasn't *his* campus, and he expected that he would find Marten here tonight. He looked around, trying to spot his old friend while studiously ignoring the interested look from a pair of young human coed students sitting at a table near the door. Several humans and timoans sat at other tables, but they ignored Carson's entrance. There was Marten, at the bar, shorter than the average human, with blue-gray hair, and where his clothing didn't cover him, finer fur the same color. He was drinking a . . . just what *was* that anyway? Perhaps feeling the attention, Marten looked up in the bar mirror to meet Carson's eye.

"Hannibal!" Marten said, as he turned and stood up from his bar stool. "What are you doing here? You should have called, told me you were coming!"

"How?" asked Hannibal, somewhat amused. Marten tended to forget that ships were the fastest method of communication between stars. This in spite of the fact that native timoan civilization, off the island, didn't even have telephones.

"How? Oh, yes, of course. But you should have called when you landed. What brings you here?"

"I did call, but you didn't answer. Must be the noise in here. Anyway, we just got in. Can we go somewhere quieter? I'll tell you about it on the way."

"Of course, let us go to my office."

∞ ∞ ∞

On the walk across campus, Carson filled Marten in. "Do you still have that talisman we found at the dig on Zeta Tucanae III? The one with what looked like a constellation?"

"Of course. It is with the other artifacts we collected. No wait, that one is in my office, along with several others I am in the process of reexamining. Why?"

"Excellent. I want to take a look at that constellation again, I suspect it's a clue to another site."

"Really? Another site on Zeta Tucanae?"

"No, I think it specifies a location in another star system"

"But the Tucani never had star travel."

"Well, neither did you, and now look at you," Carson said.

"Point taken, but a different star would be inconsistent with the cultural level. Why specify an actual stellar location by scribing a diagram on a stone instead of just writing down the coordinates or recording it on an information storage system?"

"To record it for a very long time, perhaps. Have you analyzed the material of that talisman?" asked Carson as they approached the entrance of the History Building.

"Just preliminary. I remember it is anomalously hard, but we haven't examined that part of the collection in detail yet." said Marten as they entered the building. "My office is up two levels."

"Who did you annoy?" Timoans disliked heights.

"Hah. It might look like that, but this way I get a bigger office."

They were deep in conversation as they exited the stairwell on the third floor and had taken several steps toward the office when they realized that the figure, a human, standing in the hallway wasn't cleaning staff, that he was standing by Marten's *open* office door, and that he was whispering urgently to somebody in the office.

∞ ∞ ∞

"He's back, let's get out of here!" said the figure. A muffled response came from inside. "Never mind, grab the stuff and let's go!"

"Hey!" said Marten, reacting, "what are you doing there, who are you?" Marten and Carson ran down the hall toward the man, who turned and fled. "Stop!"

Carson's longer legs took the corridor quickly, and he yelled back to Marten, "you check your office, I'll get this one." He closed on the fugitive.

"Ow!" came a cry behind him. Carson looked back to see Marten sprawled on the floor; he had been run down by another man who'd come barreling out of the office just as Marten had reached it.

The other intruder made to take off running in the opposite direction, a package under his arm. Marten rolled and grabbed his legs, tripping him. The package went flying and papers, memory sticks and other objects scattered across the floor. Carson stopped and turned back to help his friend.

"No, go after the other guy!" Marten yelled. As he did so, his intruder scrambled to his feet, kicking Marten away, and grabbed for his case. "I am okay. Go!" said Marten.

Carson turned again to pursue the first intruder just as he disappeared into the stairwell at the end of the hall. Carson rushed to the door, opened it, and saw and heard nothing. He looked up, then down the narrow gap between flights of stairs. Nothing. He quieted his own breathing and listened. Nothing. No footsteps, no heavy breathing, no sounds of doors. Up? Or down? *Damn!*

He heard a faint scuff of a foot on the stair. Down. He started down the steps, taking them two and three at a time. He rounded the corner at the landing. *Wham!* A fist smashed into Carson's face and staggered him backward. His assailant turned and ran.

Carson shook off the stunned feeling and put a hand to his lips. It came away bloody. Ignoring the pain, he grabbed the hand rail and levered himself over, pivoting across the banister to slam his feet into the fleeing intruder. The man staggered, stumbled on the steps and fell headlong onto the next landing. He didn't get up. Carson started down to check on him.

∞ ∞ ∞

Marten, meanwhile, had shaken off the kick. The intruder was still scrabbling about, picking up papers and disks and stuffing them into the case, glancing back frequently at Marten and the stairwell door that Carson had chased his friend through. Marten feigned grogginess, pushing himself up on hands and knees as though too weak to rise. The man glanced at him, then reached to pick up another handful of papers. Marten pounced, low and fast.

The impact took the man behind the knees, buckling them and sweeping his feet out from under him as he fell backward. Marten rolled out of the way, but his reactions were still sluggish from the blow to his head. The man landed on top of him. Marten's body cushioned some of the burglar's impact, knocking the breath out of him and leaving his opponent in better shape than he had planned. Still, the crook was shaken.

Marten kicked the case out of the man's grip, again sending its contents spinning. As the case slid across the floor, Marten saw another object slip out of it. He rolled and dived, landing on it and the case.

Behind him the intruder had gotten up to his knees. He saw Marten diving for the case. He dove too, hands outstretched to grab the case away from Marten, and let his weight fall on Marten again. Marten curled up into a ball, hands clutched at his knees, and rolled aside. The man hastily grabbed up his case and a handful of papers, then ran.

∞ ∞ ∞

Carson reached his man on the stairs, grabbed him by the shirt, and drew his arm back to hit him again. The man just hung limp. Carson remembered Marten; this guy would keep. He turned and ran back up the flight of stairs and through the door. He saw Marten staggering to his feet. Carson ran down the corridor to him. Papers covered the floor where the culprit had dropped his case. At the far end of the corridor, the south stairwell door was closing. He ran to check it, but the lead was too great. By the time he got there the man had disappeared. Carson ran back to check on Marten, shaking his head and muttering.

"Are you all right?"

"Yes, but I feel like a bowling pin. Just shook up. What about you? Your lip is bleeding. And where is the other guy?"

"He's on the stairs, I'll get him." Carson jogged back to the north stairwell, down the flight of stairs . . . but the other burglar was gone. He had either recovered quickly or had been faking it. *Damn it!* Carson turned back to check on Marten again.

"Here, let's get you sitting down and I'll take a look. I think you're bleeding," he said, helping Marten up.

"Just a few scratches where he kicked me" Marten said. "I was slow, too many beers at the pub." He held his hand up to the laceration on his scalp, winced, and brought it down again to look at the red residue on his fingers. "Let me get these things gathered up first."

"This is a lot of paper, Marten. Do you have something against computers?"

"I grew up with paper. And computers make inadequate beer mats."

∞ ∞ ∞

A few minutes later they were sitting in Marten's office, Marten holding a damp cloth to his head.

Looking around the office, Carson noticed several certificates on Marten's wall that didn't look like the usual academic awards. There was a trophy on a shelf. He picked it up and examined it, reading the inscription "Competitive Pistol, Second Place." The certificates were also competition awards for pistol shooting and marksmanship. Carson was impressed. He was a good shot himself but he had never done it in formal competition. And he'd thought Marten had hardly touched the things.

"Marksmanship? Pistolry? Since when have you been into firearms, Marten?"

"Oh, a little while now. Since we got back from the fiasco at the Raven, as a matter of fact. I felt rather stupid not being able to hit anything with that damn gun—I was probably more dangerous to you than the villains," he said. Carson didn't argue the point. "Anyway, I decided to join the pistol club here at the university, to get some practice in. A lot of what we shoot are antiques, at least in design, mostly brassloads."

"Brassloads?"

"Apparently up until about fifty years ago, they used a little brass can to hold the propellant, as a powder, with the slug and detonator, or primer, crimped into it at opposite ends. Humans did, that is. We timoans hadn't quite reached the gun-making stage. We just had rockets. Which I suppose is more like the ammo today, where the propellant is molded into and around the bullet."

Marten warmed up to the subject. "Brassloads make gun mechanisms more complicated, there has to be a way to eject the things once the bullet is fired, but they take some of the heat with it. The old guns seem to have had a problem with heat.

"Mind you, the ejected brass cans could be a problem too. Once, one went down the front of my shirt. I do not have much fur on my chest; it was *hot*! In my surprise I still had the pistol in my hand as I scrambled to get it out. Fortunately I did not fire again because the pistol was pointing just about everywhere but down range. The Range Officer was furious! He told me 'gun control is about keeping the gun pointed at the target' and suspended me from the range for a week. I can't say that I blame him, the whole episode was embarrassing and somebody could have been hurt.

"Once I got the hang of it, though, it was rather fun. The next thing I knew they were encouraging me to try out for competition and, well, I suppose I did reasonably well."

"Well, congratulations. I hope that doesn't come in handy."

Marten grinned. "Me too, but in our kind of field work you never know." His grin faded. "Even life in the office is getting too exciting." He looked around meaningfully at the papers and things that the intruder had tried to take.

"It looks like they weren't expecting whatever they were looking for to be hidden," said Carson, as he looked around the room. The office had clearly been hastily searched, but not ransacked. Nothing was tipped over, drawers were open but not pulled out, books were still on bookshelves.

"It was not," replied Marten.

"You know what they were looking for? What?"

"Same as you, the talisman."

Carson's face fell. "How do you kno—"

"But they didn't get it."

"What?" Carson locked his eyes on Marten's.

"I saw it drop from his bag when I tripped him, I grabbed it before he saw it."

"Good move!"

"Thanks. Then he landed upon me." Marten was leafing through the small pile of papers and memory wafers that had scattered when the intruder had dropped the bag. "These papers and memory sticks confirm it. They are from my files on that artifact and on the dig. Looks like he got away with some of the images of it, and part of my report, but I still have the X-rays, my computer data, and the rest of it."

Marten looked up from the pile at Carson and, pulling a slim, round-cornered square from his pocket, said: "What is so special about this artifact anyway?"

"Probably nothing."

Marten looked up at Carson. "Certainly. You just happen to show up on my doorstep asking about it at the same time two creeps—who must have landed within a day of you—burglarize my office and try to steal it. Come on, explain, what is the story?"

"All right. It really might be nothing, but if these markings are a, well, call it a star map," he pointed at the network of dots and lines on the face of the talisman, "then it could lead to something of potentially enormous value."

"You're joking. It is a treasure map?"

Carson grinned. "Well, no, not exactly. But it could mark the location of an information cache, or possibly an arsenal, left by the Spacefarers."

"Arsenal? We've never seen any indications of hostile activity, not with anything much more advanced than arrows and knives."

"Probably not. The description was ambiguous."

Marten looked up from the markings and stared at Carson. "Description?"

Carson interpreted the look and nodded. "Apparently so. I haven't seen the original." Carson summarized what Ducayne had told him about the translation.

Marten breathed a low whistle, looking back at the artifact. "So," he glanced up at Carson again, "when do we leave?"

Chapter 16: The Talisman

Clarkeville, Taprobane

IT WOULD TAKE them two days to get ready for departure. Marten had to arrange to have his classes covered, and wanted to be sure Carson had laid in supplies adequate to explore . . . well, they still weren't quite sure where they were going yet. They had given Jackie that problem.

"Oh, it's a supercircle," Jackie said when they showed her the talisman.

"What?" Carson and Marten both asked at the same time.

"The shape." Hadn't they heard of supercircles or superellipses? "It's not a square with rounded corners, see how the sides curve too? This one looks like a shape halfway between a circle and a square. Mathematically you'd graph it with an exponent of 2.5, a circle is—" She stopped, they were staring at her like she had grown a third eye. "What?"

"I told you she was the right person for this," Carson said to Marten. He turned to Jackie. "We hadn't noticed anything special about the shape. Is there some significance to a super circle?"

"Um, not as far as I know." Jackie had studied the math but that was a long time ago; she just liked the shape. What did she remember? "It's also called a Lamé curve, a superellipse, but this one has both axes the same, thus supercircle. We can look it up. I just think it's an attractive shape, mathematically elegant. Oh. I guess that helps reinforce the high-tech origin."

"I suppose so. So, do you think you can interpret the pattern of stones, the diagram?"

Jackie rotated the talisman, examining it from all sides. The back was plain, the only information seemed to be encoded in the diagram. "You said it was high tech. Could it be a data storage device?"

"That's possible, although what was left of the circuitry in the fragment I found wasn't very complex. From what Ducayne said, the Velkaryans seem to think that the dots and lines are the key."

"Okay, that could be a star pattern. Perhaps the different color stones represent different spectral types of stars. How old is it?"

"The fragment I found was fifteen thousand years," Carson said. He turned to Marten. "Has this one been dated?"

Marten shook his head. "Not specifically. So far what was found with it has been dated at about seventeen thousand years. That is our years, perhaps sixteen thousand Terran years. I can have the lab do a rush analysis for me if you like."

"How accurately do you need to know, Jackie?"

"To allow for stellar drift, within a thousand years would be good, if these stones represent stars." Jackie thought for a bit. What if one had gone supernova? No, there weren't any nearby supernova remnants, this wouldn't be anywhere in T-space if that were the case. If the stones were pulsars the age wouldn't matter so much, but figuring out which ones they represented would be a bitch. "Okay, yeah, five hundred to a thousand years. Anything more accurate than plus or minus a hundred years is wasted."

"All right," Marten said, "I will take it back to the lab."

"Marten, make sure they extract a sample very carefully," Carson said. "Mine showed evidence of a circuit, we don't want that damaged if we can possibly avoid it. Just drill out a tiny piece of the technetium, it shouldn't take much."

"Hannibal, I'm not a grad student. But thanks for the reminder anyway."

"Before you go," said Jackie, "let me take some scans so that I can start work on it. Maybe I can narrow it down even without the exact dating."

∞ ∞ ∞

"Damn it! You screw ups can't even pull off a simple burglary, what's wrong with you?" Hopkins paced back and forth in his cabin aboard the *Hawk*. Rico, not one of the two being yelled at, looked on in amusement. "Marten's office was supposed to be a simple in and out job, no complications, and maybe he wouldn't notice the stuff's missing for days."

"But Boss—"

"Shut up, Warshowski, I'm not finished. First you screw up a simple break in to the archeology store room—"

"We didn't screw that up, the talisman just wasn't there."

"And you let yourself get caught in Marten's office. If he hadn't have seen you he might never have missed that talisman, or figured a colleague took it. But no—"

"But boss, how were we to know he'd be back so soon? He's usually all night at the pub, when he's there," the other robber, Tuco, said.

"So what was your backup plan, to throw the stuff all over the hallway when they surprised you?"

"The little weasel tripped me! Then he must have stashed the artifact, I thought it was still in the bag," Tuco said. "But I got the papers."

"Yes, and we have pictures of the artifact." Hopkins voice lowered from a shout to more normal tones. "They're not helping us much, though. I thought that diagram was a star chart but it isn't correlating to anything. I need to get another look at it. Where is it now?"

"Not sure, Boss, but it's probably locked in a vault somewhere," Warshowski said.

"Will he take it to the ship?" Rico asked.

"Ship? Oh yes, the *Sophie*, Sophie Space Charters. What do we have on Roberts?"

"Not much," said Rico, crossing his arms and leaning against a bulkhead. "She used to fly for somebody else, got into a few incidents. Works her own outfit now, solo."

"Can we bribe her?" asked Hopkins.

"Not likely, she's pretty much a straight arrow, other than bending the flight regs once in a while. She has a mail permit, I think she's worked with Carson before. No, we probably can't, Boss."

"What about searching the *Sophie*?"

Rico shrugged. Warshowski said "Roberts and Carson are sleeping aboard, I don't think so."

"Damn it, what *can* you do?"

"I may know a guy who can put a remote tap on the ship's security system," Warshowski said. "We'll be able to listen in on everything, see a lot of it. If the object is in the open, we may see it."

Rico rolled his eyes at this. Hopkins guessed that it probably wasn't as easy as that.

"All right," Hopkins said. "Get on it."

"Got it, boss." Warshowski turned to leave, with Tuco following.

"Oh, one more thing."

Tuco and Warshowski stopped and turned. "Yes boss?"

"If it *is* still at the University, Marten is going to have to get it to the ship sometime. Keep an eye on him, pick up anything that looks interesting." Hopkins didn't want to lose it if it could be snatched easily.

"Got it boss," Tuco said with a grin. "I owe him one. I may take some of that action myself."

"Whatever, just get it done. Now get out of here!"

"On our way boss." Tuco and Warshowski left. Rico turned to follow.

"No, not you Rico, stay a moment. I've got something else for you."

∞ ∞ ∞

Jackie glared at her computer screen. One panel displayed an image of the talisman, another showed a star map. "This isn't working, Carson!" she called back to him.

Carson made his way forward to the control area. "Not getting any matches?"

"I'm getting too many matches, but none of them make sense." She gestured at the star map. "This looks like a great match, but it's nearly two thousand light-years from here. It can't be right." That would take the *Sophie* four years to cover in warp.

"Maybe they had better starships than us."

"Even if they could, why come all the way here? All of known T-space is only two-percent of that distance. Besides," Jackie touched a control and several different star maps popped up, "like I said, there are too many matches. There are over a hundred billion stars just in the part of the galaxy we can see—"

"You can't be trying to match against all of those?"

"Of course not, we don't have detailed data for that many, and certainly not to correct for sixteen thousand years of drift." Marten had called from the university with that number, older than the fragment Carson had found. "It would help if I knew the exact correlation between the stone colors and spectral type. You don't suppose those stones have changed color as they aged, do you?"

Carson looked stricken. "That hadn't occurred to me. Most gemstones don't . . . unless they're exposed to radiation. No, the talisman was only slightly radioactive, that wouldn't have an effect."

"You're sure?"

"No, I'm not sure. I'll call Marten and have him check the stones. Is there anything else we might have missed? You mentioned the shape, a supercircle. Could that have any significance?"

Jackie hadn't thought so; it was just a pleasing shape. There was a mathematical property to it. The general equation was *X*-to-the-*N* plus *Y*-to-the-*N* equals some constant, *C*. If *N* equaled one, that would be a square, although tilted to look like a diamond. If *N* was two, that would graph as a circle. For a supercircle like this, *N* would be two-point-five. Two and a half? Was it that simple? "Carson, that's brilliant!"

"What did I say?"

"Later," Jackie said, turning back to her computers. "I need to try this. Call Marten anyway, I still need to know about the colors."

∞ ∞ ∞

"Okay," Jackie began. Marten had returned to the ship and Jackie had him and Carson gathered in the eating area. She was going to explain how she had figured out the map whether they liked it or not, damn it. None of this 'just tell us where we're going' crap. Although in truth the others had far too much intellectual curiosity for that, they really did want to know how she had solved it, but they also enjoyed ragging her. "The first problem was to come up with a correlation between the colors of the stones and some characteristic of stars."

"Spectral color, right?" asked Marten.

"That was my first thought, but I couldn't make it fit anything. I ignored halo stars, correlated for drift, added halo stars back in with drift, allowed for a difference in color perception of the stones versus stars. Nothing."

"So what did work?" asked Carson.

"Consider. It's awkward trying to map points in three dimensional space to a two dimensional diagram."

"Well yes, but if you look at the sky it's just a two dimensional surface, or it seems to be."

"Ah, but we know something unique about the people who made this," Jackie said, and grinned. She'd caught something obvious that the archeologists had missed.

"And that would be . . .?"

"They're spacefarers." Jackie's smug look seemed to imply that should explain everything.

"Yes, and?" Marten asked.

"Of course!" this from Carson. "It's a 3-D coordinate system, the colors somehow representing the third dimension."

"Exactly. What we sometimes call a 2.5-D display."

"So the supercircle—"

"Was the clue that it was a 2.5-D display, yes." Jackie grinned. "Of course, even then it took a bit of playing to correlate color with distance, but I finally found a match. The cool colors represent a distance above the plane, warm colors below—something like blue shift and red shift. I had to guess at the scale and I'm assuming sixteen thousand years of stellar drift. I'm assuming that drift is constant, which it surely isn't, but it should be close enough over that time scale. There were few other things I had to tweak." In fact she had spent long hours at the console trying things. She was ready for sleep, but wanted to explain her find first. "I finally found a match near the edge of T-space."

"Where?" Carson shifted to the edge of his seat. "What did you match on?"

"You found this talisman at Zeta Tucanae, right?"

"Yes. Don't tell me that's the match."

"No, no. Completely on the other side of T-space from there. The star Beta Canum Venaticorum, also called Chara. A G0-type star just over twenty-seven light-years from Sol, about thirty-eight light-years from here."

"Chara? Greek for joy." Carson grinned. "Let's hope we have the joy of finding what we're looking for. So, is it inhabited? I assume there are planets."

"Yes, including a Terraform planet. No official permanent habitation yet, except for a lone Mennonite settlement. There may well be the odd homestead." Interstellar travel had become so easy, and so many of the nearer stars had habitable or terraformed planets, that humans had been leaving Earth and setting up homesteads around the nearer stars for over twenty years, even on planets well off the usual trade routes. Or perhaps *because* those planets were well off the usual trade routes. "There are signs of ancient agricultural activity," Jackie continued, "but nothing now." She checked her notes. "It may have just come out of an ice age a few thousand years ago."

"Did it indeed? Interesting." said Carson.

"Oh?"

"I have a theory about that. Well, more of a hunch." Several of the planets that may have been visited by the Spacefarers had had recent ice ages, but Carson wasn't sure of the significance, if any.

"And?"

"I'm not ready to talk about it just yet. I don't publish hunches."

"No, just act on them," muttered Jackie.

"So, when can we leave, and how long will it take us to get there?" asked Marten.

"Well, there's a problem," she said.

Carson looked at her, concerned. "What problem?"

"We can't get there from here. It's thirty-eight light-years, that's about twice the *Sophie*'s range."

"But—"

She held her hand up. "Relax, I'll figure out a route. But I need to take a break first, I'm beat." She got up from the table and moved to the galley door, where she stopped and turned back. "We'll be ready to go in a day or two. Marten, are you coming with us?"

"Are you joking? I wouldn't miss this." He got up too. "I am going to go back to campus and start making arrangements. I need to pick up the talisman, too."

"Okay." With that Jackie headed toward her cabin and welcome rest.

∞ ∞ ∞

The next morning Carson found Jackie at the main console, plotting their route.

"Okay, Carson," she said, "We've got a bit of a round about route. Sol and Alpha Centauri are each about one-fourth of the way there, but after that there's no place at any reasonable angle or range where we can stop to refuel."

"Damn, do I have to find another ship, then?"

"You might find a ship with a twenty-eight light-year range at Earth, but I doubt it. That's pushing the range for anything but an antimatter ship." That would leave out anything but a military ship. A few regulated commercial ships on scheduled runs also had antimatter reactors to power their drives, but that was to allow more cargo and passenger volume, not added range. "But there's another possibility. Here, look."

Roberts displayed a star chart on the main screen. "Here we are, down here," she indicated a point and it highlighted with a yellow circle around it. "And here's Chara, up here." She highlighted that one the same way. "Now, Sol is over here, and Alpha Centauri here." She highlighted two more stars.

Carson examined the display. "They're both off the direct path, about what, fifteen degrees?"

"Roughly, but that would only add about a day to the total time in warp. But look at the big gap between either of them and Chara. See?"

"Yes, but you already said that."

"Right, but look around the edges of the gap. See, this way if we go by Centauri." She highlighted a few more stars. "We can do a series of jumps, each one easily within range. All of these stars have some way or other to let us refuel."

"They're all inhabited?"

"I didn't say that. This one," she pointed at one, "has two gas giants, we can do a scoop refueling run on either of them, this ship is designed for it. And here," she pointed to another star, "this has several small ice worlds. The others have settlements where we can refuel."

"Well, that looks do-able. How much time does it add to the trip?"

"There's the problem. Not counting actual time to maneuver in-system and to refuel, that's about an extra two weeks of warp time. Add another few days for in-system time, per system. Call it a total of four to six weeks from Alpha Centauri. About the same from Sol, but on a different path."

Plus another week to get back to Alpha Centauri from here. "And if we could go direct? Just asking."

"Four weeks from here. Three weeks from Centauri or Sol, and a week to get to either."

Carson looked at the star chart, hoping to see another answer there. Jackie had drawn a series of lines representing the jumps to connect the stars. It wasn't quite a drunkard's walk, but it wandered around before reaching Chara. There were a couple of red stars in the gap; it wasn't totally empty. "What about this way?" Carson asked, pointing to one of them.

Jackie looked where he pointed. "Wolf 359?" She tapped it and a series of numbers displayed beside it. She shook her head. "Negative, that's almost twenty-two light-years from Chara. My range is twenty. That also rules out Lalande 21185; that's just under twenty but not enough to leave us maneuvering reserve." She tapped another star. "Gliese 412 is in a better position, but not suitable. It's a double star., and one of the pair is an x-ray flare star. There's nowhere in that system to refuel anyway."

"Nothing?"

"Nothing useful. If you're thinking of comets or the like, it takes time to find them and rendezvous with them. Not helpful if we're in a hurry."

Carson clenched his fists. "I'm worried about the people we've had run-ins with. What if they have a longer-range ship? They'll beat us there."

"Why would they even have any idea where to go? Anyway no fusion ship can make that in one jump. If they've got a parsec or two on the *Sophie*, they might refuel at Lalande 21185 or Wolf 359." She paused, then said "There is one other possibility."

Carson looked up at her. He was willing to try anything. "Yes? What?"

Jackie bit her lip and looked somber. "I'm not crazy about the idea. I've never done it, and there's some risk. The right gear for this ship would certainly be available at Kakuloa if we go via the Centauri system. I don't know if it's available here, although the Sapphire is a common enough model."

"Yes, but *what* gear, done *what*?"

"Drop tanks. After leaving atmosphere, we attach fuel tanks that are shaped to fit the space between *Sophie*'s hull and the inner edge of the warp bubble. We jettison them after the jump, before entering atmosphere again. It should double the *Sophie*'s range, but I'll have to double check the specs."

"And the risks?"

"Several. There's less distance between the edge of the warp bubble and the tanks, if the structure intersects the bubble while in warp . . ." That would be catastrophic; the resulting explosion would destroy the ship. "There's more power required, more load on the engine. Maneuvering in-system with all that extra mass on is a pain in the butt. And it's a one-way thing. We'll still have to take the long road home.

"Are you still interested?" Roberts finished.

"It's worth checking out. If they're available, is there any advantage to getting tanks now rather than at Kakuloa?"

"I'll run the numbers. If they can give us the full thirty-eight light-year range we could save at least a day, more like two, by not stopping in the Centauri system."

"I'll take any advantage I can get. See if there are tanks available and fine tune your range calculations. If we can, then let's do it. Time is critical."

"Okay. I'll get on it." Roberts sighed, cleared the star map from the screen and sat down to work. Either way, she was going to be cooped up in the ship with Carson for quite a while.

"Jackie?"

"Yes?"

"Thank you."

"All part of the service." That was *not* said with a cheery smile.

Chapter 17: Rico and Marten

Taprobane Spaceport

GETTING ONTO the field was the easy part. As a crew member on the *Hawk*, Hopkins's ship, Rico had automatically been issued a field pass. The problem was, for what he needed to do, he would stick out like a sore thumb. He had ways around little problems like that.

Rico slipped in to the terminal building from the field side, where nobody bothered to check him at the Employees Only sign. He looked around, went through the door marked Male and, as he had guessed, there was a locker room off to one side of the usual facilities. Opening the lockers was easy work for Rico, he had been bypassing locks for as long as he could remember. In the third one he tried he found a set of coveralls, a close enough fit to pass. He slipped them on over his clothes, then left the locker room.

This time there was a guard at the door to the field. Damn, Rico's pass was the wrong color for ground crew. He slipped back into the restroom and examined his pass closely. Ground crew passes were white, his visitor pass was similar but with a wide orange stripe printed across the top. He looked at it a bit more closely and pulled out his pocket knife. A minute or so of scraping and the printed-on orange stripe was gone, leaving only the white plastic underneath showing. Not too bad, but what if there was a chip inside?

Rico put his knife away and took out his omni. He touched a code sequence on it and two metal probes extruded from it, about two centimeters apart. He entered another sequence to activate the firmware—of questionable legality—which turned the omni into a shock rod. He pressed the probes to the card, touched a button and smiled at the resulting *zap!* and crackle of sparks from the card. So much for any ID chip.

It wouldn't pass close inspection, but the door was from an employee only area to the field, he didn't expect the guard to be especially alert. If he was, well then, too bad for the guard. He kept his omni in its shock rod configuration, concealed in his hand, and walked toward the door.

∞ ∞ ∞

Marten walked the few blocks from his office to the main street which would take him to the spaceport. He had his bag slung over his shoulder, the talisman tucked away carefully amongst his spare clothes and the other paraphernalia of travel. The sun—humans called it Epsilon Indi—was just setting, coloring what clouds he could see with pinks and oranges. He was absorbed in mentally reviewing his to-do list for the upcoming trip to make sure he hadn't left anything undone, so the metallic click didn't register right away.

"Freeze, fuzzball!" came a rough, low voice. A wiry figure stepped around the edge of the building.

Fuzzball? Then Marten looked and stifled his retort. The man held a pistol, and it was pointed at him.

∞ ∞ ∞

Rico waved his modified pass at the gate guard, who barely glanced at it and waved him through. Rico relaxed and walked out onto the field. In his Port Authority coveralls he looked just like any other ground crew member. His eyes scanned the field, looking for . . . there it was, the squat delta shape of the *Sophie*.

He sauntered over to it, computer pad in hand as though he had some routine check to do. He walked around the vehicle, looking at the various attachment points, cargo doors, fuel filler hatches, and hydraulic connectors. He leaned over as if to look at the landing gear., then ducked under the vehicle as if for a closer look.

Pretending to examine the landing gear then key something into his notepad, he surreptitiously slid a small disk, about five centimeters in diameter and a millimeter thick, slightly flexible, from under the notepad. He peeled off the backing to expose a layer of adhesive. He looked up at the fuselage of the ship and wiped his hand across one side as though feeling for a crack or a bump. His real intention was to wipe the surface clean of any dirt to ensure a good seal. He slipped the disk into his palm and, as though he were just steadying himself as he moved out from under the ship, slapped the side of the ship and the adhesive disk into place. There. To a casual glance it would look just like any other random gadget on the hull, or perhaps a hull patch.

Rico straightened up and looked around, pretending to survey the ship again but keeping an eye out for anyone who might be watching him. Nobody, the field was still clear. He made a few more perfunctory notes in his pad, then pretended to check a couple of other spots on the ship, closed his pad and strolled off toward the terminal building, again acting as though this was all just part of his job. In a way, it was.

∞ ∞ ∞

Marten stared into an enormous gun barrel, and too late the click he had heard registered on his consciousness. It had been a weapon being cocked. A similar sound came from behind him. His ears twitched at that. A second bad guy. And this was usually a good neighborhood.

"My wallet is in my pocket, I do not have much else," said Marten. He had indeed frozen, not moving a muscle, not even twitching his ears, his eyes didn't seem to focus on anything.

"We don't want your wallet," sneered the wiry-looking gunman in front of him. He looked amused that Marten seemed petrified with fear. He couldn't have been on this planet long; he was ignorant of timoan physiology. "Drop the bag."

"But—"

"Do it!"

Timoans, like the terrestrial meerkats that they were very distant cousins to, are very good at standing perfectly still. In part it evolved as a defense mechanism, so as not to attract the attention of a predator when caught in the open. But timoans, like meerkats, also evolved eating small animals and insects like lizards, spiders, grasshoppers, and crickets—fast food. A timoan could stand rigid, without moving eyes or ears yet still tracking its prey by sight and sound, then instantly explode into accurate, prey-snatching motion with no warning. And here the bad guy was even giving Marten an excuse to move.

Marten slowly reached up with his right hand to grab the shoulder strap of the bag, as though to slip it off. Using that motion as an excuse, he moved his head just enough to confirm the location of Bad Guy Two, a meter behind him. *Smart enough to stay out of arm's reach,* thought Marten, *and not directly in line with me and Wiry. Damn.* He had hoped that he could just drop down then leap straight up fast enough that they'd just shoot each other in startled reaction. He could move that fast, but the geometry was wrong. Okay, plan B.

He slowly slid the pack off his shoulder and moved his arm to hold it at arm's length, then slowly started to crouch as though to set it down gently.

"Just drop it!"

Wiry's attention was split between Marten and the bag. Marten counted on Bad Guy Two, behind him, also having his attention split. As he let go of the bag he exploded into motion.

Bad Guy Two was the more serious problem. Marten knew roughly where he was but couldn't see him to anticipate his actions, so Marten had to take him out first. He leapt backward and to the side, away from the bag, twisting in the air as he did so. He moved like a mongoose attacking a cobra. His claws raked deep across the wrist of his opponent's gun hand, slashing tendons and nerves, making the hand—and so the gun it held—nearly useless. Marten's leap finished with him beside his opponent, holding his arm and leaning low. Another half twist, bend and kick, and the timoan's foot connected solidly under Bad Guy's jaw and snapped his head back. Still holding the arm, he turned again, leveraging Bad Guy's body against his own so that Bad Guy was now between him and Wiry's gun.

But Wiry had barely moved. He'd had his eye on the bag and by the time he looked up at the commotion, it was over as far as his companion was concerned. Marten didn't give him time to think up a counter move. He burst into motion again. He leveraged Bad Guy's mass and height, running up him and leaping at Wiry from Bad Guy's shoulder as he collapsed.

Wiry brought up his pistol, squeezing the trigger. Three shots rang out in rapid succession. *Ba-ba-bang!*

The burst of shots echoed, surprising Marten—he hadn't realized it was a full-auto pistol. Then he was on Wiry, carrying him down with the impact. He slashed his claws across the man's face. He grabbed the gun arm and slammed the hand into the ground, but Wiry held on tight, trying to bend his wrist to bring the gun to bear. Blood streamed from slashes across Wiry's forehead, into his eyes.

Marten's left hand still had a vise grip on Wiry's gun arm. He reached around with his right to grab Wiry's hair, and used that as a handle to slam Wiry's head into the ground, again and again. The grip on the pistol loosened. Marten swiped his right arm around to slap the gun away and it slid halfway across the street. He jumped after it, expecting the second attacker to be right behind him. He reached the gun, picked it up and turned, bringing it up to shoot whoever was closest. But there was no threat.

The other attacker was still lying on the ground, a pool of blood around him, not moving. *Did I hit him that hard?* Marten wondered briefly. He also looked vaguely familiar. But Wiry was already running for it, and amazingly he'd had the presence of mind to grab up Marten's bag as he did so. *I should have hit his head harder*, thought Marten disgustedly. His skull must be very thick. He brought the pistol to bear, aimed carefully, and squeezed off a burst.

Wiry jumped at the noise, at the impact of the bullets, one grazing his hand as another broke the strap on the bag. He didn't stop to pick it up but began ducking and weaving as he ran. Marten grinned and ran to pick up the bag. The other thug was still on the ground. He hadn't moved,

When Marten walked up to him, the reason became clear. A bullet from Wiry's first burst had caught the thug across the neck and, from the amount of blood, must have smashed his carotid artery. He *did* look familiar; he was the guy who had run him down trying to burgle his office. And he was dead.

Marten glanced up and down the street. No bystanders. But the sound of shots would have attracted attention, people would be here soon. He started jogging away from the scene himself. Ordinarily he would have stuck around to explain things—he had acted out of self-defense, after all—but he had to get to the spaceport and, he realized, even though he hadn't done it, the gun in his hand was the murder weapon. He started to toss it away, then thought better of it. His prints and DNA were all over it. He stuffed it in his bag as he ran. He had a ship to catch.

Chapter 18: Departure

Taprobane Spaceport

AS CARSON STRODE across the field from the terminal building to the *Sophie*, he spotted Marten approaching from his left. He waved and called. "Hey, Marten!" He noticed that Marten was carrying his bag cradled in his arms rather than slung over a shoulder. That looked odd. "Marten, what's with the bag? Have you got a baby in there or something?"

They caught up with each other. "No, the straps, uh, broke." said Marten.

"Oh." Carson took a closer look at Marten. His clothing was more rumpled than was usual, his hair was mussed, and—was that *blood* on his sleeve? "What happened to *you*?"

"Had a run in with the guys from my office. At least one of them was, I never did get a close look at the guy you chased. A wiry looking guy."

"Are you all right? They tried to mug you? Did they get anything?"

"Oh, I am fine. Not mug exactly, more of a stick-up. And they got more than they bargained for, but not what they wanted. I'll tell you about it later, let's get to the ship."

"Right," said Carson. As they turned toward the ship, Carson glimpsed a motion out of the corner of his eye, as of someone ducking away so as not to be seen. Rather than turn to look, making it obvious to whoever it was that he had been noticed, Carson made to accidentally drop the papers he was carrying. "It's all right," he said to Marten, "I've got them."

Bending to pick them up, he snatched a quick glance in the direction of the motion he had seen. There were a pair of field workers in Port Authority coveralls standing talking to each other. A third stood near them, holding a note pad, as though he were part of the group, but the group didn't quite seem natural. Carson picked up a few papers, then glanced up again. Was that Rico? He fought to keep any recognition out of his face and bent down to the papers again. He was almost sure of it; it was that bastard Rico who'd kept them penned up in a tomb on Verdigris. He looked around once more as he straightened, as though checking for any stray papers. That third man was looking off in a different direction now, his face turned away. Carson recognized the profile, the build. It was definitely Rico. What was he doing here? The man darted a glance toward him, then turned his back and walked away as though he had remembered a task. Carson wondered if he had intended to jump Marten again before he got to the ship, but that opportunity had passed now.

"Come on, Marten," Carson said, "let's get to the ship. The sooner we're out of here the better as far as I'm concerned."

"Yes, I agree."

Carson signaled the *Sophie*, and Roberts lowered its boarding ramp for them.

∞ ∞ ∞

"Where do I stow my stuff?" Marten asked as he came aboard.

Roberts was doing something at the controls and called back over her shoulder. "You're in the second bunk on the starboard side."

Marten looked around and moved to put his bags on the bunk adjacent to the boarding hatch. Carson reached out a hand to his shoulder. Marten paused and turned to look at him. "What?"

"Your *other* starboard," Carson said, grinning and pointing to a bunk on the opposite side of the corridor.

"Oh. You know Carson, timoan boats have their steering board on the left side," Marten said as he put his gear on the correct bunk.

"Really? I didn't—"

"Got you! No, they've always had center-mounted rudders. Modeled on fish."

"When you boys are through joking around," interrupted Roberts, "I'd like to get the ship secure for flight."

∞ ∞ ∞

Rico hurried off the field. Had Carson spotted him? And the timoan, he was at the ship already. What happened to Warshowski and Tuco? He pulled out his omni and loaded the blackware that let him scan police channels. He listened to the police chatter for a while, then swore. He keyed in a number.

"Warshowski and Tuco blew it," Rico said when Hopkins answered. "I guess the little guy was faster and tougher than they expected. Tuco's dead."

"Dead? What happened?" asked Hopkins.

"Don't know for sure, I think Warshowski's still running. Near as I can tell from monitoring the police channels, there was a fight. Tuco's wrist was slashed and he was found lying on his gun, shot through the neck. No sign of Warshowski."

"Shot? I didn't think Marten went armed."

"Probably doesn't. The caliber matches Warshowski's gun, so maybe the timoan took it from him. Lots of blood at the scene, most of it Tuco's. They're still sorting it out."

"Damn," said Hopkins, his tone a mix of frustration and awe. "He must be good to do that kind of damage while outnumbered two to one. Good thing we've got insurance. You did deliver the package, right?" He meant the disk Rico had attached to the *Sophie*.

"Yes boss, piece of cake. I just about tripped over Carson as he was crossing the field, but he didn't see me. It's all set."

"Good. Pity about Tuco, he always was a bit clumsy." Hopkins said, in a tone that someone else might use for spilled coffee. "All we have to do now is wait."

∞ ∞ ∞

Jackie finished her *pro forma* walkaround and climbed the ramp into the *Sophie*'s portside hatch. She closed it behind her, latched and sealed it, and stepped forward to the cockpit. "Okay, gents, if you have everything secure aft, it's time to strap in," she called, looking back to Carson and Marten.

They double-checked their bunks, looked around the cabin, and came forward to strap into the seats just behind Jackie's. "All set," said Carson.

"Okay." Jackie touched several controls on her console, and the computer started prompting her as she ran through the checklist. It was quite capable of doing either or both sides of the checklist, but Jackie liked to be involved so that *she* knew what state the ship was in, too. She got her clearances—no flight plan this time—and began the take-off sequence. Aside from minor turbulence as they passed through the gathering clouds, it was a smooth lift to space.

As they cleared atmosphere, Jackie checked the navigation screen, cross checked that against what she saw out the windows, and boosted for a rendezvous orbit with the orbital dockyard. A few minutes later, as they reached orbital velocity, she cut the thrust.

"We're falling!" cried Marten.

Jackie and Carson turned to look at him. He was gripping the arms of his seat so tightly that his claws were beginning to dig into it, and he wore a terrified expression.

"Well, yes," Jackie said. They were in free fall, of course they were falling—falling around the planet, at the moment, as they had reached orbital velocity.

By this time Marten had realized that, and the look of terror was replaced by a sheepish grin. He still gripped the armrests tightly, though. "Sorry, I do not like zero gee," he said through clenched teeth.

"Okay, do you feel space sick? There are barf bags in the side pocket of the seat, I can get you some meds." As she said the last, Jackie had a sudden doubt. *Did* she have anything for space sickness in a timoan? Would human drugs help him or kill him? Well, the traumapod was programmed for all likely lifeforms, they could put him in there if it came to that.

"No, not sick" Marten gritted. "Just a reaction to the feeling of falling. It is passing." His hands were indeed starting to relax their death grip on the armrests.

"All right, then. Sorry, I guess I should have given you some warning. We have a rendezvous first, but we'll have gravity back after we go to warp." Jackie sometimes didn't bother with that unless the passengers asked for it. The small inefficiency of adjusting the warp field to leave space with a gradual curve inside the bubble didn't slow the ship by much, but Jackie *liked* zero gee.

∞ ∞ ∞

They came up on the orbital station a half-hour later, and Jackie pulsed the thrusters to match orbits. Near her assigned docking port, two large, oddly shaped objects floated. They looked like pieces of a hard-boiled egg sliced in half lengthwise, a smooth hemispherical, or rather, semi-ovoidal, surface on one side, an irregularly shaped surface on the other. They didn't match, either. They were the drop tanks.

The tanks had been on hand because one or the other of the university's Sapphires would sometimes need the extra range. Essentially they were large plastic balloons with appropriate connectors and fittings. When needed, the tanks were inflated to their pre-programmed size and shape and then rigidized. By Jackie's calculations, the pair would just give her the range to get to Chara in one long jump, with a slight reserve to maneuver in-system. It was tighter than she liked to cut it, but it would work.

The *Sophie* made fast to its docking latches, and a pair of space riggers moved out from an open airlock toward her. Roberts had radioed ahead; Carson was in a hurry.

"I'm going to suit up to go out and inspect," she told the others.

"Surely you don't need to do that," Carson said, not sure he entirely liked the idea of the captain leaving the ship while it was in space.

"Probably not, but it's *my* ship they're messing with, and if they mess up, it's only their jobs, but it's *our* lives."

"Yes, of course," said Carson.

"Back soon."

∞ ∞ ∞

Out on the hull, the riggers had already moved one tank into place and had just finished connecting the plumbing and wiring to the appropriate ports on the *Sophie*.

"That was fast," Jackie said to the riggers over the suit-to-suit. "Aren't those things massy?"

One space-suited figure looked around, saw her, and waved a greeting. "No ma'am, not very. Right now they're empty. Way too awkward to be messing with this close to a ship if they're full."

"Oh, of course, that makes sense."

They were moving the other tank into place now, pushing and pulling it into place with the practiced ease of experienced space riggers. "When we're done with this one we'll hook up the lines to fuel you from the station. Should have you filled up in an hour or so."

"Thank you."

∞ ∞ ∞

The *Sophie*, drop tanks in place and full, pulled away from the orbital dock. *Handles like a pig,* thought Jackie, *and about as pretty.* Jackie had tried to come up with an analogy for the combined shape of the *Sophie* and her surrounding drop tanks. The best she could come up with was an arrowhead stuck through a ping-pong ball, but that just didn't convey the massy, bloaty feeling that Jackie had when piloting her. Oh well, it was temporary.

She reoriented the ship, double checked that everyone was strapped in—Marten still looked rather miserable—and fired thrusters to head out to where space was empty enough to use the warp.

They reached that a couple of hours later, and Jackie readied the ship. The drop tanks added to the mass, but otherwise didn't seem to interfere with the handling, the mass was well distributed. She tapped commands into the navigation console, telling the ship to aim at Beta Canum Venaticorum, and the ship sluggishly rotated into position. She lined up the star in the targeting scope and ran a spectrum check that it was indeed the star they wanted. "Okay, sit tight, we're almost ready for warp," she told her passengers. "Secure for gravity." Another few taps on the keyboard and presses on the panel told the warp drive to ready itself. She heard the sounds of fuel pumping into the fusion reactor, of the system readying itself for the huge power demand of the warp generators.

∞ ∞ ∞

A small package on the outer hull of the ship, placed to be missed in a routine walk-around, on a spot away from the drop tanks, detected the pre-warp power surge from the ship and woke to full alertness. It queried its own inertial sensors, looked to see what stars it could see and where, and waited.

∞ ∞ ∞

"Standby . . ." Jackie checked the targeting again, scanned the board, ". . . in three, two, one, warp!" and pressed the button.

∞ ∞ ∞

The package detected another change in the ship's energy signature, and in the microseconds before the warp field formed, it fired a coded signal burst into the aether.

∞ ∞ ∞

There was a brief, half-imagined tingle as the Alcubierre-Broek bubble formed, and gravity came back. The view out the window was now a spangled black, with odd twinkles of distorted light working through the warp, and the brief flash as stray bits of space dust tore themselves apart in the tidal field of the bubble's edges. The *Sophie* surfed a bubble of warped space toward Chara at nearly 500 times the speed of light.

∞ ∞ ∞

"Boss, we just got a signal from the tracking beacon on the *Sophie*." The voice came over the speaker in Hopkins' cabin.

"Yes? So they've gone to warp? Did we get a direction?" he asked, the eagerness obvious in his voice.

"Yes and yes. Captain's just running the coordinates now, hang on." There was a brief pause, while over the speaker came the sound of talking in the background. "Looks like they're headed to a star named 'Chara', also called Beta Canorum Venti. . . . Vantati. . . Venaticum. Captain's plotting a course now."

"A course? Why aren't we just taking the same vector as *Sophie*?"

"Captain says it's too far for a single jump. Looks like they picked up drop tanks. We'll have to stop somewhere to refuel."

Hopkins swore under his breath. "Can't we get drop tanks ourselves?"

More sounds of background conversation. "Captain doesn't think so for the *Hawk*'s design, unless we get custom. When we stop at Kakuloa, if we clean out the two aft cabins and put in fuel bladders we can do the Chara run from there in one more jump, otherwise at least two."

"I'm tempted." But that would mean leaving crew behind or doubling them up. "No, screw that, two stops it is. Have him make warp as soon as possible. How long until we get there?"

"About four weeks. We'll be a few days behind."

That long? Crap. But Hopkins didn't see any alternative.

"Okay then, let's get moving. Whatever route Captain thinks fastest."

Chapter 19: En Route

Aboard the Sophie, between stars

THERE'S AN OLD saying about traveling: half the fun is getting there. That's not true of traveling in warp. There isn't much to see out the windows; after a while the sparkling black wears thin, like looking at static on a video screen, only darker. Within the gravity of a deliberately distorted warp bubble, Marten was happy. They reviewed their plans, such as they were. They checked their gear. They ate. They slept. They read or watched vids or played games on the ships computer, or on their omnis. They ate. They slept. And they talked.

"Us? No, we're not ape-descended or anything like apes," Marten explained to Jackie. "Non-arboreal. We're descended from something like your terrestrial mongoose or meerkats."

"Cats?"

"No, meerkats, social ground and burrow dwellers, related to mongooses. Go back 65 megayears and we might share common ancestry with cats, but we're closer to mongoose. Or rather, our ancestors were. Since they were ground dwellers, they stood on their hind legs a lot—like your meerkats—to watch for predators. Our—oh," Marten looked at Carson, "what is the word, scientists who study old men?"

"Old men? I don't . . . oh! Paleoanthropologists."

"That is it! Our paleoanthropologists, or should that be paleosuricatologists, think that is what freed up our hands to start using tools, to dig for food. Our ancestors claws weren't as well developed as a meerkat's are." He held out his hand for Jackie to examine. "See, more like your fingernails."

Jackie looked at the fingers and held up her own hand to compare. Narrower and sharper, not covering so much of the back of the fingertip, but yes, not quite claws either. "Not retractable, either? Cats' claws are, but I guess I wouldn't know about meerkats."

"No, ours aren't retractable." Marten said. "We do share one trait with your terrestrial cats, though."

"Oh, what's that?"

"We hate going in the water. We're not swimmers—our muscle density is high and we don't have the subcutaneous fat that you aquatic apes do."

"Aquatic apes, what?" Jackie had never heard of this.

Hannibal helped her out. "Yes, there are theories—hypotheses, really—that humans went through a semi-aquatic stage in our evolution. We have a dive reflex—physiological changes when we're in water—we float a damn sight better than most apes, and so on. No fossil evidence, of course, but that doesn't prove anything."

"So you can't swim? Some cats actually can. Tigers, I think."

"Not to save my life," Marten said, then added "well, for that maybe, for a short while. But the idea of swimming lessons is as unpleasant to us as, say, falling lessons."

"Oh, some humans do that too. It's called skydiving, jumping out of an aircraft with a parachute, or for the real enthusiasts, from space with a re-entry pack."

"What, for *fun*?" Marten looked at her wide-eyed.

"Yeah, I guess it's our arboreal heritage. A lot of people don't like enclosed spaces, though. I don't mind starship cabins or houses, but the idea of crawling down a hole in the ground gives me shivers," said Jackie.

"What about you, Hannibal?" asked Marten. "Does anything scare you?"

Hannibal looked thoughtful. Plenty of things scared him in the sense that he would rather not have them happen—getting seriously injured, losing, annual performance reviews, grading student papers—but did anything just plain give him the creeps or weird him out? "Most things that might have frightened me as a boy I've grown out of. I don't particularly like spiders, but I'll deal with them if I have to."

"Spiders?"

"Yes. Probably traces back to my childhood. When I was a kid in pre-school, oh, maybe age four, there was an older boy who liked to terrorize us little kids. He would find spiders around the outside of the building or the fence in the schoolyard and chase us with them. He liked to pull the legs off of them too. Bizarre fellow, thinking back on it. Hate to think how he might have ended up. They took him away for a psych-eval and we never saw him again. Anyway, put me right off spiders for the longest time, I'd jump at the sight of something small that looked like it was crawling, even a piece of lint."

"Really? I wouldn't have thought it, nothing seems to bother you."

"Oh, I can tolerate the beggars now. I've spent too much time in the field, crawling around in musty ruins and digging in the dirt. Can't afford the time to be squeamish about them.

"And some things do bother me. Grading assignments and bloody academic politicking, that sort of thing. I prefer the field."

∞ ∞ ∞

A few days later, Jackie checked the computer and turned to the others. "We'll be out of warp in about six hours, better get everything stowed for free fall."

Marten got an odd expression on his face. "I suppose there's no way to avoid that?"

"Sorry, artificial gravity is a side effect of warp, and we won't be under thrust until I figure out exactly where we are and where we want to get to."

"I know, I know. It was not a serious question."

They spent the next few hours ensuring that everything was stowed away and there was nothing loose to float about the cabin. They also took advantage of the last opportunity for who knew how long to use the head without worrying about zero gee.

"Okay, we've got another half hour by the clock, but we could come out early if we start hitting much dust, so let's get strapped in."

∞ ∞ ∞

It went the full half-hour, and as the timer neared zero, Jackie warned them. "Coming out of warp . . . now."

There was the half-imagined tingle of the warp field collapsing, the light of a nearby star against smooth black through the window, and they were falling again.

Chapter 20: Chara Arrival

Beta Canum Venaticorum (Chara) system

JACKIE PUT THE *Sophie* into a slow roll. The drop tanks would be more hindrance than help now. She hit the jettison control and the now-useless tanks cut loose with a muffled thump. She watched as they drifted away in opposite directions, watched as they shrank to pinpoints in the distance and disappeared. She set the *Sophie* to rotate slowly through its navigation sequence, turning to pick out selected distant stars and two nearby galaxies on its image sensors. Finally it triangulated them and determined just where in the star system she was. Tiny vagaries in warp geometry and their exact positioning at the start left a broad region of this system that they could have arrived in.

"So, where are the planets?" asked Marten.

"I'm still working that out, we need to triangulate where we are first." Jackie keyed a few commands into the computer, then muttered "Dang!"

Carson looked over at that. "There's a problem?"

"Oh, nothing really. This system is relatively unexplored. The ephemeris data isn't very precise and it's a couple of years old. I don't have a good fix on where the planets are *now*. No big deal."

"And this is no big deal because . . .?"

"Watch." Jackie keyed a few more commands into the ship's computer, then pressed a button.

There was a brief tingle as though the ship were going into warp, the windows flickered, then everything was normal again. Except that a couple of bright stars had moved.

"What just happened?" asked Marten.

"I took an image of the local sky, then did a fifty millisecond warp jump. We're eight million kilometers away from where we were a moment ago. Those stars that looked like they moved are really planets, and the computer is now figuring out their positions from the parallax." Jackie checked the computer screen. "Here we go. The bright bluish one there," she pointed at it, "is the habitable one, Chara III. The orange one near it is the gas giant, Chara IV. I think Chara II must be in line with its star, either this side or the other, and Chara I is that faint star washed out in the glare."

"Don't they have names?" said Carson.

"Not in my database."

"All right. How long to get to Chara III?"

"Give me a minute." She checked the computer, running through a couple of different possibilities. "Okay, we can jump a bit closer, then the rest of the way on thrust." She paused, glanced at the fuel readings, then nodded to herself. There was enough. "Probably about fourteen hours, maybe a bit more to get set up for orbit."

"Any sign of other ships?"

Jackie turned back to the controls and ran a quick comm sweep. "No signals. Of course if they were running silent we'd have to see them or get a radar bounce, but I don't think there's anyone here." She turned back to face the others. "There should be farmsteads on the southern continent, the data bank mentioned a Mennonite settlement, but they'll be at a low tech level."

"Well, let's go in, then."

Jackie turned back to the controls and started setting up the flight sequence.

∞ ∞ ∞

Thirteen hours later, Chara III loomed large in the forward window screens. The coloring was Earth-like, with deep blue oceans, dark green vegetation on the three large land masses, mixed with the browns of desert and the white of snow-capped mountains and polar ice. The south polar region was ocean, with patches of sea ice reflecting white. A large, roughly peanut-shaped land mass stretched from the equator to over the north pole, covering perhaps a quarter of the northern hemisphere. Patterns of white cloud swirled about the planet.

∞ ∞ ∞

Jackie brought the ship into an inclined, low orbit around the planet. They'd map the surface first and plan from there.

"Okay Carson," she said, "now what?"

"We look for a previously inhabited area, then try to identify landmarks," said Hannibal.

"Previously inhabited area? I take it you're not talking about the Mennonite settlement on the southern continent. Are we going to pay them a courtesy call, by the way?"

"Do you have any cargo for them?"

"No, I didn't want to reveal our destination, so I didn't even ask—although I should have according to my courier license." She hadn't been too worried about that. The odds of packages destined here from Taprobane were minimal; it would all have been sent to a closer jumping off point, probably Sawyers. "I do have net updates, if they even have a net. I'll hail them when we're in range—assuming they have a radio they keep on."

"Sure, as long as it doesn't slow down our search."

"For a previously inhabited area. What exactly do you have in mind?"

"I'm assuming that the Spacefarers wouldn't have come here unless there'd been an intelligent species for them to interact with. Of course I could be wrong about that. Since we know there are no intelligent natives now, we look for where they've been. There should be some signs even after this time. We look for straight lines, areas that look like they were once cultivated, and so on. I'll feed the images from the multispectral scanners into the archeological software."

"What multispectral scanners? This isn't a survey ship, professor, it's basically a yacht. But—"

"What? Oh, damn, of course. This will take forever if we have to eyeball it. What sensors do we have?"

"As I was about to say, we have conventional imaging. We've got infrared, and radar, but they're not registered to each other, the sizes and pixels are different."

Marten interrupted. "Not a problem. I have worked with imaging before. If you have a standard software load, I can create a set of software filters to combine those into a format Hannibal's program will take."

"Okay," Jackie said, "you can use this terminal. Let Carson know when it's ready to roll. Carson, you and I *really* need to talk about your plan. Let's get all the hidden assumptions out now."

∞ ∞ ∞

"No response from the colony to my hails," said Jackie several orbits later. "That doesn't surprise me, there's no reason for them to keep their comm gear powered on, assuming they have any. No echoes from network pings, either. They take this low tech approach seriously."

"Some sects more than others, I think," Carson said. "But they probably don't want to rely on something they can't easily replace."

"I suppose. It's just a little creepy, though. I've taken expeditions to some pretty isolated spots, but there are always signs of other people in the system. Radio chatter, automated beacons, something."

"Well, we didn't come here to chat. Anything interesting on the scans?"

"Not so far. Next orbit takes us over the colony anyway, then the middle of the northern continent."

∞ ∞ ∞

"Carson, take a look at this." Jackie's voice held a mix of curiosity and urgency.

"What is it, did we find something?" Carson pulled himself into the cockpit area, gliding in above the chair Jackie was strapped into. Marten followed, hand over hand along the corridor grab rail.

"No, these are scans of the colony site," Jackie answered. "I know what cultivated fields look like from orbit, and these aren't it. Look." Jackie put several images up on the main screen.

"You know what they look like if they're cultivated with automated machinery, but . . ." Carson's voice trailed off as he examined the images. "That's odd, these fields are overgrown. Marten, what do you make of this?"

"Hard to make out from this altitude, but you're right, nobody has worked these fields this season. The vegetation is too random. The paths are becoming overgrown. What about the buildings?"

Jackie tapped out a sequence and several different images came up on the screen. "This is the area around the fields." She pointed at the side of one image, where there were several smaller rectangular shapes. "There, buildings on that side."

"Can you zoom in?"

"Somewhat, we don't have a lot of resolution." She zoomed the image. "No obvious damage."

"No. In fact that looks like it might a person walking between those two buildings. See the shadow?"

"Show us the rest of the area around the buildings," said Marten. "Perhaps you just happened to see a fallow field in the first image."

"Fallow?"

"Yes. No industrial or bioengineered fertilizers, right? So they probably do crop rotation, leaving fields unplanted for a season to recover. Check the other side of that village."

"I don't think there are enough buildings down there to call it a village, but okay." Jackie had been flipping through images as she talked. She put another one up on the main screen. "I guess you're right, these fields look more cultivated. Still a bit ragged, but like you said, Carson, they won't have modern equipment. I don't see anything that looks like people, though. Where is every-body?"

They scanned through several images. Individuals would barely register at this scale, but they ought to be able to pick out their shadows. But there were none.

"That's just too weird, Carson. Something is wrong down there."

"I agree," Marten said. "There are no signs of people or ani-mals either. In an agrarian colony, people should be out at this time of day, judging by the sun angle."

"Could they be hiding from us?" Carson asked. It didn't seem likely, but it was a possibility.

"I doubt it," said Jackie. "They might have known we were here if they'd heard my hails, but why not answer? And the light-ing is wrong for them to have seen us from the ground. It's day-time, their sky is too bright right now. Why hide even if they did see us?"

"What about that figure we saw earlier?" asked Marten. "We know there's at least one person down there."

"Do we? All we saw was a shadow," said Carson.

"What else would cast a shadow like that?"

"A scarecrow."

"Okay, that's just too weird. We'd better land and check it out." Jackie looked at the navigation console. "We've done about a third of an orbit since we overflew them. I'll land next time around. De-orbit burn in about twenty minutes."

"Do we have to?" Carson asked. This was more wasted time. "What do you think we're going to find?"

"Yes, we do. If there's somebody down there that needs help, we have a duty to assist."

"But, right now? Surely a few more days won't make a difference."

"It might. But aren't you curious to know what's going on?"

"Of course I am. But I'm more curious about the possible alien archive, or arsenal, or whatever it is. That's why we're out here, remember?"

"And we're still looking for it. Who knows, maybe the colonists found it and zapped themselves with alien tech."

"What?" It sounded like Jackie thought she was joking, but as Carson thought about it, it wasn't something he could just dismiss. "Oh, all right. We'll land and take a quick look to find out where the colonists went, or what happened to them. But if we find a post or a tree with 'Croatoan' carved on it . . ."

Jackie and Marten both stared at him. "What in the world—" started Jackie.

"—are you talking about?" finished Marten.

Carson just sighed and shook his head. "Never mind."

∞ ∞ ∞

The de-orbit burn was routine and Jackie had plenty of delta-vee to adjust for how much the planet had rotated under their orbit track. She brought the *Sophie* in for an inspection pass at 2000 meters above the settlement.

"I still don't see any people. Things do look well-maintained, though, except for those fallow fields." She scanned the area looking for a place to set down. She needed a clearing far enough from the buildings to not cause damage with her exhaust, but didn't want to land in the fields. If there were still people here, she didn't want to piss them off. There was one, a small meadow, with a broad stream along one side where she could refuel. "I'm going to set down there," she told the others as she turned the *Sophie* and reduced altitude for an inspection pass. "Anyone see any cows or anything?"

"No, you're clear."

She glided the ship in, flared to a near stall twenty meters from the stream and touched down with just a brief burst of thrusters.

"Okay, we're down, but nobody goes anywhere until I check the atmosphere. It should be breathable but we don't know what happened to the colonists."

"I don't think you need to worry about that, Jackie," said Carson.

"Yes I—" but there'd been something ironic in Carson's tone. She turned to look at him. "Why not?"

He grinned and pointed out the portside window. "We've got company."

Crossing the field from the direction of the settlement was a trio of figures, clearly human, bearded, wearing broad-brimmed hats, white shirts and black trousers.

"I think we found the settlers," Carson continued. "Or rather, they seem to have found us."

∞ ∞ ∞

A few minutes later, Roberts and Carson were standing at the foot of the *Sophie*'s boarding ramp as the three men approached. Jackie could see several others at the far edge of the field.

"Hello!" she called out as the men approached the ship. "I'm Captain Roberts, this is my ship the *Sophie*. Nobody answered my hails. We landed to see if we could render assistance."

The three looked at each other, then back at her. One of them, who looked older than the other two, perhaps in his fifties, took a step forward.

"I thank thee, and bid all of you welcome. We have no radio. Who would we talk to? And why do thee think we need assistance?"

"Uh, we couldn't see anyone from orbit. The place looked empty." Jackie looked around in confusion. "Why weren't you working the fields? Where was everybody?"

The two men to the rear of the elder looked at each other. Were they smirking?

The elder drew himself up a bit straighter, as if offended. "Madame Captain," he said, "today is Sunday. We were in *church*."

Behind her, Carson made a choking sound. *Is he laughing at me?* thought Jackie. At least he had the grace to stifle it.

"But I do thank thee," the elder continued, "for waiting until service was over before roaring in here in that noisy machine of yours."

∞ ∞ ∞

Their visit to the settlement was brief, but enlightening. Carson got the impression they didn't particularly want visitors, at least not outsiders, although they were certainly polite enough. For his own part he wanted to resume the search for something archeologically significant as soon as possible, and here they had been quite helpful.

"I don't know about what it is thee is looking for," the elder had said to him, "but the other continent showed signs of long ago cultivation, terraces and the like. One of the reasons we settled here is to be far away from all that."

"You were concerned about contact?"

"Not specifically. There were no signs that the natives were still around, but we thought it best to separate ourselves on the chance that there were."

"Probably a wise idea. Do you have coordinates?" asked Carson.

"That we do not. But it was mid-continent, along the western edge of a central plain."

"That gives us a place to start looking. Thank you."

∞ ∞ ∞

It was on the third orbit after leaving the settlement of New Conestogo when the computer, checking for regular features as they scanned, alerted them to a possible site.

"I think this is it." Carson had a magnified image up on the main screen. The others huddled around. "Look here . . . and here" he said, pointing to several vague rectangular outlines in gently rolling plain in the northern continent, near the foothills of a north-south mountain range. "I think these are fields. The radar shows these areas as much smoother than the surrounding plain, and the outlines are more distinct. I think they cleared these of fieldstone and made stone fences—it's typical of agricultural fields in a once-glaciated area. And here, see these parallel lines following the contour of this hill? I'm sure that's terracing."

"But why terrace the hills when they could just expand farther out onto the plain?"

"Hmm, a very good question. That's a keen observation. I haven't a clue."

"Maybe there were some plains-dwelling creatures they'd rather avoid," Marten suggested.

"Or perhaps the land was too swampy, or a lake."

"Huh. What about the landmarks?" said Jackie.

"There's a stream cutting a notch through this hogback ridge *here*," Carson said, pointing it out. "And this peak" he tapped the screen "looks high enough and is in line with the notch. Of course we won't know for sure until we go down for a closer look."

"Okay. Assuming that is the right place, where's our destination?"

"There'll be a large structure, most likely a pyramid, but it could be something else, a monolith perhaps. It will be on high ground, a level area. There's something near the peak of this mountain," Carson pointed at the screen again. "The lighting is wrong in this image so I can't tell if this shadow is from something artificial or just the rocks. We'll have to go down and take a look. Can you land us near there?"

Jackie examined the images thoughtfully. "Not on the mountain, no, and I don't see any clear area except near the stone fences."

"What about one of those valleys?"

"The mountain winds will be too unpredictable to try any of those narrow valleys, even if the valley floor is smooth and level enough, which I doubt."

"How about flying slowly past it on the way in?"

"That I can do. Anything else?"

"Not for now. Let's just get down there."

"Right. Okay everybody, strap in and prepare for de-orbit."

∞ ∞ ∞

The *Sophie* cruised at a thousand meters above the old settlement. At this height, Jackie could make out the low stone fences outlining the fields they'd seen from orbit. A cluster of small, rocky rectangles, overgrown with the scrubby bushes that dotted the landscape, indicated what had probably been houses, storage areas, or perhaps a meeting hall.

"Okay, this looks like it," Carson said. "Can you set her down and we'll check it out from the ground?"

"Right. That field to the southeast looks clear, and it's near the stream so I can top up. I'll set down there."

Jackie throttled back as she banked the ship around to line up on the field, then flipped a switch. She heard and felt the usual series of clanks, vibrations and a muffled hum as the gear doors opened and the landing gear lowered. She brought the ship in over the edge of the field at about twenty meters, then pulled the nose up to kill their forward speed, throttling up the ventral thrusters as she transitioned to a hover. The view below showed that the area was clear of large rocks, small trees, or other obstacles, and she set the *Sophie* down with a gentle thump in the middle of a cloud of dust kicked up by the landing jets.

The aft port-side thruster had started a small fire in the grass—or whatever passed for grass on this world—but a quick blast of water routed past the jet nozzle put that out.

They were down.

Chapter 21: Expedition

Surface, Chara III

JACKIE PORED over the aerial photographs they'd taken on the way in. She muttered to herself, then cross checked something against the radar altimetry data. "It's no good," she said, looking up at Carson. "There's not enough room on the summit, and the ground nearby either slopes too much or has too many trees to land safely. We'll have to leave the ship here and hike in."

Carson studied the images, tracing out possible routes with his fingers. He noticed a clear area about a third of the way to their destination. "What about this valley here?"

"No, too risky. Look at the topography; the floor slopes, and it's littered with small boulders. The winds will be unpredictable around those ridges, too. I'd rather walk than risk the ship by setting down in there."

"Okay, you're the captain." Carson paused, turned to Marten. "That's what, a two day hike?"

"Perhaps three. It's unfamiliar territory and we have to climb a mountain at the end," Marten said. He turned to Jackie. "Are you up for a hike or are you going to stay with the ship?"

"Oh, I'm coming. I'll lock the ship down and rig a proximity alarm to scare off any animals." She turned to a different screen and checked a reading. "Tanks are full, I need to reel the hose in."

"Fair enough. Okay, let's get the gear pulled together. The bad guys may show up in a few days, we need to make time."

∞ ∞ ∞

Two hours later the trio were following the creek upstream through the notch in the hogback, keeping to the course Carson had plotted out and downloaded into their omnis.

The rocks on either side of the notch showed heavy folding and layering. Millions of years ago this had been the bed of an ancient sea, building up layers of sediment. Carson wondered what sort of fossils might be found if they had time to look. If any at all—this planet might have been more recently terraformed. Then the sea had dried up or drained as tectonic forces had caused the continental rock to fold up, to buckle and crack, forming the mountains they were headed toward. Carson scanned the terrain with a practiced eye—he was no planetologist, but any good field archeologist knows some geology. The rock looked like limestone, weakened by folding. There might be caves or springs in the area. It reminded him of the eastern foothills of the Rocky Mountains back on Earth, in central Colorado; there might even be hot springs.

∞ ∞ ∞

Behind the hogback, a long narrow valley stretched out in both directions, perpendicular to their path, parallel to the ridge and the foothills ahead. The valley floor was uneven, with rolling hummocks and odd rock outcrops, cut across by the stream bed. A few hundred meters away they could see a small herd of grazing creatures which from this distance resembled deer or antelope, although given the terrain they might have been more like mountain goat. The animals ignored them and continued munching on the grassy ground cover and occasional small bush. The trio ignored them and kept to their path.

"What sort of predators do you suppose preys on those things?" asked Jackie as they hiked.

The others looked at each other, then back at Jackie. "Probably some sort of cat analog, or maybe something canine like a wolf or coyote," Carson said.

"Dangerous to humans?" She saw Marten's look and added "or timoans?"

"It wouldn't know what either was, so probably not—but don't act like food. And feel free to make noise to encourage that impression."

Jackie started whistling, and as she did so, slid her pistol out of its holster. She thumbed the status button and confirmed that it was loaded, then tested the action. As she slipped it back into the holster, she heard the others working the actions of their sidearms, too.

∞ ∞ ∞

As the ground began to slope upward, away from the rolling plain on the valley floor, the grassy vegetation gave way to scrubby bushes, then to a full fledged pine forest with deciduous trees mixed in. Most of the latter were small, spindly trees that looked something like aspen, but the leaves were more fan-shaped, like ginkgo leaves. They still followed the small creek bed upstream, and the burble of water tumbling over the rocks accompanied them. To Carson's irritation, so did the occasional whine of insects. The air smelled of pine and damp earth.

∞ ∞ ∞

It was on the back slope of one of the foothills, Pyramid Mountain still ahead, when the saber tooth attacked.

Carson was in the lead, Roberts following, with Marten bringing up the rear as they walked along the wooded trail. At intervals on either side of the trail, and from what they could see, back into the woods, large slab-like boulders littered the ground. Carson had said that they were the remnants of a harder stratum of rock that had collapsed like this as softer layers beneath eroded out from under. Marten had fallen back a little, and as he walked the path next to a boulder—this one higher than his head—the animal pounced.

There was no scream, the animal just leaped. Marten sensed motion and flinched, which was enough to throw off the animal's timing, and the slash of the sharp, fifteen-centimeter teeth—like daggers—missed his neck. The animal was nearly Marten's size, about a meter and a half long, with two saber-like teeth and claws far sharper than Marten's. It screamed now in frustration and circled to leap again. Marten took a step back to give himself room and stumbled as he backed into another rock outcrop. He was cornered.

∞ ∞ ∞

Carson kept up a steady pace on the trail. They were rounding a boulder when he felt a pinprick stab on the back of his neck.

"Ouch!" He smacked at it and brought his hand around to see the squashed remains of a small insect and a smear of blood, *his* blood. "Damn it, Jackie, I thought you said there were no mosquitoes on this planet!"

"There aren't," she said. She looked around. There were small dark flecks silently weaving in the air. She took Carson's hand and examined the chitinous remains on it. "That's a black fly."

"Lord. What stark raving lunatic would deliberately populate a planet with carnivorous insects?"

"Well . . ."

"No, that was a rhetorical question. Don't tell me about whatever particular ecological niche they fill, I don't want to know." Carson shook his head, then muttered something about "accursed vampiric vermin." He looked back along the trail, past Jackie. A hundred meters farther back it curved around some boulders, and the trees on either side were sparse. Something, some*one*, was missing. "Where's Marten?"

Chapter 22: Sabertooth

In the mountains, Chara III

THE CARNIVORE jumped, again going for Marten's neck, its claws reaching to grab and hold. Marten ducked under the leap, but felt a searing pain across his left shoulder as the animal's claws slashed him. He twisted and repaid the beast by slashing his own claws across its belly. It yowled, but Marten knew he hadn't hurt it much. He again tried to get space, to get time to draw his pistol. The animal wasn't having any of it.

It pounced again, lower this time, perhaps instinctively knowing that Marten's torso wouldn't move as fast as a limb or head. Marten anticipated the move, but there was nowhere for him to go. *Where are the others?* The civet-like beast's jaws came toward him, mouth impossibly wide, saber teeth menacing. With the uncanny speed of Marten's kind, and with no other option, Marten grabbed a fang in each hand. The pain startled him, the teeth had an edge as well as a point, but he hung on; his life depended on it.

The civet was even more startled; this was a tactic it had never encountered. It was like its teeth were jammed in something. It pulled back, pushing forward with its clawed forepaws for leverage, snarling.

Marten cried out as the claws raked his chest, but still he held on. *Damn it, where are Hannibal and Jackie?* He couldn't hold this thing forever. He felt its hot breath on his face, it stank of old meat. "Hannibal! Jackie!" he shouted. His hands were bloody, his fingers on fire from the serrated back edge of the fangs, and his grip was slipping as the animal struggled.

Suddenly the animal jerked violently, spasmodically. At the same time, Marten heard a gunshot. Another shot, two, and the great sabertooth hung limp. Marten raised a foot to its chest and kicked it away as he released his death grip on the fangs. "About time you showed up," he said to the others, a dozen meters away with weapons drawn.

∞ ∞ ∞

Roberts tended to Marten's injuries while Carson kept watch, pistol drawn, in case the beast had a partner. "It doesn't look too serious," she said.

"If you were on this side of my skin," said Marten, "you wouldn't be saying that. It hurts like hell."

"I'm sure it does. But luckily he only got his claws in where you have bone underneath, your shoulder blades and ribs. A little lower and we might be trying to figure out how to stuff your guts back in." Roberts was cleaning those scratches as she said this.

"Oh, charming. Thank you very much. Just what *was* that thing anyway? Those teeth! I felt like my fingers were going to be cut off." He flexed his blood soaked hands. "Still feels like it."

Carson glanced at the animal's body, then resumed his lookout. "Looks a bit like a saber tooth cat or tiger," he said, "they evolved several times on Earth. Body is more like a civet than a cat, though, although they're related."

"Let me finish these scratches then I'll take care of your hands," said Jackie as she pulled a packet of topical antibiotic out of her first aid kit. She paused, "maybe I better use yours," she said, "I don't know how you'll react to this stuff."

"Don't worry, it's the same. Timoans are tolerant of most common human drugs."

She applied the antibiotic and bandaged the wounds. "How are the muscles? Some of those scratches were deep."

Marten took a few cautious deep breaths, carefully shrugged his shoulder, swung his arms, and winced. "It still hurts, but I will manage. Thank you."

"No problem. That was pretty amazing, grabbing its fangs like that. Why, *how*, did you do that?"

"I didn't have much choice, I didn't have anywhere to go and there were these two great spear points coming at me. It was just reflex, I grabbed them so they wouldn't come any nearer."

"Well. I'm just sorry we didn't get it recorded; nobody's going to believe it."

"Maybe I should remove the fangs and hang them on a necklace?" Marten grinned.

"Maybe on the way back," Carson said, gathering up his pack. "Come on, let's get going. I'd like to put distance between us and the cat, in case it had a mate."

∞ ∞ ∞

They pushed on for another hour. They were climbing again, Marten was holding his own despite his injuries, but was thankful when Jackie gave them an excuse to call a halt.

"Hey guys," Jackie's breathing was labored. "Have we come far enough for today? My leg muscles are killing me. Too much zero gee time, I guess."

Carson thought for a moment. They hadn't made as good time as he'd hoped because of the saber attack, but the sun—Chara—was getting low in the sky. It would be dark soon, especially here in the shadow of the mountains. They'd have to stop.

"All right. It looks like a clearing ahead, maybe there'll be enough breeze to discourage these damn black flies. We'll set up camp there."

∞ ∞ ∞

Hannibal pulled a small green cylinder from his backpack and placed it on the ground. It rather resembled a smoke grenade complete with a pull-ring, but lacking the handle. He looked around. The area was clear of rocks, twigs or sharp stones, it would do fine. He pulled the ring on the package and stepped back. He always got a kick out of watching this. The cylinder extruded a rod a meter tall and the collapsible tent began assembling itself, first opening like an umbrella then followed by a sequence of unfoldings and unrollings almost too quick to follow. Within a minute it had assembled itself into geodesic dome nearly three meters in diameter. "Tent's up," Carson called to the others, "you can stow your bags."

He looked over at Marten, who despite bandaged hands had gathered small pieces of deadwood and branches and dropped them down in a pile. "What's that for?"

"A campfire, of course." Marten was surprised at the question.

"We've got self-heating meals, you know, and the tent has a light."

"Sure, but it makes things cozier, and it will discourage animals."

"Fine, I've nothing against a fire, so long as we don't burn down the forest." It wasn't really that dry, and the ground here was clear of leaf litter. "But just to be sure about the animals, I'll set up a perimeter alarm." Carson dug into his pack again and pulled out a small electronic device. It would sound if anything bigger than a tree rat came within twenty meters of the camp. The hope was that the noise would scare the animal off as well as alerting the campers.

Jackie returned from a trip into the bushes, and they sat down to a quick dinner of food bars and instant hot chocolate, too tired to bother with even the simple self-heating meals. After cleanup, they all crawled into their sleepsacks and, worn out from the day's exertions, fell quickly asleep.

∞ ∞ ∞

Carson woke in the night to take care of a biological necessity and found Jackie sitting outside the tent, her back to the dying fire, looking at the sky.

"Hey, what's up, Jackie? Is everything all right?"

"Oh, sure. Just a touch of insomnia. I came out to look at the stars."

Carson looked up. Chara III's moons were both below the horizon, and the dark sky was filled with brilliant pinpoints. Toward the east there was a grouping that looked familiar. "Is that Orion?" he asked. "The belt looks wrong." Most of the bright stars in the constellation Orion were far enough from T-space that the constellation looked much the same from Earth, Sawyer's World, or Tau Ceti. But here the leftmost star in the belt was out of line, as if the sword were dragging that side of the belt down, and one of Orion's shoulders, Bellatrix?, was dislocated.

Jackie looked where Hannibal was pointing. "Yes, that's Orion. He's starting to look a little different out here."

"Yep. Can we see home from here?" They might be on the wrong side of the planet, or of the sun.

Jackie grinned. "Whose?" She pointed at a bright star about halfway across the sky from Orion. "Okay, that's Sirius, an easy landmark because it's so bright. Follow a line of about four medium bright stars to the right, to the two that are close together," she pointed, "the upper one is Sol. Up from that, about half the angular distance from Sirius at a right angle, that's Tau Ceti." She lowered her arm a few degrees. "Down from Sol about the same distance, that one is Alpha Centauri. Well, it's two of course, but too far from here to see that without a telescope." She gestured again. "Go right from there about half that distance, that medium star near a couple of others, that's Epsilon Indi."

"You know your stars."

"I *am* a starship captain," she said.

Carson held up his hand at arm's length. He could just about cover the rough triangle around Sol that their various home stars made. *A long way from home*, he thought. A movement overhead caught his eye, and he turned to look. A bright star moved steadily in a straight line from south to north. "Jackie," his voice serious, "look there, is that what I think it is?"

Jackie looked in the direction Carson was pointing and muttered a curse. "Crap. That's way too bright for anything we left in orbit. I think we're going to have company."

"How soon?"

"Hard to say. It's nighttime, so they won't pick out *Sophie* unless they're looking hard, with active sensors. Even if they do, I doubt they'll try a landing in the dark. I wouldn't, not in unknown territory. Best case they won't be down until sometime tomorrow. Then they'll have to figure out which way we went, if they follow. They might just wait for us to get back to the *Sophie*."

Carson weighed that. "Not much we can do about it now anyway. All right, we move out at first light."

∞ ∞ ∞

Aboard the *Hawk*, they had indeed been looking hard, and had spotted the *Sophie*.

"It's in a clearing near the foothills of that mountain range," the pilot said, pointing at a display. "The ship is mostly powered down so they may be away from it."

"Probably hiking into the mountains," said Hopkins. "Okay, prepare to land. Set us down nearby."

"Now? It's risky landing in unknown terrain at night."

"Yes, now. I don't want to give them any more lead than they already have. It was good enough terrain for them to land, so can you. Switch on the window's light amp, that's what it's for."

"It's not—" the pilot began, then broke off under Hopkins' glare. "Very well." He touched a control and announced to the ship, "Prepare for reentry and landing."

Chapter 23: To the Pyramid

The mountains, Chara III

JACKIE AWOKE the next morning to a mountain obscured by fog or low lying cloud. A fine dew had settled over the camp. The outside of the tent was wet, and everything felt clammy and more than a little cold.

"Oh, lovely morning," she said, her voice dripping sarcasm in much the way the tent dripped dew.

She seemed to be in a sour mood, but Carson knew her well enough by now to recognize that as a symptom of coffee deficiency as much as anything else. He had already heated water for instant, and he handed her a cup as she sat up.

Roberts took a sip and made a face. "Ugh, that's vile stuff. Thank you." She took another swallow. "It's still an ugly day," she said, but in a slightly more mellow voice.

"I think it's just morning mist," said Carson. "It should burn off once Chara rises a little higher in the sky. I expect it will be clear enough by the time we're ready to go again." Carson was already starting to pack his gear. He had obviously been awake for a while.

"You're probably right." Jackie crawled out of her sleep sack and looked around. "Where's Marten? How's he doing?"

At that point Marten, who'd been taking care of business, came back into the tent. "Right here. I'm doing rather well. Shoulder and ribs still hurt like blazes if I move the wrong way, and my hands are a little tender, but I'm good to go. I heal quickly."

"Good, glad to hear it." Jackie looked at Carson. "So what's for breakfast?"

"Well, let's see. We have food bar, food bar, or, for variety, food bar."

"What, no ration bar? I'm disappointed. I guess I'll have the food bar, then."

Carson tossed one to her. "Eat up, I'd like to be out of here soon. We're wasting daylight, and company may be coming."

Fifteen minutes later, the tent was down, all the gear stowed, the fire doused and the ashes stirred, and they were breaking trail again. They could see blue sky through the thinning, patchy cloud.

∞ ∞ ∞

The vegetation had thinned out. At this altitude, the trees were scrubby little imitations of their brethren on the lower slopes. The ground was more lichen-covered broken rock than it was soil or pine needles, and the going was getting steeper.

"Hey Hannibal," Roberts called up the path. "I've been meaning to ask you something."

"Yes, Jackie, what's that?"

"Why would anybody build a pyramid near the top of a mountain instead of down on the plains where it would be a lot easier to build? Not to mention easier to get to?" They were taking more frequent rests now.

"Good question. It *could* be because they wanted it to be difficult to get to, so that only the most persistent would be worthy, and they had to prove their worthiness. And I think that it proves that they used advanced technology to build it. No dragging great stone blocks up here."

"Ah. I guess we're proving ourselves worthy, then. I hope it appreciates the effort."

Marten chuckled. Carson ignored him. "There are other possibilities. When the pyramid was built, the plain below could have been a lake, or a shallow sea, or covered with ice."

"Ice?"

"This planet has polar ice caps and we saw snow on the peaks at lower latitudes. It may have come out of an ice age not many thousand years ago. If so, that whole plain below, and a good chunk of this mountain, would have been under a few hundred to a thousand meters of ice. Or water, if it were warmer. They probably put it up here because they could be sure of it staying dry and accessible. Kind of makes you wonder what's hiding under the ice or on flooded continental shelf on other planets."

"That's what neutrino tomography is for, to—"

"The resolution isn't fine enough," Carson said, interrupting.

"Okay," Jackie continued, "but they could have built it closer to the equator, where the climate is more consistent."

"She's got you there, Hannibal," said Marten.

"Not really, you're more likely to find a civilization at these latitudes, where there's some seasonal variation to encourage agriculture. Life is too easy, too constant at the equator." It was hard to tell from Carson's voice whether he was extemporizing or really meant it.

"Uh huh. Still damn silly if you ask me," said Roberts.

"I didn't."

"Oh, right."

The ascent continued.

∞ ∞ ∞

They were nearing the peak now. As they trekked up the rocky slope, they would catch occasional glimpses of the structure ahead of them as it came into view above the rocks. Their breath was coming shorter—they'd been climbing steadily, and the air was thinner at this altitude. There was also the anticipation.

Finally they reached the last ridge, and the rough ground they'd been walking on gave way to a level area—still with a few rocks, gravel and a few small, hardy, alpine plants. Before them rose a high-peaked, four-sided pyramid. Beyond that the mountain rose higher. This level area looked like it had been deliberately leveled, carved out of the side of the mountain just below the peak. But it was the—what, building? temple? tomb?—that caught their attention.

It was constructed of a pinkish rock or what looked like rock. It wasn't granite, or sandstone, or marble, or anything any of the three could readily identify. For the most part the sides were flat, once polished to a high shine but now—after who knew how many thousands of years—starting to show a little wear. The sides were also decorated with relief carvings, geometric shapes—rectangles, squares, and circles—in different groupings and patterns. One large rectangle might have outlined a doorway, but there were no obvious gaps or cracks to prove that it was.

"The stonework is excellent!" said Carson.

Marten examined the surface closely, running his fingers over the surface. "Is this stone?" He tried scratching the surface, first with his claws, then with his knife, although from the absence of weathering, he was sure it would be pointless. It was. So was his knife, now. "Very hard stuff. Not natural stone, anyway."

Carson grunted an acknowledgment. He was examining the carvings around the presumed doorway. "If this is a library, they surely meant for there to be some way to get inside, but nothing too obvious. The clue will be in these carvings."

"Or it could just be solid, like the pyramids," Jackie pointed out.

"Which pyramids?" There was a note of irritation in Carson's voice. "In any case, whether you're speaking of Egyptian or MesoAmerican pyramids, I'll remind you that both sorts are actually complex structures that possess inner chambers, passages, and the like."

"Yes, Professor. Just wondering out loud."

Carson caught himself. "Oh, sorry."

∞ ∞ ∞

They began examining the carvings around the base of the pyramid. Some of it seemed to be related to astronomy. There were star diagrams, representations of this planet's two moons, and a stylized Chara-centric diagram of the Chara planetary system. Might this be the key? A problem to solve? Carson pushed at a few of the carved planets at random, as though they were push buttons. Nothing.

Jackie watched this idly. There was what might be the rectangular outline of a door, with simple geometric figures carved nearby. Something looked familiar about one particular shape. "Carson, never mind the buttons," she called out.

"What do you mean?"

"I think there's an easier way in. Where's the talisman?"

Marten spoke up. "I have it."

"Okay, try it in that recess," said Jackie, pointing.

Carson and Marten looked at the recess, and they recognized the rounded square shape of the talisman. Marten pulled it out of his pocket and examined it. "Let us hope that the dating sample we took didn't damage it." So saying, he fit it into the recess.

The niche wasn't deep enough to hold the talisman, just a shallow recess to show where it could be placed. Marten held it there. Nothing happened.

"It doesn't seem to—" Carson began, but Marten, still holding the talisman in place, raised his other hand to silence him.

"I think I hear something. Wait." A dim light illuminated on the door. After a few moments, the crack marking the edge of the door deepened, and then the door itself swung up.

Chapter 24: Within the Pyramid

The Pyramid

AS THE DOOR lifted, Marten snatched the talisman back, and the door finished opening to reveal a tunnel leading into the interior of the pyramid. This was it. Marten slipped the talisman back into his pocket.

"Well, shall we proceed?" said Carson.

"After you, you're the senior investigator."

"So I am. Thank you." Carson pulled a hand light from his pack and walked forward a few paces into the tunnel. He stopped to look around, at the walls, the ceiling, and the tunnel leading onward. He took out his omni, touched a control and waved it around. It was silent. "No radiation, nothing toxic that the omni registers." He took a few breaths, sniffing. There was a faint stale smell to the air. "It looks solid, and I don't smell any obvious gases or fumes in here. Let's go."

The others followed. The tunnel zigzagged at slight angles, but couldn't have been more than twenty meters in total length. At the end it opened into a larger room, although it was still small compared to the overall size of the pyramid. Arrayed around it were several large stone—or whatever it was—blocks, like tables or altars, or perhaps even sarcophagi. One table supported a cylindrical metal device, a bit over a meter long and twenty-five centimeters in diameter. A metal rod or tubing wrapped around it in helical fashion for perhaps a third of its length, and near its other end were projections, possibly handles, with what were probably controls. It suggested the product of advanced, and non-human, technology.

"Lads and ladies," said Carson in a hushed, awed tone, "I think we've found what we came for."

"So, what exactly *is* a Cosmic Maguffin?" asked Jackie. While it looked like a kind of tool or perhaps weapon to her, she figured this was the archeologists' area of expertise.

"Haven't a clue, to tell you the truth," said Carson. "I wasn't even certain there'd be one. Given where we found it and they way those handle-looking projections fit, it could be anything from some kind of artwork, to a death ray, to a healing ray, to—and this would be the classical archeological presumption—some kind of religious icon or fertility idol."

"Fertility idol? With two, ah, penis-like projections?"

"I've seen stranger. Although truth to tell I think a lot of what the old terrestrial archeologists labeled fertility symbols were really just that culture's equivalent to pornography." Carson looked as though he was about to say more, then thought better of it. "Anyway, I think on that particular gizmo they're just handles, and it's a tool of some kind. Please, try to avoid turning it on until we figure out what."

"I wouldn't think of it, Doctor Carson," a voice called from the gallery entrance.

Carson and the others whirled to look. He thought he had recognized the voice, and his fear was confirmed when he saw the man's face, and the armed men flanking him.

"Hopkins!"

"Ah, so you know my name now. That saves introductions. And you've met Rico already." Hopkins nodded toward one of the other men, one holding a familiar-looking assault rifle. There was another man, similarly armed. And no doubt more outside the pyramid.

"This is becoming too much of a fucking habit," spat Carson disgustedly. "Damn it, this really does belong in a museum!"

"Come now, Carson. I know as well as you do that *this* particular artifact will never end up in a museum even if I did let you take it."

"What? That's absurd."

"Don't lie to me, Carson, you're nowhere near as good at it as I am. Does the name 'Ducayne' ring a bell?"

"No, but 'Quasimodo' might." Carson was too annoyed to care that pissing off the guys with the guns might not be a good idea.

"Enough! Now, lie down on the floor, slowly, and put your hands behind your heads." Hopkins ordered. "Men, watch them carefully, especially the timoan; they're fast."

Grudgingly the trio did so, any thoughts of fighting it out dashed by both the tactical position—there were men with guns between them and the door—and the fact that Hopkins called three more men in from outside.

Their sidearms were removed from their holsters, and they were given a perfunctory pat-down before being tied up and dragged out of the way, over against a wall of the chamber.

Hopkins pulled out a camera and took a few quick photos of the room and the gadget on its pedestal. He put the camera away. "All right, men, pick up that device—carefully!--and anything else interesting, and let's go."

There wasn't much else interesting. They gathered a handful of smaller artifacts which could have been anything from hand tools to replacement batteries for the larger device, but that was all. The men started to leave, with Hopkins trailing. Carson and the others were still trussed and in a heap against the wall.

"Hey, Hopkins!" Carson called. "What about us?"

"Sorry, Dr. Carson, this time I don't need a write up to increase this baby's value. I'd just as soon you stayed here."

"Damn it, man, you can't just leave us here!"

"Why, certainly I can. Goodbye Dr. Carson, gentles." With that Hopkins turned to leave, then paused and turned back. "Oh, and by the way—although you don't look like you'll be getting free any time soon, if you do happen to, you might want to stay clear of the door." And with that, he left.

∞ ∞ ∞

"What the heck did that mean, 'stay clear of the door'?" asked Jackie. Now that nobody was pointing a gun at her, she was trying to wriggle her bonds loose.

"I don't know. Maybe he has Rico outside with a rifle, but I've got a bad feeling about it." said Carson. "Come on, maybe we can work each other's ties." Carson wriggled around to try to get back to back with Jackie or Marten.

"If you can get your hands near mine," said Marten, "I think I might be able to slash the cords with my claws. I just can't reach my own."

"All right, let's try that." Squirm, wriggle. "That's it, up a bit." Twist, bend. "There."

"Okay, Hannibal, hold still, I don't want to scratch your wrists too."

"Right."

Then with no warning at all, there was a sharp, incredibly loud *BANG!* and they felt the concussion through the pyramid. If it echoed at all in the enclosed space, they couldn't hear it, their ears ringing so much from the initial explosion. The ringing faded but the noise didn't. A crashing, rumbling roar followed. A cloud of dust drifted in from the tunnel. Hopkins had blown up the tunnel entrance, sealing it. They were trapped.

His ears still ringing from the blast, Carson thought he heard Roberts say something like "Oh, so *that's* what he meant."

Chapter 25: Trapped

Within the Pyramid

THE RUMBLING echoes of the rockslide died out, and the three looked around, seeing nothing in the pitch blackness.

"Great, now what?"

"Hang on." Jackie's voice. The sound came of clothing rustling, then a bright light.

"Ow, hey, warn a guy before doing that, will you?" Marten said.

Carson and Marten both shielded their eyes, blinking in the sudden brightness.

"Sorry, I'll turn it down." Jackie did so. "I'm just not a big fan of dark spaces."

"What, like outer space?" said Marten, who had no problem with dark spaces.

"Dark, *enclosed* spaces."

"Well, so now we can see our tomb." The disgust in Carson's voice was clear.

The zigzag of the entrance tunnel had kept most of the rocks and rubble, which blocked the entrance, in the outer part of it. A few had bounced in as far as the room they were in, and it was obvious from the lack of light that the entrance was blocked.

"No good. Any other way out?" Jackie asked.

"You looked around in here as much as we did, did you see anything that looked like another way out?"

"No, but—well, you guys are archeologists. Don't old tombs and pyramids sometimes have hidden passages?"

"Some of them do, yes, but this isn't a tomb. Well, not originally anyway. The entrance was difficult enough to open, why would they deliberately conceal another?" said Marten.

"Hang on," said Carson. "You may have a point there, Jackie." He paused for a moments, sorting out his thoughts. "Marten, this library—archive, whatever—is empty, correct?"

"Eh? Of course. There's nothing in here, there was just the cylinder."

"But the entrance was closed, and there was a puzzle to get in here."

"Yes, but what's your point?" asked Marten.

"So how come it's empty? Would someone who'd cleaned the place out bother sealing the entrance again? What if this is just another part of the puzzle, a false library?"

"Hmm. Something like the false chambers in some of the Egyptian pyramids?"

"Along those lines, yes."

"Wait a minute." Jackie hadn't quite been following the archeologists' conversation, but now she thought she understood. "You think there really is a hidden passage, another exit?"

"There's no guarantee. Even if we do find another passage, it might just lead to a library chamber, not an exit. But we won't know if we don't try. Look for anything that might be an activation mechanism, look for cracks in the wall that might not be just joints. Heck, tap the walls for different sounds—it's not uncommon for doorways to be plastered over to really conceal them."

There followed an intensive examination of the walls, floor, and every ledge and glyph sculpted into the walls.

∞ ∞ ∞

Carson finally stopped, and swore in disgust. "This is futile. If there were a secret door we'd have found it by now. And why would there be? This is no library, just a store room for that . . . that damned Maguffin!"

The others stopped their searching and looked at him. "But that doesn't make sense," said Marten. "Why go to the trouble of building this, the elaborate puzzle carvings on the outside, when that's all that was in here? Where's the easy stuff to help a developing civilization get started?"

"Uh, guys?" Jackie said, but Carson was already talking.

"Maybe that gizmo was an education ray or something. It could implant knowledge directly into the brain," he said.

"Of an alien brain?" asked Marten.

"Guys . . ." Jackie tried again.

"What?" Carson and Marten both turned to her and asked, simultaneously.

"Um, you didn't solve the puzzle to get in here, remember? We used the talisman. Could that be significant?"

"Significant? Roberts you're a genius!" Carson scrambled to his feet and hurried over to the rubble-choked entrance.

"Carson? Now what?" asked Marten.

"We used the pass key. Now just maybe that opened a different door, one to, oh, a janitor's closet, perhaps," said Carson, explaining over his shoulder as he began to examine what he could of the entrance passage.

"Some janitor. But even so . . ."

Marten had caught on, and filled in the explanation. "Then maybe there's a door from the passage into the proper first gallery. Maybe we can get to it."

"That's a lot of maybes," Jackie said, but she was already in the passage way and beginning to move rocks away from the wall so they could search it for doorways. "Tell me you still have the talisman."

A shocked, sudden silence as Carson and Marten looked at her, then at each other. Marten started frantically slapping at his clothes to check his pockets, then he dug into one.

With a triumphant smile, he pulled out the talisman and held it up to show it. "They were just looking for weapons when they patted us down, so they missed it."

"I think they were too interested in patting *me* down," said Jackie. She shivered briefly at the memory. "Remind me to take a shower at the first opportunity."

"They what?" Carson bridled.

"Forget it, Hannibal, let's just get out of here," she said, and turned back to moving rocks. The others joined her, occasionally stopping to examine the wall.

After several minutes of this, Carson shouted. "I think I've got it. Marten, bring the key." He used his fingers to clear dust and bits of gravel from a recess in the wall. The recess matched the supercircular shape of the talisman. Marten handed it to him.

"Hadn't we ought to clear some of these boulders out first, they might block the door."

"If you like, but I'm ready to try it now." Carson placed the talisman in the niche. Jackie took a hasty step back out of the way as some of the rocks slid a little farther. The door opened.

They entered the new room and shone their lights about. It was another gallery, with carvings on the wall and simple mechanical models on the pedestals. From the diagrams and models, it looked like lessons in basic mechanics and machines: the lever, the pulley, the screw, the hammer.

"The hammer's not a separate class of machine," said Jackie.

"Isn't it?" asked Carson. "Maybe we don't consider it so, but it isn't a lever. Think of a pile driver. It provides a mechanical advantage in momentum, is all"

"I suppose you're right. That might have led them to some interesting insights on physics."

Carson shrugged. "That could be, but I think physics is physics."

Marten, meanwhile, had been examining the walls, focusing on the corner near where they came in. If there was an outside door, it ought to be about here. There! It was another talisman-shaped niche. "Over here!"

Again Carson applied the key, and the door began to slide up, this time with a horrible scraping and screeching. As it rose, rock and rubble slid in underneath it, and they jumped back to avoid crushed feet or broken ankles. The door stopped, jammed about halfway up, with the opening obstructed by more stone and rubble.

"Damn it, the slide has blocked both doors."

Chapter 26: Exploring

Within the Pyramid

CARSON AND ROBERTS sat on small boulders. Marten had hopped up onto a pedestal where he too sat. It had been several minutes since they'd found the second door and the blockage behind it. Marten toyed idly with a model gearbox.

"Carson," said Roberts.

"Yes?"

"If that first room *was*, as you put it, the alien equivalent of a janitor's closet, what do you suppose that Maguffin was?"

"Good question. Could have been anything from a floor polisher to the router used to engrave the walls."

"Ah, I hadn't thought of that last one. The floor polisher had occurred to me. But that would make it advanced technology. What could shape or carve whatever this pyramid is made of?"

"Yes." Carson sat up straighter. "A disintegrator, perhaps. Yes, whatever it is, we've got to get it back."

"Sure. How?"

"Well, first thing is to get out of here."

"Sure. How?" asked Roberts again.

Marten spoke up. "This room is all mechanics. That can't be all the Spacefarers wanted to teach. There must be more galleries or rooms. Maybe they'll have a way out."

"Exactly!" said Carson. "Look for doorways, access key niches, puzzles. You know. Spread out." The others were doing that as he spoke, examining the gallery walls carefully.

It didn't take but a couple of minutes before Carson called out. "Found it!" He showed the others a carved picture depicting a balance or lever on an off-center fulcrum, with a rectangle on the short end. Near the other end, connected to the lever by dotted lines, were three other rectangles: smaller, the same size as, and larger than the balanced block on the lever.

"What do you think, a simple multiple choice question in mechanical advantage, right?"

"Like, 'a block on the short side is going to be balanced by *what* on the long side?'" said Jackie.

"A smaller block," Marten said.

"Exactly," Carson said as he reached over and pushed on the smaller rectangle. There was a click and, with a hum, a door slid up.

∞ ∞ ∞

A long dark passage sloped downward, curving to the left as it descended. They looked at each other, hesitant.

Carson turned to the others. "Any better ideas?" Not getting a response, he started walking cautiously down the passage. About a meter in, panels set in the wall near the floor lit up dimly, lighting the way.

Jackie hung back. She *hated* tunnels, especially dark ones, the thought of all that *solidity* around her was . . . disturbing. But at least this had some light and was obviously man—or intelligent being, anyway—made.

"Come on, let's see what's down here." Marten tried to encourage her. Maybe we'll find the treasure, or at least a way out."

"Treasure?"

Marten shrugged. "I don't know, isn't that what the lost temples of ancient civilizations are supposed to contain? Although in real life, looters more often get to it first."

They moved to catch up with Carson, who had rounded the curve and was out of sight. "Come on down here!" he called back, "There's another chamber!"

∞ ∞ ∞

The ramp spiraled down through a full revolution, ending abruptly as though the corridor had been just walled off. To the right, leading off the spiral ramp, was an open gallery. Ahead, Jackie could make out the faint outline of a door.

"How come there's no niche for the talisman in this door?" she asked.

"Who knows? Maybe the janitor didn't need access. Maybe the problem is so simple, if you can read the symbols, that they thought it was redundant."

"Simple? What, like 'what is two plus two'?"

"Quite possibly, yes."

"Great, so we just have to figure out the symbols. Yeah, simple."

The gallery walls were covered with carvings. What could be best described as low tables were arranged around the room. On several of these were placed objects, artifacts of different kinds, although they looked more artistic than functional. Most of the tables were engraved with passages of what might be text or hieroglyphs, as well as diagrams and pictures.

"It looks like a museum," said Jackie, "although this stuff is kind of simple. No Cosmic Maguffins here."

"I think it might be more of a classroom," said Carson. "Look over here, it starts out with simple mathematical concepts —counting, positional notation. I think it's supposed to teach their numbering system. Base eight, octal, by the looks of it."

"Yes, octal," said Marten. "Here it progresses to geometry." He pointed to a carving showing a right angle triangle, with squares on each side. The smaller ones were divided into a three by three grid and a four by four grid of squares. The large one on the hypotenuse was five by five, but that grid was also overlain with shading to show it was the sum of the two other squares. "It's an illustration of Tevarki's Theorem. Pythagorus, on Earth. And look, here it's getting deeper into geometry and trigonometry." He gestured at a different set of carvings, diagrams and text.

"It's a math classroom then. These artifacts," Carson picked up a dodecahedron from a set of regular geometric solids, "are just to help with the lessons." He set the object back down.

"All right, what does that buy us?" asked Jackie. "We didn't come here for a math lesson, and it's certainly not going to get us out."

"Don't be too sure of that. Look, the markings on the outside of the pyramid were astronomical, right?"

"Yes, so?"

"Well, the puzzle we were supposed to solve to open it was based on astronomy, it could only be opened by someone who'd learned basic astronomy, which they could do by looking at the sky. With me so far?"

"Well maybe, but we used a key." Jackie shook her head. "Anyway, with that level of astronomy they'd have this level of mathematics, too."

"We solved a puzzle for the door that led us here. Mechanical advantage. They'd probably know that if they knew astronomy too. I think . . ." Carson paused. "Yes, this is deliberately simple to establish a pattern, to make sure the basics are covered."

"To what purpose?" asked Marten.

"Remember the wall at the bottom of the ramp? It had a door in it, and several of the carvings were definitely mathematical," Carson said. "I think the text was based on their numbering system, and perhaps whatever symbols they used for mathematical operations."

"So there's another puzzle to open this door, one based on mathematics?" asked Jackie. "As simple as 'two plus two', I think you said."

"Yes, almost certainly. Anyway, we have nothing else to try. First we need to decode their symbols, we ought to be able to understand the mathematical concepts. Marten, give me a hand here, we'll start with the very basics."

∞ ∞ ∞

It went quickly. These carvings were *meant* to be understood by someone with no native knowledge of the language, so it built upon itself progressively. Marten, Jackie and Carson were all familiar with these elementary mathematical concepts. At least at the beginning. By the time they got to spherical and hyperbolic geometry, Jackie, with her background in astronavigation, was going it alone for the most part. Marten and Carson filled in with translation and building up their mathematical vocabulary.

"Whew," Jackie said, rubbing her eyes. "I'm beat, let's take a break." She sat down on the floor. "Between the lighting, the low tables, and the brain-strain, I'm bushed." The others made mumbling agreement noises. "Can we try the door now? Do we have enough to figure out what the puzzle is?"

Carson shrugged. "Perhaps for now. Who knows what we might need later. But it doesn't hurt to check." He got up, signaled to the others. "Come on, let's take a look, the more eyes the better."

Now that they could read Spacefarer numbers and math symbols, the puzzle was amazingly simple; they could have stopped their efforts some time earlier.

"Oh hell," muttered Jackie at this realization, "bloody archeologists."

Carson pressed on a sequence of raised squares marked with carved glyphs, and the outline of the door deepened, then the whole rectangle moved inward a centimeter or two and slid sideways. The opening revealed a continuation of the downward spiraling ramp, again illuminated with dim lights along the wall.

The three looked at each other, waiting.

"Well gentlebeings," said Carson, breaking the tension. "Shall we proceed?" and he started down.

"I'm just worried about what the next lesson is going to be. Sooner or later we'll find something that none of us know anything about, and then where will we be?" said Jackie.

"I am hoping it will be near an exit," Marten said, with a not quite sincere note of cheerfulness in his voice.

∞ ∞ ∞

The theme of the next "classroom" would have been obvious to any high school science student. Even though the presentation was a bit different than the customary human way of displaying it, the model of the periodic table was a dead giveaway. Chemistry.

"Kind of obvious, this one," said Jackie. Look, we've got chemical samples here, and information about their structure." Indeed, the shelves held small blocks of metal, and easily recognizable small blocks of carbon, and sulphur. Globes of glass—or a similar hard transparent substance—held what was probably the various gases; the reddish-brown bromine and the yellow-green chlorine were obvious. The engravings beside the samples matched the symbols in the rectangles on the periodic table model. The model was interesting. Rather than the flat chart Jackie was most familiar with, this was as though the chart had been rolled into a kind of stepped cylinder or spiral, which widened at the points where the Mendeleev table inserted extra columns.

"Hey, Carson, did you ever study science fiction?" Jackie asked.

"That sounds like an oxymoron."

"No, I mean stories about scientific ideas. I had to do a semester of it at spaceflight school, mostly stories about alien contact. I think it was because they didn't really have any idea how else to prepare us for what we might find out here."

"That's one approach. What's your point?"

"This place reminds me of something from one of the stories we studied, a team exploring ruins on Mars—"

"We haven't found any ruins on Mars," Carson pointed out.

"This was written before the first landings. Anyway they're looking for a way to translate Martian texts and find a chemistry lab. The periodic table is their Rosetta Stone, their omnilingual. That's the name of the story, 'Omnilingual'."

"Very clever. Do you think you can do that here?"

"Maybe." Jackie began examining the model more closely. Chemistry had been one of her favorite subjects, she had a natural talent for it, and she still remembered where some of the elements belonged in the table. She started singing under her breath, pointing to appropriate locations as she did so: "There's mercury and thallium and indium and gallium." Start there, over one, up two, three. Then up one more, over and down: "Aluminum and silicon, germanium and stannium." That last was tin. The chemical symbol came from the Latin name *stannum*, but the latter didn't scan any better than the old British "aluminium" did. What was next? Something leading into the rare earth elements, in a row. "And cesium and barium and lanthanum and cerium." What came next? She couldn't remember, and skipped on a bit. "There's gold and silver, copper, zinc and cadmium," those were in some kind of order, up over and down. "And rhenium and osmium, iridium and platinum." Enough! Rhenium? Ah, right, that was in this row along with the other three, the platinum group. What next?

"What was that?" asked Carson.

"What was what?"

"That tune you were singing."

"Me? No, I wasn't . . ." Jackie said, but there was no use denying it. "Okay, it's just a mnemonic for the elements, a song I learned back in school. We used to play a study game of pointing them out on the chart. I've forgotten a lot of it now."

"Ah, catchy tune. Sounds like something from Gilbert and Sullivan."

"Who? Oh, Gilbert—didn't they manufacture chemistry sets for kids? My dad had an antique he'd inherited from someone. Never let me touch it of course."

"No," Carson said. "Something about a modern major general, from *The Pirates of Penzance*, an operetta."

Jackie just looked at him blankly.

"Never mind." He shook his head. "It's obvious what this is set up for. Let's just figure out what we need to translate to open the next door. Come on." He turned to go to it. "Marten!" he called across the room, "Let's just copy down the symbols we need from the door and translate those, not much for us to learn here."

They began examining the door to the next level. Carson and Marten examined the symbols and diagrams to determine which they would need to translate, and Jackie occasionally contributed the element names she had already determined from looking at the periodic table. She sat on the floor, leaning against the wall, and idly studied the door, putting in her bit when asked but mostly just daydreaming, humming that damn element song, or whatever the tune was. Her gaze fell upon a recess carved in a familiar shape. At first glance it looked like part of the decorative carving that framed the different areas of the door holding the puzzles, just as the previous door had. But there was something about the shape and size . . . Jackie scrambled to her feet, surprising the others at her sudden motion.

"What's up, Jackie?" asked Carson. "Did you sit on an anthill?"

"No, look!" she pointed at the supercircle-shaped recess. "Who has the talisman?"

"I do" said Marten.

Carson was now at the wall, examining the recess with growing excitement. "Dig it out, give it here!"

Marten fished it out of a pocket, and passed it over to Carson. Carson held it up close to the recess—the shape and size looked like a match.

"What are you waiting for?" said Jackie.

The recess wasn't deep enough for the talisman to stay in it unsupported. Carson held it in, and a second later there was an audible hum and click—the same sound they'd heard when they'd solved the puzzle on the last door—and the door started to slide open. Carson let the talisman fall from the niche into his hand, and the door continued its movement until fully open. Beyond it lay another downward ramp.

"We should have guessed, based on the first door, or at least noticed it sooner," muttered Carson.

"Too many other interesting things to look at," Marten said. "But exploring the rest of this structure should be easy."

"Let's hope there's no place off-limits to the pass," said Jackie.

∞ ∞ ∞

The going went faster from that point on. The security pass talisman did work in subsequent doors, so they didn't have to waste time solving problems. They did, however, make brief excursions through each gallery or "classroom" to determine what each was about and see what useful items there might be. The galleries covered more complex subjects, and in greater depth, as they descended. There was optics, mechanics, basic biology, genetics—it was interesting to note that the Spacefarers were apparently related to terrestrial life too. "Or maybe they just studied the local and flora and based the lesson on that," pointed out Jackie to the others' chagrin.

∞ ∞ ∞

Farther down they went. They found galleries describing fluid mechanics and aerodynamics, biochemistry, static electricity, geology, electromagnetism, nuclear physics, astrophysics, and more.

"Is that a Feynman diagram?" Jackie wondered aloud, examining a wall carving which depicted a series of bent lines with a chain of small circles connecting them.

Marten and Carson looked at the diagram, then at each other. "What's a Feynman diagram?" Marten asked.

"It shows the interaction of subatomic particles by their paths and energy exchange. This line of circles might represent energy waves." She studied the other diagrams. They had a familiar feel, with a difference she couldn't quite put a finger on. "I think this gallery might be quantum mechanics, but it's a little off. I don't know if I've forgotten more of my QM than I thought or if the Spacefarers had a different spin on the theory."

"That would be strange," Carson said, deadpan.

"But charming," Marten added.

Jackie gave them a dirty look and wondered if Marten was really ignorant of Feynman diagrams.

They had also noticed that the foundations of the structure had cracked. There were several places where cracks showed in the walls. There were also places—presumably on the outer walls of the structure—where the not-quite-stone material of the structure gave way to the actual rock of the mountain. In all likelihood, the builders had dug a deep foundation and at the lower levels, just filled in cracks in the rock with their equivalent of concrete, leaving areas where the native rock was smooth and defect free to serve as the wall itself. Except that after these thousands of years, the rock was no longer defect free. But the ramp kept going, and the pass still worked, and they needed to find a way out somehow. They continued downward.

Chapter 27: Descent

Below the Pyramid

THE DESCENDING ramp followed the usual pattern, except as they rounded the curve, this one dead-ended, with a single doorway. Other than minor cracks in the wall—they'd been seeing those for the last couple of levels—the corridor just ended, with no sign of a concealed door or engravings for a puzzle to solve. There was just the usual gallery off to the side.

"Well," said Jackie, "Ground floor. Hardware, appliances, and small furry animals."

Marten shot her a look.

"Everybody out," she finished.

They fanned out to survey the gallery, occasionally remarking to each other at a particularly interesting carving on the wall or some small object on a shelf or dais.

"Hey Carson," Jackie called over to him, "there's been a passage on to the next level beside every gallery so far. If this is the bottom level, what do you suppose they used to get to the next level from here?"

"There is no next level, this is it."

"That's exactly my point. So where's the transporter? We'll just beam out of here."

Carson looked over at Roberts, saw the silly grin, and just rolled his eyes and shook his head.

"With our luck it probably wouldn't work anyway," she continued. "Speaking of work, do you suppose the device Hopkins made off with, whatever it is, still works?"

"The doors and lights do, and it might pick up power from the environment, even if the creators didn't have batteries with a ten thousand year shelf life—which we know they did."

"Point taken."

"So how do we get out of here?" asked Marten.

"That's a valid question. Okay, we need to do a *thorough* search of this level. Look for any hidden doorways. If that doesn't work I guess we go back up and see if we missed something at the main entrance level. Maybe the talisman is still good for something."

"What about the chemistry gallery?" Roberts asked. "Maybe I can rig up something explosive from that element collection."

"I think we'll keep that as our last resort, Jackie."

"Spoil sport."

They fanned out around the room, each checking a separate wall in detail. The cracking in the walls they'd seen earlier was more prevalent here, some of the cracks quite wide, but with solid rock behind. Jackie had about given up when she heard Carson's shout. "Over here, I think I've got something!"

The other two came running. "What have you found? Another door?" But Carson wasn't examining the wall engraving. He was on hands and knees examining one of the cracks in the wall, first peering into it, then listening at it.

"Come down here. See this gap in the crack? Put your hand there, what do you feel?" said Carson.

Jackie knelt down and waved her hand in front of the crack. Was that a draft? She put her face down next to it. She definitely could feel a current of air blowing across her cheek, coming out through the narrow channel. She thought she could hear a faint, distant roaring, too. "What is that?"

"I think there's a cave, this crack connects to a cave system," said Carson. "These mountains must be riddled with them. It's the right kind of rock."

"So we could get out through a cave? But, we can't get through this crack, not unless we can find a shrink ray of some kind."

"Yeah, good point. Still, there's hope now."

"Let's check farther, maybe there are more cracks, perhaps we can loosen a couple of rocks."

Marten had been examining the wall around the crack, then scanned the adjacent floor and ceiling. "I do not think so, this material is very strong," he said, replying to the last comment. "But I also do not think we'll have to." He pointed at an area of the floor a meter from where they were gathered. "Look."

In the floor was a recess, in the shape of a supercircle.

Chapter 28: The Gizmo

In the Mountains

"BOSS? AREN'T WE going to test the gizmo?" Rico had been itching to see what it did ever since he had first laid eyes on it, and here they were almost halfway back to the ship. Hopkins had set an aggressive pace, but they were slowing down.

"Test it? We don't even know what it's supposed to do, how would we test it?" Hopkins asked.

"Well, the handles are obvious. It's got controls, knobs and sliders, and a pretty obvious pushbutton on the handle, that's got to be a trigger."

"So you think it's a weapon?"

"Well, what else would it be?" Rico thought in terms of weapons a lot. "Anyway, how about we just point it at a tree or something and press the trigger?"

"Are you volunteering?"

"Ah," Rico thought about it for a moment. He *had* wanted to try firing the thing, but on the other hand they really *didn't* know what it would do. Even firing a hand-held missile could be dangerous if you didn't know what you were doing. He wasn't that stupid. "No. How about we rig up some kind of mechanical actuator and do it remotely?"

"We shouldn't tamper with it," Hopkins said. "Look, I'm curious myself as to what this device is for, but if we damage it our customer would not be at all happy at that." Rico thought Hopkins was going to let it go at that, but Hopkins continued: "And in this case an unhappy customer could be hazardous to all our health."

That last puzzled Rico, and he wondered just who this customer was. But he still wanted to know what the gizmo did. "Who said anything about tampering? I don't wanna take it apart, just push some buttons. Anway, maybe after all this time the power supply's dead."

"Maybe."

"Besides," said Rico, going for his last, best argument. He *really* wanted to see what this could do, and there would never be a better chance. He wouldn't see it after they turned it over to Hopkins' "customer". "What if it's the wrong gizmo?"

"What?"

"Well, what if there are secret tunnels in the pyramid and Carson found them? What if this thing is a decoy? Are you going to tell your boss you didn't even test this?"

"All right, but not here. When we get back to the ship we'll do it properly." Hopkins looked up at the gathering clouds. "Let's hustle, it looks like rain."

"Okay." Rico turned to the others. "Let's step up the pace," he called, and started toward the back of the group to encourage the stragglers. As he went, he pondered Hopkins's lack of reaction when he used the phrase "your boss". That was an interesting development.

Chapter 29: Down and Out

Below the Pyramid

THIS TIME THE passkey opened a trapdoor in the floor, which slid aside to reveal a rough-hewn passage. A few meters farther in the passage widened to a large cave tunnel. Rock sloped down away from the door to form a ramp down into the cave. A cool damp breeze blew up from it, and they heard a distant roaring noise.

"They must have discovered this cave here when they excavated to this level," said Carson. "I wonder why they didn't just seal it off altogether."

"Who knows," said Marten. "Maybe to monitor the cave, to make sure it wasn't creating a structural hazard."

"Judging by the cracks, they got that wrong."

"Well, ten thousand years can make a difference. But maybe they had another reason."

"Well, we won't find out sitting here, so we might as well get going."

"Going where?" asked Jackie.

"Down into the cave, of course."

"You guys go ahead. I'll go swing by the chemistry room and blow the main door open. Meet you back at the ship."

"Come on Jackie, this has to lead out. There's a breeze. That means it opens up somewhere. And it sounds like water—remember the springs we passed on the hike up? This mountain must be honeycombed."

"We can't get out through a spring."

"There'll be other openings. Come on, we need to at least give it a try." With that, Carson slid his feet into the opening and eased himself down the rocky slope. Marten followed, and Jackie, hesitating, brought up the rear. The trapdoor opening faded to a small dim rectangle behind them.

∞ ∞ ∞

Jackie hesitated inside the cave entrance. She had become used to the dim tunnels of the Archive, but it was *dark* in here, utterly black. And noisy. A continuous loud roaring filled the cavern, much louder than the faint background noise they had heard in the artificial passageways of the Archive. Jackie couldn't bring herself to go on, and crouched, paralyzed, just inside the broken wall leading back into the Archive. Marten had already walked on ahead, unheeding.

Carson turned back to her, shouting to be heard over the roar. "Come on Jackie! Let's go!" Jackie didn't move. Carson yelled down the tunnel. "MARTEN, HOLD UP! WAIT!" Jackie could barely hear him over the roaring noise, but Marten stopped and turned. He came jogging back up the narrow rock trail.

They gathered around her. "What's wrong?"

"I'm sorry. It's the dark, and the noise. What *is* that, anyway?" Jackie couldn't seem to get enough oxygen. She breathed heavily, almost panting, and her skin felt cold and clammy. She recognized it as a cold sweat rather than just the humidity of the cave.

Carson was staring intently at her face, his light shining on her. "Good gosh, you're as white as a sheet. I didn't know you had freckles."

"Wha, what?" said Jackie, confused by the apparent non- sequitor.

"Your face. It's so white I can see your freckles, they don't normally show up."

A part of Jackie's mind realized that Carson was trying to distract her, talking about something entirely different and mundane to reduce her near panic. When she realized that she *was* near panic, she felt a mixture of shame and anger at herself. Loud noises didn't bother her. Darkness didn't bother her. Why was she paralyzed like this? And what *was* that noise anyway?

"You didn't answer my question," Jackie was starting to calm down now, the anger at herself replacing the panic, "what *is* that noise?"

Marten answered. "There's a waterfall, up ahead in the passage."

A waterfall? At this point Jackie finally noticed the small stream flowing along one side of the tunnel floor. "Must be huge to make all that noise!"

"Less than two meters. Sounds are magnified in here, and carry farther. It's like being in a speaking tube."

Jackie had never heard of a speaking tube, but she could guess from context. As she adapted to the noise and dark she began to relax. Knowing what it was helped. "Okay, I'm . . . I think I'm okay now," she said to the others. She breathed more slowly now, her heart didn't pound so much. "Just give me a moment to get used to the noise and get my bearings."

Carson nodded. "Sure, take your time." Turning to Marten, he asked: "This waterfall, can we get by it?"

"Oh, easily. The stream is not deep and there are rocks we can step on. The cave roof drops enough that we can use it for hand holds. The path kind of crosses the stream there. The tunnel curves so I couldn't see any farther than that."

"Good enough. Jackie, how are you doing?"

Jackie took a deep breath, the air cool and damp. The roar of the waterfall was just background noise now, still loud but something she could ignore, like that of jet engines or rocket thrusters around port. Her eyes had adapted to what little light they had, it was no longer just pure black noise. "Okay, I'm fine now." She straightened up. "Sorry about that. Let's go."

They sensed her embarrassment at her near panic attack, and saw no reason to discuss it further.

"Okay, let's get across the falls and see what's around the corner," said Carson. "Marten, you take the lead, then Jackie, I'll take up the rear. Stay close." And they led off down the tunnel.

∞ ∞ ∞

The cave turned out to be fairly easy to follow, without a lot of twisty side passages. Mostly they could just follow the stream, and what side passages they saw were smaller, with a regularity, a sameness, perhaps due to the homogeneity of the rock and the process by which the cave had formed.

The main passage, except for occasional areas where it broadened, was taller than it was wide, with the bottom narrowing in a way that sometimes made walking difficult. At times the passage narrowed to where they couldn't proceed except by walking in the trickling stream on the tunnel floor. Despite this, Carson felt they were making good progress.

Up ahead the tunnel turned sharply to the right. The tunnel itself opened up and widened at the bend, with curving walls and a higher ceiling. Carson considered this and wondered what the turbulence in this elbow bend would be like in a flash flood. He tried to remember what the weather had been like, if a storm or rain had been imminent. No, the skies had been clear.

"Carson, you know some geology." Jackie's voice broke his train of thought. "Why are there no stalactites in this cave?"

Carson had been too focused on just getting out to have noticed, but now that Jackie mentioned it, there was indeed a distinct absence of stalactites, or flowstone, or any similar features usually found in caves. "Perhaps it's just a young cave, they haven't had time to form."

"It was here before that ten- or twenty-thousand-year-old pyramid above it. What do you mean 'young'?"

"Caves are often much older than that, but you have a point."

"Unless they came back later, after the cave formed and put in the trapdoor," Marten said. "Although I don't think that is likely."

"No," said Carson. "Given this stream, it probably means that this passage frequently fills with water. Stalactites won't grow in tunnels that are underwater or often flooded." He regretted the words as soon as he'd uttered them.

"What do you mean, 'frequently'?" Jackie asked. Carson heard concern in her voice.

He had been hoping not to worry the others about that. "Torrential rains, spring thaws, I don't know. We should be fine, the weather outside was clear."

"You're not a pilot," Jackie said. "There was a system building up offshore to the north-west when we landed. That was almost two thousand klicks away so I didn't pay a lot of attention to it. I don't know the weather systems here, but on similar planets that kind of thing could build into a storm system inland."

"If it did, when would it get here?"

"Too many variables. It's been a couple of days already. Depends on the jet stream, mountain ranges, whether there are high or low pressure areas building to the east. Worst case it's already raining outside."

"I didn't need to hear that," Marten said.

"The stream doesn't seem to be flowing any more than when we started, but that's all the more reason to step up the pace." So saying, Carson quickened his stride down the passage, and Jackie and Marten hustled to keep up.

∞ ∞ ∞

About an hour later, after a particularly difficult stretch of clambering over a series of irregular boulders, they reached an area where the cave widened and had a broad stretch of dry floor, with the stream off to one side.

"Hold up, rest break!" Carson called back, and heard his voice echo strangely in the cavern.

The others made appreciative noises, settling down on the flat, gently sloping rock floor. After resting for a few minutes, Jackie stood up, pulled out a knife, and turned to the wall of the cave. She began scratching at the rock.

"Carving your initials?" Carson asked. Then he noticed that Jackie had scratched out an "A", not a "J".

"Sort of." said Jackie, continuing to carve. She finished and stepped aside so the others could see her handiwork.

"AS? What is AS?" asked Marten.

Jackie just grinned. She looked over at Carson. "Do you know?" she asked him.

Carson gave her a blank look. "Why would I know?"

"How about 'Arne Saknussemm'?" hinted Jackie.

Saknussemm, Saknussemm. The name sounded damn familiar, but Carson couldn't quite—then he had it. "Jules Verne, *Journey to the Center of the Earth*. You're sick, Roberts."

Jackie just grinned.

"But shouldn't you have done it in runes?"

Jackie's grin dropped. "Dang it, you're right."

Marten looked from one to the other. "What are you two talking about?"

"Character in a well known book," Carson said. "Ask me to explain later."

Jackie smiled wryly, as at some inner joke. "I'm surprised you're not going to add something like 'TS + BT', Hannibal."

Carson looked back at her, puzzled. "What? Who are TS and BT, and why would I want to do that?"

"Well, given your name and all, I thought you'd make the connection."

"Hannibal? Elephants? Alps? We're crossing a mountain, but —"

"No, no. Hannibal, Missouri, Earth. Don't you read *anything* besides your archeology journals? Come on, Carson, I hate having to explain jokes."

"Then find better ones. What about Hannibal, Missouri?"

"The Mark Twain cave. *Tom Sawyer*, the cave where Tom Sawyer and Becky Thatcher get lost."

Carson groaned. "Roberts, you are *worse* than sick! And before you get started, let's not even mention Ali Baba or *King Solomon's Mines*, all right?"

"If you sesame so, chief."

Marten had been mostly ignoring the banter; the cultural references obviously meant little to him. Instead he'd been staring at the stream flowing along the cavern floor. "I hate to interrupt," he said, "but am I mistaken in thinking that the water level has risen since we stopped to rest?"

Chapter 30: Getting Wet

The Surface

RICO SWORE AS the cold rain drizzled down the back of his collar. He'd been one of the few who had even thought to bring a rain poncho, but his was wrapped around the gizmo, keeping it dry. Hopkins had appropriated a poncho from one of the others, so most of them were trudging along, wet and miserable.

"Hey boss," he called. "How about we double-time it for a while? Warm us up and get us back to the ship sooner."

"Works for me." Hopkins raised his voice to the others. "All right, let's pick it up. But watch your step. I don't wanna slow down for a twisted ankle or broken leg." With that he moved out in an easy jog, taking the lead.

"You heard the man," Rico said, "let's double time. Move it!"

∞ ∞ ∞

Carson and Roberts both peered at the stream. It didn't look any different to Carson, but he hadn't looked at it closely when they'd stopped. He got to his feet; they'd better keep moving. "All right. Roberts, you seem to be *too* rested anyway. Let's go."

Jackie moved to take the lead, and they began again to descend the cave, following the stream. *Was* it running a little fuller? He couldn't be sure.

There was something else bothering Carson. "By the way, Jackie, they took our weapons. Where'd you get the knife?"

"What? Oh. Boot knife. They were looking for guns and big knives, not this little thing." Her grin faded. "Besides, they were more interested in checking my boobs than my boots."

"Oh. Sorry I asked." Carson clenched his fists. That was something else Hopkins would answer for.

They pressed onward, quickening their pace.

∞ ∞ ∞

They continued their descent into the blackness, their lights co-cooning them in little bubbles of illumination as they went. Somehow this reminded Carson of warp bubbles. Perhaps it reminded Jackie, too. She said: "I will be so happy when we're back aboard the *Sophie*."

"So will we all. I'll be even happier if we can somehow get the Maguffin back. But let's get out of this cave first." The tunnel here averaged about two meters wide; sometimes high enough to walk comfortably, sometimes the ceiling came low enough that he and Jackie had collected some nasty knocks on the head. Marten had managed to avoid those. The stream on the floor of the tunnel was fifteen to twenty centimeters deep at that point, perhaps a meter wide, and flowing swiftly with the downward slope of the tunnel. But all things considered—the bumps on the head, Marten's wounds from the cat attack—the going was fairly easy. At least they weren't doing a belly crawl through mud.

"Carson, how do we know this stream doesn't just end in an underground lake or a tunnel full of water with no way out?" Jackie asked.

"There's still a slight breeze in the tunnel, and the water has to go *somewhere*, otherwise it would have just filled up the whole mountain." Carson knew that water could seep out through cracks or small openings that no human—or timoan—could ever hope to squeeze through, and also aware of the possibility of a sump, a dip in the cave tunnel that was filled to the ceiling with water even if the tunnel ahead were clear, like the U-shaped trap in the drain pipe under a sink. He avoided mentioning any of this to Roberts.

"Anyway," Carson continued, "remember the springs we saw on the way up? There'll be others, bigger ones."

"If you say so," said Jackie, "I hope you're right."

So did Carson.

∞ ∞ ∞

Hopkins' party had reached the foothills when the rain began to let up. "Okay, rest break," he said, and pushed his poncho back to check his omni.

"How much farther, boss?" Rico was breathing hard, but nothing like the heavy panting that was coming from a couple of the team members. *Wimps*, Rico thought.

"Just a few klicks, we're almost there. How's the gizmo?"

"Fine. Nice and dry." *More than I can say for myself.*

"Good." Hopkins checked his omni. "Okay, men. Ten minutes and then we go."

∞ ∞ ∞

Marten had the lead when he suddenly stopped and called back, "Hey, I think I see daylight ahead! Just a glimmer."

"Really? All right, everyone stop. Let's douse our lights for a moment," Carson said, and switched off his own. The others did so in succession, the cave growing darker—but not pitch dark. There was a paler patch ahead; they could actually *see* a vague, not quite so dark outline of the cave wall ahead against the darker black near them. They must be near an exit; farther back in the cave there had been only one shade of dark—pitch black. Carson hoped it wasn't just some small gap impossible to squeeze through.

"Great," he said. "Not much farther now, let's go." He turned his light back on, the others doing likewise, and they continued down the passage, a bit more spring to their steps.

They continued another fifteen or twenty meters down the tunnel. The light from ahead was now bright enough that their flashlights made little difference. The flat area between the edge of the stream and the cave wall had narrowed, and the sideways angle of the floor was steeper. Carson was in the lead. He heard Jackie's surprised yelp from behind him, and a splash. He whirled at the sound.

"That is freaking cold!" Jackie was standing in the stream, the water up past her knees, shaking water from her hands.

"What happened? Are you all right?"

"I'm fine, I just slipped. Good thing this stream isn't any deeper." She reached a hand to Carson. "Here, help me up."

The footing was awkward. He leaned across the narrow stream and braced his left hand on the opposite wall of the cave, then reached out to Jackie with his right. They grabbed each other's wrists and with Carson's help, she pulled herself up and out.

"The stream bed slopes downward faster than the cave floor," she said. "And the water's too cold to walk in for long anyway, we need to keep to the ledge."

Carson nodded. "Right. Like me, feet on the ledge, brace yourselves against the opposite wall." He demonstrated, leaning across the passage at an angle, doing a sideways shuffle with both feet and hands to keep out of the stream.

"That's easy for you primates. My arms and legs are shorter," Marten grumbled. He dropped himself across the tunnel, bridging the stream at a shallower angle than Carson or Roberts. "Never mind. I'll manage."

A few meters farther on the cave ceiling lowered to where Carson and Roberts had to duck their heads. The second time Carson banged his head on the rock overhead, he said to Marten, "You know, there are advantages to being short." But the light was getting brighter. They had to be close to an exit.

As they rounded the last corner, daylight reflected through the water and made patterns on the cave walls and ceiling. Carson looked back at the others.

"It looks like we've got some good news and some bad news," he said. Indeed. There was a day-lit opening that should be large enough for them to escape through. But the cave roof sloped down, and that opening was under water. "I think you're going to have to go for a swim, Marten."

Marten muttered an oath under his breath. "I do not swim," he said in a louder voice.

∞ ∞ ∞

Jackie moved up to where Carson was standing, and examined the opening. The stream filled the whole width of the cave—less than two meters at this point, and the ledge on the left side that they were crouching on just merged with the wall. There was a ridge descending from the cave ceiling, parallel to the wall. Jackie put her hands on it to steady herself as she leaned across the stream to peer beyond it, and saw another ledge on the opposite side, a dozen centimeters below the water surface. "Hang on, I'm crossing over." She followed word with action, taking one large step across and standing, feet wet, on the other side. She crouched down even lower, trying to see that part of the cave mouth that the dip in the ceiling blocked from the others.

Was that a gap above the water surface? Jackie inched her way forward and looked again. Something was touching the surface of the water, but . . . it was leaves! There was a gap of perhaps twenty centimeters between the surface of the water and the roof of the cave on this side of the exit, and vegetation—a tangle of vines or bushes—grew from the outside rock above and hung down over the entrance down to the water level. But how deep was it?

"Here, take my light," Jackie said as she passed it across to Carson. "There's a gap on this side, I'm going to see how deep the water is." Steadying herself with her hands on the wall and low ceiling of the passage, Jackie eased one leg off the ledge and down into the pool. The coldness of the water bit into her leg and she sucked in a breath. The bottom sloped away and she groped around with the toe of her boot, the water up to her thigh now. Nope, she couldn't quite touch bottom; it was deeper than that.

She shifted her body to sit on the ledge, back to the wall, leaning a bit forward to steady herself with her hands on the opposite ceiling, where it dipped. Her butt was wet now, sitting on the underwater ledge, and the water was *cold.* She braced herself. *Here goes nothing*, she thought, and slipped off the ledge, stretching her legs down and anticipating complete submergence.

She slid down as far as her waist, and her feet touched bottom. *Yes*! She took a few quick breaths, panting as her legs numbed to the frigid water.

"Okay, it's about waist deep here, I'm standing on the bottom, I'm going to check out the exit." Jackie called back to the others as she eased herself forward toward the lowering ceiling and the leaf covered exit. She bent over, trying to keep her head and as much of her torso out of the icy water as she could, but her shirt wicked up the water, leaving her chilled. As she reached the exit, she took a deep breath, held it, and waded forward. She felt the leaves brushing her head, the ripples from her motion splashing against her face, and she was through.

She stood up and wiped water and muddy leaves from her face with her hands. She was about to let out a whooping cheer when she remembered that somewhere out there there were

Hopkins and his thugs, and she had no idea if they were in earshot. She stifled the yell.

She turned back to tell the others, ducked her head to go back into the cave, and stopped. It was pitch black in there, her eyes were now used to the outside light and she couldn't see a thing. She couldn't yell into the cave from here, she might be heard by somebody else. But it was so damn dark. No, she remembered, there's plenty of light in there. *Just sit here a moment with eyes closed and adapt to the dark. Ignore the freezing water. Okay, deep breath, in you go.*

It was only a couple of steps until she could stand up straighter, and yes, there was light in here. Carson and Marten were still waiting patiently, anxiously. "What kept you?" asked Carson.

Jackie ignored the question. "There's a way out. It's a little overgrown and the water's going to be about chest high on you, Marten, but there's a small gap between water and roof all the way out. It's only a few steps, no problem."

"All right. You lead. Carson, can you follow close behind please?" said Marten.

"Of course. Here, give me your stuff, keep your hands free."

Marten did *not* like the water, and cursed bitterly about how cold it was, but they managed the exit without serious mishap. They were all soaked, and cold, but forced themselves to do a quick reconnoiter of the area. They found no sign of Hopkins or his men. Above, the overcast was breaking up. Blue sky showed through, together with a few rays of sunlight.. Safe for the moment, they found a clearing where the ground was already warming in the sunlight and sprawled out to dry off, savoring their freedom.

∞ ∞ ∞

Carson didn't give them time to rest. "Come on, we have to get a move on. Hopkins has already got the Maguffin, but there may still be a chance to get it back."

"What chance? For all we know he's already off planet by now. And besides, he's got a half-dozen armed men, we've got nothing."

"With that many men he had a bigger ship, which will take more time to refuel, and—"

"Not that long, they've had time."

"—and," Carson went on deliberately, "it will have taken them a couple of days to get down from the pyramid. We may even have taken a shortcut."

"It would help if we knew where we were."

Carson looked around. Pyramid Mountain was *there*, and *that* hill looked like one he'd seen from the trail up. "I do. The hogback we landed near is over this hill and across the valley. Three, maybe five, kilometers tops. Let's go."

Jackie looked at Marten. "Does he really know that? How?"

Marten nodded. "Probably. Same way you know your stars."

"Okay then, let's go." Carson strode out, leaving Jackie and Marten to pick up their meager possessions and jog to catch up.

They caught up, and after walking a hundred meters or so together, Jackie spoke up. "Hey Carson," she said, "you didn't say what we'd do about the half-dozen armed men."

"You're right, I didn't."

"Well?"

"Well what?"

"What are we going to do about a half-dozen armed men?"

"I'll figure that out when we get there."

"Oh, great."

∞ ∞ ∞

Back at the *Hawk*, Hopkins directed his men to stow the gear and generally make ready for takeoff.

"Sir, we ought to top off the tanks. You were in such a rush to get after Carson when we landed, and it was dark . . ."

"Very well. Run a hose out to the stream. Rico, post a guard, just in case Carson does show up."

"You don't really think . . ." asked Rico.

"No, but he can keep an eye on the hose, too."

"Okay, boss." Rico turned and signaled to one of his men. "Joe, guard duty. Walk the perimeter, I'll have someone relieve you in two hours."

"I hope to be out of here in two hours," said Hopkins.

"Boss? What about testing the gizmo?" Rico had been looking forward to it.

"Oh, all right. Rig up some kind of remote for it. And we'll test it away from the ship. Might as well set up cameras for the test too. But I want to lift by tonight. We leave in five hours, you've got four."

"Got it, boss. Thanks."

Chapter 31: The Test

The Hogback

JACKIE CREPT UP to the ridgeline of the hogback and peeked over. Their landing area lay below. The *Sophie* was where she had left it, still secure. But that wasn't all. Hopkins was also down there. At least his ship was. It—Jackie could make out the name *Hawk* painted on its side—was parked near the stream. A thick hose snaked out from under the ship's belly and into the water. One of Hopkins' goons wandered around the ship, casually holding an assault rifle, apparently standing watch. Jackie backed away from the edge of the hill and returned to her companions.

"They're refueling their ship, piping in water from the stream. I see one guard walking perimeter, no sign of the rest of them. They're probably in the ship," she told the others.

"Maybe they're not back yet," Carson said.

"They are. I think I recognized the guard, he was at the pyramid."

"Damn. And the *Sophie*?" asked Carson.

"She looks okay, we'll have to get down there to be certain. If I still had my omni I could log in to the ship's computer from here, but . . . Well, never mind."

"So, what *is* our plan?" asked Marten.

"Plan?" Jackie shrugged. "I have no idea. Hannibal?"

∞ ∞ ∞

Carson had been thinking about that since they reached the ridge. "Give me a moment," he said. "It looks like they may have been waiting for us to come back. Perhaps Hopkins thought we might find a way out."

Carson considered the implications. They'd be expected, although if he were Hopkins, he would have left someone or some gear to monitor the pyramid and the trail back, to alert them. Carson smiled a wry smile. This gave them a slight tactical advantage, the opposition would be expecting some warning of Carson's approach that they weren't going to get.

But could he and the others get to the *Sophie*? And if so, then what? "Jackie, if you can get to the ship, how long to prep it for takeoff and be ready to go?"

Roberts thought out loud. "Key the door code, wait for the hatch to open, get through it, and close. Initiate the emergency takeoff checklist on the computer. Spool up the thrusters." She paused to add up the times. "About two minutes. But won't they be shooting at me?"

"Not if our distraction works, they'll be headed in the opposite direction."

"What distraction?"

"I'm still working on that. I'm making this up as I go along."

"And how do you get aboard?" asked Roberts.

"The theory is that we distract and run, and you come pick us up. It'll be tricky . . ."

"Damn right."

"All right, listen up. Marten, can you take the man on watch? Sneak up on him, take him out?"

"Yes, that should not be problem."

"Good." Carson outlined his plan, filling in details as the others raised questions.

Suddenly Marten raised his head and looked around. "Did you hear that?"

Carson hadn't heard anything, but timoan hearing was more acute. "Better go check," he said, gesturing toward the top of the ridge.

"Okay."

∞ ∞ ∞

Marten crept up to the top of the slope, crawling along the rocks, blending with the bushes. He reached the edge and peered down. Crap! The door to the bad guy's ship was open, he must have heard its mechanism. Hopkins and two men came out, carrying the Maguffin between them. Marten turned and scrambled back to his companions.

"They're outside, Hopkins and two others . . . no, three with the guard. They've got the Maguffin!"

"What in bloody hell?" Carson said. "If they mean to test it . . . Come on, let's get up there." They all three scrambled back to the top of the ridge.

∞ ∞ ∞

Carson and the others peered over the edge. He saw that they'd set the Maguffin up on a tripod made of branches, about thirty meters from their ship. There was—it was hard to make out at this distance—a box with a lever or mechanical arm, fastened to the Maguffin's handles. Wires trailed back to where Hopkins and his men were, near their ship. Two recorders on tripods were aimed at the Maguffin.

"It looks like they've rigged up a remote activator or something," said Jackie. "Smart."

"Still rather stupid to activate it at all without knowing what it is, if you ask me," said Marten.

Carson thought for a moment. "Perhaps not. The thing has handles and hand controls. It's not likely to be extremely dangerous to the operator if it's meant to be held while in use."

"A backpack nuke has handles too," remarked Jackie.

They all slid a little farther back from the edge of the ridge, and hunkered down flatter, but kept watching. Carson whispered a question.

"Jackie, if that thing *is* a disintegrator ray, how would it work?"

"How would I know? The only disintegration I've ever seen is dust particles kamikaze-ing the front of the warp bubble," said Jackie, then realization hit her. "Oh!"

"Oh?"

"Warp bubble. If the makers figured out a way to generate a small, stationary warp bubble, that might do it."

Down the slope, Hopkins gesticulated at one of his men. Rico? He pointed at something Rico was holding—it had wires dangling from it, it was the controller for the remote activator—then at the Maguffin. Rico shrugged, and went back to check the gizmo.

Carson still wondered about the disintegrator. "How would that work, and wouldn't it just zoom off somewhere?"

"Making a tiny warp bubble? I have no idea. But matter at the event horizon of the bubble just tears itself apart from tidal force. Dumps a burst of radiation, too."

Below, Rico finished making an adjustment to the alien device and rejoined his group.

"How much radiation, if you did it in standard atmosphere? What would happen?" asked Carson. "Assuming it even worked that way."

Hopkins raised his hand, and he and his men hunkered down a little more. So did Carson and the others on the ridge. Hopkins started rhythmically waving his hand, it looked like he was counting with his fingers.

"Looks like he's doing a count down," said Jackie, then she thought a moment about Carson's question. "A lot of radiation, think how much matter's involved. A big pulse of x-rays, probably, just like—" Roberts's eyes grew wide, realizing the implication.

Carson, seeing her expression, made the same connection. "A nuke," he said.

Simultaneously, Roberts and Carson flattened themselves to the dirt, trying to merge with it, at the same time yelling "duck and cover!" Marten flattened too, and they buried their faces in crossed arms, hands over their heads, just as Hopkins finished his countdown.

∞ ∞ ∞

They felt the light more than they saw it, although there was a red glare even through closed and covered eyes. Just a little at first, accompanied by an ear-piercing shrieking whistle, then a sudden bloom of light and a wave of heat swept over their heads and shoulders, followed in a split-second by a huge *BANG!* that shook the ridge and squeezed their lungs. Then it was calm and silent, save for the echoes booming back from the mountains.

Jackie was already on her feet and running. "To the *Sophie*! Now's our chance!" Carson paused long enough to check that Marten was up and moving, then followed close behind her.

The cloud of dust raised by the blast was still settling, and a circle within about five meters of where the Maguffin had been the vegetation was aflame. The Maguffin itself lay on the ground about twenty meters from its original location. Carson couldn't tell if the wisps of smoke came from it or the scorched vegetation it lay on, but its coils seemed intact and its housing was undented. One of the guards lay on the ground broken and bleeding. Hopkins and the others staggered to get up; some were holding hands to their eyes. Carson heard shouts of "My eyes!" and "I'm blind!" mixed in with screams of pain.

The trio was two thirds of the way down the slope of the hogback now, running pell mell, barely keeping their balance as they charged down the steep hill. Hopkins and his men were down but not out, and others in their ship would be coming out to investigate. They ran for their lives.

"What . . ." Marten was panting too hard to talk easily. ". . . happened?" He took a more breaths, still running. He slipped, stumbled, recovered. Kept running. "Felt like . . ." he took a few more panting breaths, "a bomb."

Slightly ahead of him, Jackie scrambled and recovered, running for the *Sophie*. "Close . . ." she gasped as she ran, "I'll," a quick dance to recover as she stumbled over a rock, ". . . explain later." She reached the bottom of the slope just ahead of him, and ran flat out now, the *Sophie* just meters away.

Marten darted a glance toward Hopkins's crew. They still staggered, dazed and flash-blind. *They haven't noticed us yet*. But where was Carson?

There he was, turning from the straight path to the *Sophie*. What? Carson ran toward the slightly smoking Maguffin, lying not far from Hopkins.

It looked like Hopkins himself had recovered. He staggered to his feet, turned to survey the area. He reacted when he saw Carson.

"Stop—" Hopkins winced as if in pain and clutched a hand to his side. Rib injury? Marten wondered. "Stop him!" Hopkins managed to shout. He still blinked fiercely, his face tear streaked, but he seemed to be recovering. Not so his goons, who were still stumbling about, but the door to their ship was sliding open.

∞ ∞ ∞

Carson heard Marten calling. "Carson! Never mind the device, just get to the ship!" Carson checked the *Sophie*. Jackie was already ducking aboard through the opening hatch. He ignored Marten's shout. He had to get the Maguffin. He dodged around one of Hopkins's staggering minions, giving him a kick for good measure as he passed. The man went down. He heard Marten again "Carson, gun! Behind you!" He looked back. At the hatch to Hopkins' ship, a man was leveling a rifle at him. He dived for the ground and rolled. The man fired a burst.

As Carson rolled, shots hit the ground where he had been a moment before. He scrambled to his feet, and now the Maguffin was only a few meters away. He dove for it, grabbed it, and almost dropped it in surprise. It was hot. Ignoring the pain in his hands he held onto it, rolled into a runner's crouch and was off again.

∞ ∞ ∞

The gunman fired another burst, shifted aim, fired again. Damn it, it was like trying to shoot a jackrabbit. Every time he brought the gun to bear, the guy bounced away in a different direction. *Time to rock and roll*, he thought, and turned the selector from burst to full auto.

∞ ∞ ∞

Marten saw that Carson was vulnerable. Carrying the Maguffin slowed him, and at the rate the gunman was firing, he would get a lucky hit soon. Marten glanced around. Jackie was already aboard the *Sophie*. Most of Hopkins's men were still incapacitated. Where had that guard been? There!

In two bounds, Marten covered the four meters to where the guard's rifle lay and snatched it up. Without pausing to aim, he fired several shots at the gunman, coming close enough to startle and distract him.

"Carson! Run!" Marten called out.

The gunman turned toward Marten, gun raised. Marten squeezed off another burst and ran for all he was worth, ignoring the renewed pain from his earlier chest wounds.

∞ ∞ ∞

Jackie had the *Sophie* on line and fired up the hover thrusters. As Carson and Marten ran toward her, she began drifting the *Sophie* toward them, kicking up clouds of dust. She turned to present the portside hatch toward them. There was enough space between the jets that they could scramble aboard while avoiding the hot jet wash. Jackie looked out to see Marten turn and fire again toward Hopkins's ship, keeping the gunman's head down as Carson raced up the boarding ramp. Marten fired once more then dropped the rifle and leaped for the ramp. Jackie started to lift as soon as he hit the ramp. He dove through the hatchway hollering. "Go! We're aboard, let's go!"

Jackie banked the *Sophie* away from the *Hawk* and put her into a climb as it turned, retracting the ramp and closing the hatch as she went. As the hatch closed, Jackie applied full power and the *Sophie* blasted toward the clouds.

They'd made it.

Not quite. As Carson and Marten scrambled up from the entrance hatch to strap themselves in, an alarm light lit up on the control board. Jackie glanced at it and swore. In bright orange letters it flashed "FUEL CONSUMPTION" and "POSSIBLE LEAK."

Chapter 32: Dogfight

Aboard Sophie

"WHAT'S THE problem?" asked Carson.

"All that shooting must have punctured a tank. Damn it, this ship is supposed to be bulletproof." Well, meteoroid proof, anyway.

Carson raised an eyebrow at this. "Maybe he was using armor piercing rounds. Marten fired enough shots at their ship, I hope he returned the favor. What do we do?"

"I'm not going into warp until we figure out how bad the problem is and how far we can get. And I don't want to leave atmosphere until we're sure the rest of the hull is airtight. We need to set down somewhere so I can inspect."

"How critical is it?"

"Shouldn't be a problem, we've got plenty of fuel if we're not warping. The board's green otherwise. I'll run a pressure check on the hull." Jackie pressed a couple of keys on the console as she said this.

"I hate to interrupt," said Marten, who was watching the view aft on another screen, "but Hopkins' ship just lifted. He's after us."

Jackie moved the control yoke and cursed at the ship's sluggish response. She muttered while keying something in to the control pad. "Water's a nice dense fuel source, but it's also heavy as hell." She made another turn with the controls. "Damn thing flies like a pig, and has all the gliding properties of a brick." She looked around her. "Sorry *Sophie*, I didn't mean it." She took one hand off the yoke and touched a sequence on her console.

A button illuminated with the words FUEL JETTISON and Jackie stabbed it down. The *Sophie* vibrated and shook, surging forward as the outboard tanks dumped their water as fast as they could. It flashed to a misty cloud as it hit the slipstream, leaving a thick contrail behind them. Hopkins's ship swerved to stay clear of it.

"What are you doing?" asked Carson.

"Lightening the load. Don't worry, there's still plenty left. Three more tanks."

Jackie again gave the controls an experimental wiggle. The *Sophie* was definitely more responsive now. "That's better," she said, and closed the dump valves. They still had the inboard tanks, if they could avoid the *Hawk* that was still enough to reach space and get far enough out to enter warp. She could cut the warp short and double back to refuel after the *Hawk* had given up on them.

"All right," said Marten, "how did you know that would happen, the explosion?"

Jackie scanned the console as she talked, climbing for altitude and keeping an eye on the cabin pressure. It seemed to be holding. "Carson asked me about that gadget, how it might work if it was a short-range disintegrator." She quickly recapped her comparison with a warp bubble.

"But why design a tool like that?"

"Who knows? There has to be more to it than that. Maybe Hopkins had it set to full power. When they turned it on it just sucked air in, turned it to energy, created a vacuum, sucked more air in, and so on. That would explain the shriek."

"And the bang?" Marten asked. "Carson said something about a nuke."

"A nuclear bomb creates an x-ray pulse, which heats the air to a plasma, and *that* is what gives off the light and causes the blast," Jackie explained.

"Ah, so a big burst of x-rays from the device—"

"—would be like a nuclear grenade," she finished.

"Oh my."

"How did you know it would do that?" Carson asked.

"I didn't. I was expecting a flash, like a fusion thruster, but hadn't thought beyond that. I just figured we'd better be ready for the worst case."

"Yes," said Marten. "That was a good diversion, by the way."

"Thanks," said Carson, who was now looking at the rear screen. "Jackie, I don't suppose you have a way to toss a nuclear grenade out the back, do you? Hopkins' ship is coming up fast."

∞ ∞ ∞

"Is it armed?"

Carson scanned the screen, examining the *Hawk*, looking for gun ports, a laser turret, or some other sign of weapons on the closing ship. "I don't think—" he broke off as a pod lowered from the underside of the ship, and with a flash two missiles launched from it, streaking toward them leaving a trail of fire and smoke, as the pod retracted. "Yes! Two missiles at six o'clock! Evade!"

Jackie snap-rolled the ship inverted, ignoring the rattle and crash of loose items falling about the cabin, and pulled back hard on the control yoke, pulling the upside-down *Sophie* down through a split-S maneuver, coming out of it right side up below and flying in the opposite direction as Hopkins' ship. She snapped the controls about quickly in a series of jinking maneuvers. "Missiles?" she asked.

∞ ∞ ∞

The first missile had been confused by the *Sophie*'s sudden maneuvers, and lost her. It continued on its original path, twisting and turning to try to pick up the trail, its exhaust leaving a corkscrew spiral of smoke.

∞ ∞ ∞

Carson said: "Lost one, the other's still tracking."

Tracking *what*? Radar? Infrared? Jackie hoped the latter. "Hold on!" She reached out to the control panel with one hand, the other still moving the yoke in a jinking pattern, and in quick succession hit the ENGINES OFF and FUEL JETTISON buttons, then pushed the controls to put the *Sophie* in a diving glide. Hundreds of gallons of water dumped from valves near the exhaust nozzles, cooling them and creating a great cloud of steam and water droplets where the *Sophie* had been.

∞ ∞ ∞

The second missile, which had been following the bright infrared spot that was *Sophie*'s starboard thruster, was confused by the bright hot spot suddenly being replaced by a larger, diffuse glow, but it plunged on.

∞ ∞ ∞

Jackie banked the *Sophie* left to change direction again and spared a glance at the screens. "Status?" she asked Carson.

Carson saw the missile continue on course, waver a bit as though seeking, then disappear into the cloud. "Lost it, I think."

"Where's the *Hawk*?" Jackie asked. *Sophie* was still in an engine-out glide, not a good position for a dogfight.

"I don't see it. Wait! It's high, about four o'clock."

Jackie took a quick look at the rear view screen. Hopkins's ship was maneuvering to line up another shot after Jackie's first evasive turn, and cutting across the curve she had made. It approached at an angle, lining up for an intercept.

∞ ∞ ∞

The missile exited the spreading cloud, still seeking a target.

The Hawk's weapons pod began to lower again.

The diffuse glow from the cloud cleared from the missile's sensor. It resumed its hunt for the target.

∞ ∞ ∞

The *Sophie,* still in a gliding descent, was rapidly losing altitude, worse now as Jackie made evasive turns as they went, costing precious lift. She would have to restart the engines soon. She extended her finger toward the START ENGINES button.

∞ ∞ ∞

The *Hawk,* almost directly behind them now, lowered its nose toward them.

The missile saw the heat plume of a ship's exhaust. Its guidance system gave the robotic equivalent of "tally ho!" and locked on.

The *Hawk* was now lined up, its pilot reached to the fire control.

The missile flew on into the portside main thruster of the *Hawk*, and committed spectacular suicide.

∞ ∞ ∞

At the first flash of the explosion, Jackie stabbed her finger down on the START ENGINES control and put the *Sophie* into a hard diving turn away from it, praying that she had enough altitude for the thrusters to kick in before she hit the ground. The altimeter unwound like a crazed backward clock.

Debris from the *Hawk* rained around them, and the ground was getting close.

Jackie pulled up the nose, and felt the thrusters come up to power. She leveled off just as she was brushing the treetops, and a memory flashed of the time in flight school when she had come back with leaves stuck in her landing gear. "Whee, that was fun," she said, exhaling the breath she'd been holding.

Behind them, off to their right, the remains of the *Hawk* crashed to the ground.

Chapter 33: Pyramid Redux

In the Plains

"WE'D BETTER LAND, I need to check over the ship, patch that bullet hole," Jackie said, climbing above tree top level and turning toward to a clear area, near the stream but at some distance from their earlier landing site. That was farther away than she remembered coming, but there had been distractions.

"Fair enough, you're the pilot."

"And Captain, Carson. Don't forget it." She felt better now that she was back at the controls of her ship; she just hoped the damage wasn't serious.

"I wouldn't mind standing on solid ground for a while," said Marten. The air combat maneuvering had been particularly unnerving to him.

Jackie brought the ship in and landed easily about twenty meters from the stream. She went through the shutdown sequence and turned to Carson. "Okay, I can refuel here but I'll need to patch the tank first, and check the whole ship over for other damage."

"What can we do to help?"

"Not much with the ship. You and Marten grab rifles from the weapons locker," she turned back to the console and touched the control to unlock it, then turned back to Carson, "and guard my back while I inspect the hull. If any of Hopkins' men weren't aboard and saw his ship go down, they may decide that we're their ride home. We don't need that."

"No we don't. There might be something out there like Marten's saber-toothed friend, too," Carson said. He got up and made his way to the hatch. Marten had already pulled two rifles and ammo packs from the locker. Carson took one of rifles, checked it over, then took the offered ammo pack as they left the ship.

Jackie turned back to the console and set up the ship's computers to run extended diagnostics. She started them running and got up and went to the tool locker. She pulled a portable console from its rack, and grabbed a handful of essential tools and a tool bag, which she slung over her shoulder. As she descended the boarding ramp, she muttered to herself. "Okay *Sophie*, let's see what ails you."

She began her walk around going forward, taking a clockwise direction around the ship. She knew there was damage somewhere aft, given the fuel leak, but she would get to it. Sticking with routine made it less likely to overlook anything. She looked under the ship at the landing gear. There was a nick in the portside gear door—they'd been shooting up at *Sophie* as she took off—but it didn't look like anything serious. There was also a scrape along the side, probably from when they'd been shooting at Carson. She patched both with thermal foam to preserve the heat shielding capability.

Jackie continued her inspection, walking around the forward end of the ship checking the hull for any indications of damage. She pulled off inspection plates even if they didn't seem harmed, just to be sure. If nothing else, they had a long trip ahead and the inspection needed to be done anyway. At intervals she jacked the console into a probe port on the hull to query its integrated systems. It was midway back on the starboard side she found the bad news.

A bullet hole big enough to put her finger into penetrated the hull deeply. Jackie knew the layout of the *Sophie* as well as she knew her own body, that hole pointed directly at the lower right warp generator.

Jackie tried to ignore the sudden knot in her stomach. If the warp module were damaged they wouldn't be going anywhere, and there was no way to call for help. This is what every starship pilot dreaded. But that's why warp modules were armored, to prevent accidental damage—although meteoroids rather than bullets were the expected hazard. Still, tough as a warp module might be, a sufficient shock could damage it enough to be unreliable, and *something* had possessed enough energy to make a hole in a hull she had been assured was virtually bulletproof. Jackie's mouth was suddenly very dry.

∞ ∞ ∞

Carson's gaze swept the plain again, then he turned to face the mountains, checking everything in that direction. Chara III's larger moon, looking about half what Earth's Moon does from Earth, was low in the sky above the mountains. It would be setting soon. A bright spark of light near it caught his attention. Was that another planet in this system? Or the smaller moon? He dropped his gaze for a moment to scan the area again, then looked back. Had it moved? It was hard to judge movement against the cloudless sky, but it looked farther from the big moon than it had before. Hannibal held up a fist at arms length, and measured off against the big moon. Two fists, about twenty degrees.

He waited a minute, scanning the ground, then looked again. He held up his fist to measure again, convinced now that it was moving. A fist and three fingers. It was definitely moving. And it was descending. A ship?

"Jackie! Marten! It looks like we're going to have company." He pointed up as the others turned toward him, and they looked.

"Are you expecting anyone?" Jackie yelled at him. She stood up from where she had been squatting by the *Sophie*.

"Of course not," he called back. The spot of light was getting bigger, and the motion more apparent.

Jackie started back toward the ship's hatch. "I'm going to hail it. Do you guys want to stay out there or come back and sit in the target?"

Hannibal and Marten, at opposite ends of the ship, turned and looked at her, then at each other. They shrugged. If the incoming was hostile, they wouldn't be going anywhere without a ship anyway. "The ship," they nodded at each other in unison, and headed back for the hatchway. Jackie was already inside, working the communications at the control panel.

"What have you got?" asked Carson as he came up and sat down in the seat beside her.

"Nothing. No response to hails. I swept the bands, no radio traffic. No transponder. I think I'm getting a skin paint with the radar but it doesn't make much sense."

"Communications failure, perhaps? It's coming this way for help?" Marten said, half suggesting, half asking.

"Unlikely that they'd all fail simultaneously, but weirder things have happened," said Jackie. "Should we take off? We can't make orbit but we can leave the area."

Carson thought for a moment. "I don't know. If they're not in trouble they might interpret that as hostile. Can you get a visual on it?" It was starting to show as a bigger dot on the screen now, but the blurry shape didn't make much sense.

"No, the alignment scope won't reach that angle unless I move the ship." She turned back toward Marten, halfway between her and the hatch. "Marten, grab the binoculars from locker seven and take a look outside."

Carson followed Marten out, almost bumping into him as he'd stopped just outside the hatch and was looking up at the light. "Well, what do you see?"

Marten hesitated. "I see . . . I'm not sure what I see." He handed the glasses to Carson and called to Jackie. "Get out here, you need to look at this!"

Carson looked. The binocs were out of focus, the fuzzy shape didn't make sense. He groped for the control.

Jackie, now at his elbow looking through another pair of binoculars, let out a long, low whistle.

Carson touched his autofocus button and the image snapped clear. It still didn't make sense. "A *pyramid*?"

"Good, that's what I thought I saw," said Marten.

∞ ∞ ∞

They took turns with the binoculars, watching the flying pyramid, or whatever it was, for several minutes until it settled behind a mountain peak.

"What the hell was that?" said Carson.

"It's no starship, that was way too big," said Jackie. In the excitement of the moment she had forgotten her concern about the warp module, but the memory was back, and her voice held a grim note. The size of that pyramid had been beyond the theoretical limits for a warp bubble, so even if whoever—or whatever—

was flying it was friendly, they couldn't hitch a ride home. She needed to check the diagnostics; maybe her warp unit was okay.

"Maybe they know something about warp technology we don't?" ventured Marten.

"Even if they did, where'd they come from? If our exploration of the archive triggered an alarm or something, they got here so soon they had to be nearby. There's no such thing as faster-than-light radio." *Unfortunately,* Jackie thought. "Anyway, I need to finish checking out the *Sophie*, we may have a problem." She turned and went back into the ship, dreading what the diagnostics would tell her.

∞ ∞ ∞

Carson and Marten looked at each other. "Problem?" Carson asked.

"I don't know."

"It sounds like there might be something wrong with the ship. You stay out here on watch, and I'll go ask her."

"Very well."

Carson turned and entered the hatch. Jackie was at the controls, her elbows on the panel, head propped on one hand, shoulders slumped. She started at Carson's entrance, and sat up quickly. "Problems?" Carson asked again.

"We took a bullet, heavy caliber, to our lower right side. Where the warp unit's housed."

Carson didn't like the sound of that. He didn't understand all the implications, he knew that starships typically had three warp units, but the tone of Jackie's voice said it was bad news, and, were her eyes red? "And that means?"

"It should have meant nothing, but the diagnostics say that the module's broken. They're tough, but hit it hard enough and the shock will damage the nanostructure. The thing's shot." She grimaced at the unintentional pun.

"But aren't there two others?"

"Yes, but we need all three to balance the warp geometry and control against Finazzi instability."

"Whose what?" Carson knew what it was, but he wanted to help Jackie focus; she was visibly shaken.

"Finazzi instability, named after one of the guys who pointed out that quantum effects could destabilize a warp field. Never mind. The point is we need three, we only have two, and we're not going anywhere. We're stuck here on Chara." Her shoulders slumped again. "Unless . . ." she raised her head, looked at him. "Did you let Ducayne know where we were going? Will he come looking for us if you don't report?"

Carson paused, thinking. Things had been chaotic in their rush to leave Taprobane. "Yes and no. I did send a report in, couched in rather ambiguous terms in case it was intercepted, but Ducayne should be able to figure it out."

"That's great!"

Carson held up a hand. "But that doesn't mean he'll come looking for us. I didn't give him an ETA. Heck, I didn't know if we'd find anything here or not. Between whatever circuitous routing it takes my report to get to him, and the expected travel times of the kind of exploring we're doing, it would be at least months before he decides it might be worth looking for us, and who knows how long before he gets here, if he does."

"Well, that's it then. We're stuck here." Jackie turned to the controls and started aggressively flipping switches and slapping control pads.

"What are you doing?"

"Finishing the diagnostics and inspection. I can at least make *Sophie* airworthy. There's that settlement on the other continent. If I'm going to be marooned I'd rather be somewhere a little more civilized than here."

"From what we saw before, I think 'little more' pretty much describes it." Carson turned to leave, then turned back. "Look, what about the other ship?"

"Hopkins' ship? It's destroyed."

"No, I meant the flying pyramid. But come to think of it, yeah, what about Hopkins' ship too? Sure it crashed, but could we salvage parts?"

Jackie looked thoughtful. "Perhaps. A crash might be a gentle enough shock that the warp modules wouldn't be damaged. The rest of the ship would take the impact. Oh, the one nearest the explosion would be wrecked, but . . . ." her voice trailed off.

"So could we swap out the warp units?"

"Too many unknowns. I've got sufficient tools to remove and replace *Sophie*'s, not that that's something I ever planned on doing myself, but removing them from a wrecked ship is something else again. That's even assuming they're the same model; they can't be balanced if they're not. I didn't recognize the make of Hopkins' ship. It wasn't a Sapphire, that's for sure."

"So, not worth the trip, then?"

"I didn't say that. There are only a few different models of warp unit, so there's a chance. That is, *if* at least one survived the impact, and if we can extract it from the wreckage, and swap it out for *Sophie*'s."

"What will it take?"

"Let me finish with *Sophie* first. We can do a flyover of the wreckage and get a better feel for whether anything survived."

"All right, then that's our plan."

"Carson?"

"Yes?"

"What about the pyramid?"

"Good question. You're sure it wasn't a starship?"

"Unlikely, but if it was alien, who knows? We know there's technology out there we don't understand. And it was flying."

"Yes, so?"

"Carson, it was flying *without rockets or wings*. That implies anti-grav. We can't do that."

"We can do artificial gravity."

"That's a byproduct of the warp balancing, we can't do it without the warp on and you saw what happens if you try *that* in atmosphere." She made a gesture to where they'd stowed the artifact.

Carson nodded. "You're right. Jackie, we have to get up there. They have to be aliens, and spacefaring, starship or not. How soon can *Sophie* be ready to fly?"

"You want us to fly up there?" she gestured toward the mountains. "We don't even know if they're still there, and we know there's nowhere for *Sophie* to land."

"We can at least do a fly-by."

"What about the warp drive? Can we focus on one thing at a time?"

"Jackie, this could be the most significant event in our history, meeting another spacefaring species."

"Don't let Marten hear you say that."

"You know what I mean. If they built the archive—and they must have—they've had space travel thousands of years longer than we have. Besides, didn't you ever want to be in a first contact situation?"

"To tell you the truth, no. There are too many opportunities for mistake, and possibly for dying horribly. Remember Captain Cook."

"Cook?"

"*HMS Resolution*, Hawaii, Earth? Killed by the natives."

"Oh, him. That wasn't a first contact, that was second. Anyway, the aliens seemed friendly enough from the archive."

"That was then. Anyway, there's not much daylight left and I need to work on *Sophie*. The aft fuel tank still has a bullet hole in it. Let me get that fixed and then we'll see about your flying pyramid."

Jackie gathered her tools and portable console and returned to the hole in the hull by the warp generator. If they could replace it, they'd have to remove this whole section of the outer hull. In the meantime she applied a temporary patch over the hole to maintain an aerodynamic shape while they were just flying in atmosphere. She continued her inspection around the aft end of the ship, finding another hole that was still dripping water. The fuel leak.

Jackie set to work removing a section of hull to access the tank. She got the hull plate off and examined the tank behind it. There was a hole about a centimeter in diameter, still dribbling, with a spiderweb of cracks radiating from it. She took a small cylinder from her kit and inserted it into the hole, the water squirting out around it and soaking her sleeves. She pressed the stud on the cylinder's end. Inside the tank the cylinder unfolded like an umbrella and she pulled it back to seal against the wall of the tank. The water slowed to a trickle then stopped. She twisted the protruding rod and the outer surface folded back flat against the outside of the tank, anchoring the patch. She finished up by covering the whole thing with sealant. It wouldn't hold hydrogen again without a proper repair, but it was at least water-tight. She secured the hull plate over it again and patched that, then finished her inspection.

Carson and Marten still walked the perimeter, rifles held casually, but one or the other of them always had an eye toward the mountain where the pyramid ship had descended. They hadn't seen it again.

"Okay, I'm ready to start tanking up, somebody want to give me a hand with the hose?" Jackie had returned her tools to the ship and now had a panel open on the side, from which she was unreeling a spool of hose.

"Sure thing," said Marten, and started dragging one end toward the stream near where they'd landed. The sun was starting to set and it was getting dim, but to Marten there was still plenty of light.

"How long to tank up?" Carson asked.

"Couple of hours. It'll be well dark by then."

"Any problem with flying after dark?"

Jackie thought about that. There was no technical problem, she had hundreds of hours of night flights and hundreds of night take-offs and landings. With the windows in night-vision mode she didn't even need landing lights. Still . . . "We've had a long and busy day, I'd just as soon be well rested before taking off again. We can do it if we have to, but do we have to?"

Carson paused before answering, running a hand across his chin, thoughtful. "I'd really like to get up there and see what's up with that pyramid. But you have a point. Could we do one quick high-altitude pass tonight?"

Jackie considered. She did a few checks on the control console, came to a decision. "Okay." She pressed a button on the console, and the sound of the pump stopped. Another button, and she said, "Marten, change of plans, bring the hose back please." Her amplified voice could be heard through the hull.

"So what are we doing?" asked Carson.

"We've got enough fuel for a short flight. I'll give you fifteen minutes, but we leave now. Night vision or not I don't want that other ship to think we're trying to sneak up on them in the dark."

"Good thinking."

"That's why you're paying me," said Jackie, a smug grin on her face.

∞ ∞ ∞

"Prepare for takeoff. Is everything secure?" She heard the confirmations and started touching control pads on her console. The outside lit up as Jackie turned on landing and navigation lights, then brightened even more as the thrusters powered up. The *Sophie* rose into the air, then accelerated forward and banked toward the mountains. "I sure hope they're friendly," Jackie muttered to herself.

Ten minutes later they were cruising a thousand meters above the pyramidal building they'd spent the last few days hiking to and from, the latter part of that journey within a cave in the mountain. There was no sign of any other pyramid, ship, or anything else.

"Damnit, they're gone." Carson's frustration was clear. "There's not even a sign they were anywhere near here."

Jackie had been scanning all around, not just looking at the ground; she didn't want to be taken by surprise if the other vehicle was in flight. So it was Marten who noticed.

"Not quite true." He pointed at the archive. "They cleaned up the rubble around the entrance, where Hopkins tried to trap us."

"So they did. Why, I wonder? There's no native species left here that could use it."

"A sense of neatness, perhaps? But where did they go, we never saw them leave."

"They may have stayed below the ridgeline," said Carson. "Or teleported, for all we know. Don't look at me like that, we don't know what they're capable of."

Jackie banked the ship to circle the archive. "I'll do an expanding spiral search pattern to see if we see anything, but just for ten minutes, then we need to head back."

Carson banged a fist on the arm of his seat. "Damn it. Opportunity of a lifetime and we missed it." He took a breath. "All right," he said, his shoulders slumped, "let's take a look." His heart wasn't in it.

Chapter 34: The Hawk

The Landing Area

THE NEXT MORNING Jackie and Marten ran out the refueling hose at first light. They'd found nothing else the night before, and had returned to their landing spot just after dark. Carson hadn't said much, although he had moaned about the lack of pictures. "Nobody will believe it," he muttered. Jackie wasn't sure if she were relieved or frustrated that the pyramid ship had already gone.

The *Sophie*'s tanks were just about full, and Marten was preparing breakfast, when Carson roused from his bunk. "What's the plan, Captain?"

Jackie gave him a look, then said, "Hopkin's ship went down in the trees a few kilometers north and a bit east of here. We fly *Sophie* over the wreckage and check it out. If there are pieces big enough that a warp unit might have survived, we find the nearest place to land and check it out on foot. Otherwise I guess we plot a course for the Mennonite settlement and early retirement."

"Could we head up to the archive again?"

"What for? We can't land there."

"Carson, let it go," said Marten. "The other ship is gone."

"But what if they left something behind?"

"What would they leave? No, Jackie is right. We can't land there, and we have to focus on the immediate priority. If there is a good warp unit we don't want it damaged by rain or wild animals while we're off on a wild moose chase."

"You mean goose chase," Jackie said. She knew that if there was an undamaged warp generator, rain or animals weren't likely to bother it much, but she kept that to herself.

"More likely to find moose around here than geese, there are no lakes," Marten replied, and grinned at her.

Carson looked from Marten to Jackie, back to Marten. His shoulders slumped a bit. "Okay, you're right. Let's focus on getting out of here. We can always come back." He paused, straightened a little. "Perhaps we can figure out how to set off the burglar alarm again."

∞ ∞ ∞

The wreckage of the *Hawk* was easy to find. It had plowed a swath through the trees. A few hundred meters to the south of the main impact site, the remains of the portside engine had started a fire when it came down, and there was a considerable blackened area.

"I'm glad it isn't any drier, a wildfire would have been all we needed last night."

Jackie brought the *Sophie* in high and they descended slowly, keeping a watchful eye out for any movement on the ground. *Sophie* already had too many bullet holes in her, if any of Hopkins' crew had survived they might want to take pot shots.

She put circled the crash site, keeping the *Sophie* banked over. The *Hawk* was a mess, all right. A large chunk of the port side was just gone, and the hull was banged and torn from bow to stern along that side. The other half didn't look too bad, though, notwithstanding several clear dents and scrapes from where it had hit tree limbs.

"Okay, the starboard side looks like it's a big enough piece that it might still have a warp generator intact."

"Is it the right kind? What make of ship is that?" said Carson.

Jackie looked at him. "It's broken, dented and beat up. Sorry, I don't recognize the model. Best I can say is that I don't *know* it has the wrong kind." She leveled the ship and climbed for altitude, looking for a clear area to set down. The edge of the treed area was about two kilometers away. Jackie flew out over the plain then circled back and landed close to the edge of the woods.

"Maybe you should stay with the ship. Marten and I will go reconnoiter," said Carson as he began pulling gear together.

"Do you know what a warp generator looks like?"

"Actually I do, but more to the point I know what a man with a gun looks like. If any of Hopkins' men are still around and dangerous we want you ready to get out of here. If it's all clear then you can come and help get the warp generator out."

"Okay, fair enough," said Jackie. "Oh wait a moment." She went to a storage drawer and rummaged a bit, then came out with a couple of wristbands. "Here," she said, handing one each to Carson and Marten, "communicators and locator beacons, seeing as Hopkins trashed our omnis."

"Ah, thanks." Carson slipped the commloc over his wrist, then pulled something from a pocket. "Although these days I've taken to packing spares." He held up an omni.

∞ ∞ ∞

The forest was no match for the jungle of Verdigris, Carson was pleased to note, and it seemed to lack the black flies that had plagued him on the hike up to the pyramid, but the going was still tough.

"No trails through this mess," observed Carson, stepping over the rotting trunk of a fallen tree. "Obviously there are no moose on this planet."

"What are moose, anyway?"

"What? From your joking earlier, I thought you knew."

"I know they're Earth mammals. I've never seen one."

"They're large antlered herbivores. They live in wooded areas, trample trails."

"Ah, like *prendal*," Marten said, referring to similar creatures from his home planet.

"If you say so." Carson raised his wrist, and spoke into the commloc: "*Sophie*, what's our bearing?"

"*You're tracking a bit to the left. Angle to the right a bit,*" came Jackie's reply. She had taken a bearing on *Hawk* when she landed, and the *Sophie*'s direction finder was locked on Carson's signal.

"All right." Carson looked through the thicket of trees ahead, looking for signs of broken branches that would indicate they were near the *Hawk*. "No sign yet, so far everything is quiet."

"*Roger that.*"

Fifteen minutes later Marten noticed something in the bushes. "Carson, look at that." There was a meter-long piece of metal, bent and torn, lying on the ground. Looking upward they saw shredded leaves and a recent scar on a thick tree limb. "A piece of the ship, blown off when the missile hit. We're getting close."

"You're right," said Carson. He unslung his rifle and checked its readiness. "Let's take it slow from here, just in case."

A dozen meters farther on they found more metal scraps, and they could begin to see a clearing in the overhead branches ahead. The air smelled of charred wood and the foul odor of rotten meat.

"There's one who didn't make it," Marten said, pointing at something wedged in the crook of a tree branch.

Carson looked where Marten was pointing. A body, or most of one, dangled from the branch, its clothing torn, one arm missing, the body starting to bloat. "Poor bastard He must have fallen out."

They held their rifles at the ready and scanned all around them. Survivors aside, the body could have attracted predators.

"This is not going to be pleasant," said Marten.

"I never expected it would." They went a little farther and the wreckage became obvious. There was debris from the ship and broken branches scattered everywhere. The torn side they'd seen from the air, but the rest of the hull looked intact. Cautiously they drew closer.

"Let's do a circle around, check for survivors."

They didn't find any. They did find several other bodies scattered near the wreck, mangled and broken. As they approached the hull, they saw the pilot still strapped into the control chair, a broken tree branch impaling his chest and the seat back. Then they heard a moan.

Carson scrambled across the torn edges of the hull to get to the pilot, then realized that the poor fellow wasn't doing the moaning and never would. The moan came again, from somewhere aft in the ship.

"Marten, I think there's someone in back." He made his way down a short corridor from the control area. There was another groan, and was that . . . yes, someone strapped into a seat.

The man was in bad shape. His face and shirt were dark with dried blood, there was a pool of vomit, also dried, in his lap.

There was a gash on his left arm, which is where some of the blood had come from, and the edges were angry red with the beginning of an infection. Despite the mass of bruises and scrapes on his face where it wasn't obscured by dried blood, Carson recognized him. "Rico."

"Wha'? Whozere?" Rico's voice came tired, slurred. "Help. Need water." In the dim light and with his eyes crusted with dried blood, there was no way he could see much.

Carson had mixed feelings about helping Rico, but he pulled a water bottle from his gear and held it to Rico's mouth.

Rico took a sip, swished, and spit it out. "Thanks. Mouth tastes like shit. More." Carson held the bottle up again while Rico drank. After several swallows, Rico spoke again, his voice still slurred but sounding a little less tired. "Who? Wha' happen?"

"It's Carson."

"Carson!" Rico's voice held more surprise than anger or fear.

"Your ship got hit by one of its own missiles and crashed. We haven't found any other survivors yet."

"Tol' those idiots not use missiles. Wha's wrong wi' me?"

Carson looked him over. The seat was rear-facing, against a bulkhead, but it was no crash couch. Rico had large cuts on his scalp and arm which had contributed most of the blood, but there was also a large bruise and swelling on the back of his skull. Carson touched it gingerly.

"Ow! Wha' fuck are you doin'?"

"You've got a bad bang on your skull, probably concussion. That'd be why you threw up. Can you move your arms and legs?"

"Strapped in. Buckle won' release. Can't reach knife. Can't *see* knife, all blurry." While saying this, Rico had wiggled his legs and right arm. His left moved a little but it seemed limp.

"You've got dried blood in your eyes." Marten handed Carson a strip of cloth he had pulled from somewhere in the wreckage, and Carson poured water on it and wiped Rico's face, getting the worst of the blood and vomit off.

"Thanks Doc. Still blurry, got flashblinded."

Marten gestured to Carson, indicating he wanted Carson to come with him. Carson handed Rico the cloth and the water bottle and followed Marten farther back into the remains of the ship.

"What?"

"What are we going to do with him?"

"I don't know yet. He's badly concussed. He'll probably die in a few days if we don't get him help."

"He can't even see anyway, how will he get food and water?"

"If it's from the flash, his vision will come back. If it's brain damage—"

"Do we care? He's one of the guys who tried to entomb us in the pyramid, shot at us, and fired missiles at us."

Carson was sorely tempted to just leave Rico to his fate, but there was another factor to consider. "He may also know more about who they're working for and what their plans are. Ducayne could use that information." Carson looked at Marten, who looked sullen. "Besides, he wasn't doing the shooting and he says he told them not to launch the missiles."

Marten shook his head; his facial muscles couldn't quite handle a sneer. "Probably because he's smart enough to know not to wreck the Maguffin. But sure, let's see what we can get out of him."

"That's not what I meant. We won't get anything out of him right now, we need to get him back to the *Sophie* and into the traumapod."

"Oh for . . ." Marten turned away, then back. "All right. Maybe we can lock him in there for the trip. *If* we get a working warp pod and are going anywhere at all."

"Okay. I'll go check on Rico. You look around for other survivors and take a look at the warp modules."

There were no other survivors. Marten came back to report that from what he could tell without dismantling the wreckage, at least one warp module should be intact. Carson helped Rico clean up, then finished bandaging the worst of the cuts and cut him free of the seat belts. There wasn't anything he could do about the fractured skull, though, unless he got Rico into *Sophie*'s traumapod.

"You really ought to be on a stretcher or in a mobile, but we don't have that choice. You're gonna have to walk, but don't get any ideas."

"No fear, Carson. Was never anything personal, jus' business. Looks like I'm out of business for now."

"It's the 'for now' that concerns me."

"I'll be good."

∞ ∞ ∞

They radioed Jackie to have the traumapod standing by. She prepped it and came out to meet them with the pod's stretcher. By then Rico needed help walking, he was periodically overcome with dizziness and nausea. They got him on the stretcher, which immediately started warning about his low blood pressure. They carried him the rest of the way to the *Sophie* and slid him into the traumapod. The pod's half-dozen robotic arms went to work, attaching sensors, cutting off his clothing, swabbing his skin in preparation for any necessary surgery, and inserting IV lines.

The pod display listed dehydration as well as numerous cuts and contusions, but the most serious injuries were the skull fracture and a corresponding subdural hematoma, a bleeding into the brain. The pod's medical computer recommended immediate surgery and, not receiving any countermand, got to work.

"Well, that's going to be a while," said Carson, turning away from the pod and moving to sit down at the small galley table where Jackie and Marten were already seated.

"Right," said Jackie, "and we've only got the one traumapod so nobody break or cut anything until then. Meanwhile," she continued, changing the subject, "what about the warp modules?"

"Their starboard side was relatively undamaged," Marten said. "We'll have to cut to get it out, though."

"Okay, I have tools. What about bringing it here?"

"The ground is more or less flat," Carson took up the explanation, "and the underbrush isn't too bad. There's the occasional old log but we can probably rig up some kind of travois to drag it. It can double as a stretcher to lift it whenever we need to."

"Perhaps Rico can help, although I do like the idea of just keeping him in the pod until we get back to civilization," said Marten.

"He'll be in there a day or two at least. He's in for a few hours of surgery and then a while to recover. I don't think he'll be in any shape to help for a couple of days. I'd just as soon get started now."

"Sounds good to me," Jackie said. "We've still got a few hours of light, I'd like to take a look at the wreckage. Marten, can you stay with the *Sophie*? Just call if anything comes up."

"Certainly."

∞ ∞ ∞

As they rounded the tree, Jackie saw her first glimpse of the wreckage, with the pilot's impaled body still strapped in the chair. Flies were buzzing around it. Jackie caught a whiff of the rotten-meat odor and gagged, nearly throwing up. "Geeze, Carson," she said when she'd recovered, "you could have warned me."

"Sorry, Jackie. It's bad, isn't it? I'm surprised. It usually takes longer for the smell to get this bad."

"Yeah. Well we're here now. Let's check it out. But we bring masks next time."

Jackie made her way to the aft starboard side of the wreckage, Carson following close behind her. "The hull is intact on this side, just as Marten said. That's a good sign." She walked around the ship, examining its surface.

"Is there something in particular you're looking for?" Carson asked.

"Inspection ports. Inside we'll have to pull the interior panels to access the module, but there should be inspection hatches on the hull. If I can—Ah, there." There was a small door outlined on the hull with a smaller circle beside it. Jackie pushed the circle in with her thumb, and the door popped open, revealing a covered data interface port. "This looks like it. Carson, hold this for a moment." She held out her portable terminal to him. A small hex nut held the cover of the data port secure. She took out her pocket-wrench and unfastened the nut, then took the cover off the data port. From another pocket she pulled out a cable and plugged it in. "Okay, hand me the terminal." She took it back and connected the cable.

"Will that work without ship's power?" Carson asked.

"It should. The terminal can power the interface and if the warp module is intact it will have reserve power." Jackie touched a few controls on her terminal. A data display began to update itself. So far so good. Then "Damn!"

"What? Is the module damaged?"

Damaged might have been easier to take. "No, the module seems to be in great shape."

"Then what?"

"It's the wrong freaking model. Same internal design but the power interfaces and mount points are all wrong. We can't use this."

"Could we adapt it somehow?" From the tone in Carson's voice, he probably knew better.

Jackie snorted. "Sure, Carson. We'll use duct tape. So what if it vibrates a little in flight and we end up lost."

"Could we use the fabber to make proper mounting brackets?" That was what the fabber was for, to make simple devices or parts for repairs. It was limited in the complexity of the materials or circuits it could fabricate, though.

"Mounting brackets, perhaps. But not power connectors that could hold up to the current." She unplugged the data cable from the wreck. "Or do you have some superconducting cable in all that gear you brought? Two-centimeter thick ought to do it. " She handed the terminal back to Carson, then turned and slammed the hatch cover closed with a fist. "Damn it!"

"Do we really need three warp modules?"

"What?"

"Isn't there any redundancy? Can't we warp with two?"

Jackie was quiet for a moment. In theory only one module was needed to generate an Alcubierre-Broek bubble, but only in theory. "It's not that simple. You need at least two to balance the Finazzi instability, although two doesn't give you much margin of error and you have to go slower."

"How much slower?"

"Ah, speed would be square root of two-thirds," Jackie thought for a moment. "About eighty percent, call it four hundred cee. We would get more range powering just two modules instead of three, but that's not the only problem.

"The warp fields have to be arranged symmetrically, radial symmetry around the axis of travel. The *Sophie* is configured for three, if we only power up two we'll shoot off at an angle and end up who knows where. Just like if one is loose."

"Could it be recalibrated? Take short hops?"

"No. Not reliably and that would reduce our effective speed even more." Jackie picked up her wrench and toyed with it, rotating it in her hands. "I don't suppose the settlement on the south continent would have anything useful."

"The Mennonite colony? They don't even have a radio. I suppose we could fly there and ask. I think it would be a waste of time, but if it's our only choice . . ."

Jackie looked at the wrench in her hand, then back to the wrecked ship, then at Carson. "There is another possibility. Marten won't like it."

"What's that?"

"At one time Mitsubishi considered an option on these Sapphires to have four warp modules, to add reliability and speed. It was never very popular, the speed increase wasn't significant and the extra power consumption cut the range. But the hull was built with the mount points in place."

"Wait, are you saying we could reposition the warp modules?"

"In theory, but I've never done it. We'll need to open up all the paneling. We can leave the dorsal module where it is and move the lower port module down to the ventral mountings."

"So why wouldn't Marten like it?"

"With just two diametrically opposed modules we can't bias the warp the way we can with three. It will be absolutely symmetrical."

"Does that mean--?"

"It means no artificial gravity. The whole trip will be in freefall."

"You're right. Marten's going to hate it."

∞ ∞ ∞

"You want to do *what*?" Marten shouted when Carson told him.

"You'll survive. Would you rather be stuck here?"

"You could come back for me with a working ship." He raised a hand to forestall the protest. "No, never mind, that wasn't serious. I wonder if you could put *me* in the traumapod for the duration."

"Oh come on, Marten, it's not that bad. You know you get used to it."

"For a couple of days of in-system travel, maybe. And it's more 'learn to tolerate' rather than 'get used to'. But yes, I suppose I'll manage." He sighed, resigning himself to the inevitable. "What do we need to do?"

"Well, first we're going to fly back to the Mennonite colony. In a pinch Jackie says we could do the work ourselves, but she'd rather have a few extra hands to help with some of the heavy lifting."

"That's the other side of the planet. I don't suppose we're staying in atmosphere for that?"

"Sorry, that would take too long, and it's not really the kind of flying the *Sophie*'s designed for. No, we'll be doing a fractional orbit. About forty-five minutes, only twenty of that weightless."

Marten sighed again. "It's a good thing we found that pyramid, otherwise I'd really be regretting I ever came on this trip. So, you said that's the first thing. What else?"

"Oh, then you'll need to clear your gear out of your berth. We're going to take the walls off and pull up the floor."

∞ ∞ ∞

With Mennonite help, the work took several days. It was less time than Carson had expected. The ship was designed to facilitate repair, with morphic fastenings on the panels that let the whole panel be removed or replaced with the touch of a button. Jackie spent more time on re-routing and checking the power and control cabling than it had taken them to unmount the heavy warp module from its original position and secure it to the mounting points beneath the floor panels.

"What about the alignment?" Carson asked. "If it's not exactly parallel to the ship's axis, won't we end up nowhere near our target?"

"If they're badly aligned, yes. One AU per arcsecond of misalignment per parsec. But these babies," she patted the module she was connecting a cable to, "are self-aligning as long as they're correct within a tenth of a degree. Once I get this one locked down I'll run the calibration. The modules will send signals to orient themselves with each other, then use the data to compute the timing offsets in the Higgs generators."

Carson looked at her for a moment. He'd understood each word, and thought he had an idea of what she meant, but . . . "Okay, good. I'll leave you to it. How much longer, do you think?"

"The warp drive will be ready to go by this evening. We'll still need to reassemble the paneling but that should only be a few hours. Unless there's a glitch we can depart tomorrow morning."

"Wonderful."

∞ ∞ ∞

"Everything secured for takeoff?" Jackie double-checked with her passengers. "All loose items secured? Tray tables and seat backs in an upright position?" She did a quick walk through of the cabin to confirm it, she had already done the outside walk around and the cabin hatch was secure. She got affirmative responses from Carson and Marten, and went forward to strap in to the control chair.

As she started flipping switches and pressing buttons on the control panel, prepping the ship for takeoff, Marten asked: "So, where is it we're going?"

"Oh, did you miss that conversation? Carson wants to report in to Ducayne, but a straight run to Alpha Centauri is past our range from here. There's a star, Lalande 21185. It's a red dwarf two-thirds of the way there with an ice plutoid we can refuel at."

"Ah. Are we going to hide the Maguffin there too?"

"Undecided." Carson joined the conversation. "I'm still of two minds about that. Ducayne will want it as soon as possible, but by taking it down to Sawyer we risk it being hijacked—"

"But Hopkins is dead. He blew up his ship."

"I don't think he was working alone."

"Well no, he had a half-dozen henchmen with him."

"That's not what I meant," said Carson. "He implied that he already had a customer for the gizmo, that it was specifically what he came for, not just ancient pottery and stonework. Whoever sent him is very likely watching for our return."

"Ah, so potentially we could be jumped any time after arriving in the system."

"Right. But that's not the only reason not to take it to Sawyer, either. Do we really want to bring this alien gizmo of undetermined power—and demonstrated destructive capability—down into a city, or even a heavily inhabited planet? And if Ducayne's tempted to test it, I'd just as soon he did it off world somewhere."

"Another very good point," said Marten.

Jackie had only been half listening; she had talked about it with Hannibal earlier, and was finishing up the preflight checklist. "Okay, gentles, everyone strapped in? We're about to lift."

There came the sound of the thrusters powering up. The ship lifted a little, settled while Jackie checked the final pre-takeoff items. "Okay, lifting!" They felt gently pressed down into their seats as the *Sophie* quickly ascended to a dozen meters above the ground, then, still rising, began to transition to forward flight, pushing them back in their seats now as the ship accelerated forward and Jackie pulled back on the stick, pitching the *Sophie* upward as it leaped for the sky.

Chapter 35: Snowball

Lalande 21185

THEY CAME OUT of warp in the outer reaches of the Lalande 21185 system. The ship was on a night time cycle. Hannibal and Marten were asleep in their bunks and the cabin lights were dim, but Jackie was at the controls for the break out. She checked a few readings on the control panel, the data display on the computer. Everything seemed proper. She dimmed the lights all the way down and turned on the window. Jackie wasn't prepared for what she saw and gasped in amazement, then let out a quiet "Wow."

After admiring it quietly to herself for a few minutes, she thought to wake the men up. She brought up the cabin lights and turned off the window, then sounded the usual morning wake-up call. *Oops, better have the galley make coffee*, she thought, and told it to do so.

A few minutes later, Carson and Marten were gathered in the cabin with Jackie, wondering just what was going on.

"What's the emergency?" asked Hannibal.

"Oh, no emergency, or I'd have used the emergency wakeup and you wouldn't be floating there sipping coffee. No, there's something outside I thought you'd like to see." She started to dim the cabin lights.

"Outside? What?"

"Look." She turned on the windows.

There were a few moments of silence, then a couple of subdued "wow"s and "that's amazing"s as they all took in the scene again.

Lalande 21185 was a bright spot against an almost black sky, but the eye-catching feature was the enormous, glowing comet trail that spiraled out from a tiny bright dot near it. It circled, or spiraled, around the star three or four times before it broadened and diffused and the fuzzy-edged laps around the star began to blend together, forming a larger and more nebulous disk that covered a good thirty or so degrees of viewing angle. As the disk faded toward black at its outer, ill-defined edge, a distinct circular gap could be seen in it.

"That's fantastic!" said Carson. "What causes it?"

"This star has a gas planet in what's called a 'torch orbit' around it. It's so close it orbits in a couple of days, and the star's heat is boiling its atmosphere away. The stellar wind trails it out just like a comet's tail, but the orbit is so fast you get the spiral effect until it's diffused out."

"Sure is pretty. But it can't last long, can it?"

"No, probably only a few thousand years; we're lucky to see it. I've been to other stars with torch planets, but they've lost their atmosphere long ago and there's only a gas halo left. This is the first spiral I've seen."

"What is the gap?" asked Marten, pointing out the window and making an elliptical motion with his finger.

"There's a small rocky planet farther out in the system. That will be its orbit. Its gravity is scooping a lane clear. This system has a couple of Jupiter-sized planets too, but they're too far out to see."

They watched, admiring the scene for a while longer, then Carson said: "All right, where to from here? You said there was a place to refuel?"

"Yes, near the edge of the gas disk there's an ice planet."

"What's so nice about it?"

"What? Oh, no, I said 'An. Ice. Planet,' not 'a nice planet.' Technically though it's only a plutoid."

"Oh, right, of course."

"Here, let me switch the windows to infrared." So saying, Jackie touched a control and the view out the window changed, the spiraling disk broadening out and blurring, and covering a larger part of the visible sky. Beyond where the original, visible-light disk had faded out, another gap could be easily seen in infrared. "Okay, that's our ice world's orbit. I need to locate it and lay in a course. The galley's open if you want breakfast."

Marten didn't seem enthusiastic. "No thanks, I think I'll go back to my bunk and strap in. I'll eat after we land, to celebrate the return to gravity." So saying, he pushed off in that direction.

Jackie shook her head. "Poor guy. I thought he was getting used to zero gee."

Carson shrugged. "It's mostly the transitions. He manages all right if it's prolonged. He's been okay on this trip since the second day out, but putting up with it is tiring for him. Anyway, I'm for breakfast." He turned toward the galley. "Want anything?"

"No thanks. After I work out the course maybe." At that, Jackie pulled herself into the control chair, strapped in, and started tapping out commands on the computer panel.

∞ ∞ ∞

Landing on Dirty Snowball—as they'd dubbed the ice-covered worldlet formerly known only by an index number in a database—was easy enough, and even the one-tenth gee surface gravity was enough to make Marten happier.

"I'm going to suit up and get the refueling under way," Roberts was telling the others. "Carson, you need to figure out what you want to do with the Maguffin." Jackie already had her vac suit out and started to don it as she said this.

"Can't you do it all from inside?" asked Carson. "I thought the refueling probe was automatic."

"It is, but I like to check it when it deploys. I also want to check the landing gear to make sure it didn't freeze into the ice."

"Oh, okay. That sounds like a good idea."

"That's why you're paying me the big money."

It was a lightweight suit, not intended for major surface explorations. The basic suit was more for emergency decompress use, with additional layers as needed. There were gecko boots and pads for working outside the ship in free space, and surface boots, the traditional "moon boots," for walking around on a body's surface. Jackie slipped a pair of these over her suited feet, then shrugged on the life support backpack and connected its hoses and cables. She pulled her helmet over her head and latched the neck ring, then ran through the suit checklist on her heads up display. Everything came up green except pressure; she still had her gloves off. She tugged those on and secured the wrists, double checked the pressure seal, then grabbed a pair of outer gloves in her left hand. She would put those on outside. She keyed the suit's external speaker. "Okay gentlemen, I'll be back soon. Don't go anywhere without me," then stepped into the airlock and closed the inner door.

She ran through the suit checks once more, checked the airlock inner door seals, and started the airlock cycle. She could feel her suit inflate slightly and stiffen as the airlock vented. The airlock pressure reached zero, and she opened the outer hatch.

The ground beyond thirty or forty meters from the *Sophie* looked like dirty sea ice, or a glacier. It was a lot of ice, with large cracks and crags, and covered with layers of dust left behind when the ice around it evaporated in sunlight and vacuum. Near the *Sophie*, though, everything was shiny white and smooth. Her hot exhaust had melted and vaporized the ice and blown away the dust, and water vapor had refrozen and settled out as a fine snow after the engines shut down.

Jackie walked over—carefully, but the ice was too cold to be slippery—to a landing pad and examined it. There was a dusting of ice crystals on it and the bottom was embedded in the ice, but she this didn't worry her. The *Sophie* would melt and break that in a few seconds when it blasted away. The cleared, polished white area around them might be an issue, though.

"Carson, this is Roberts" Jackie called the ship over her suit comm. Then felt a bit silly. Who else would it be?

"Yes Jackie, what's up?"

"If you're thinking of burying the Maguffin out here somewhere, you might consider how you feel about having it at the center of a great big white bull's eye."

"What?"

Jackie explained the surface phenomenon around the ship.

"Oh, I see." Carson turned on the windows. "Yes, I really do see. Okay, I'll think about that while you're setting up the refueling. Aside from that, how does it look?"

"No problems. A little bit of ice around the foot pads but nothing *Sophie* can't handle. Let me get started on the fuelling, I'll talk to you later."

"All right, Carson out."

∞ ∞ ∞

Roberts continued around to the aft end of the ship where the ice boom was stowed. She opened a panel to expose a keypad, then tapped in a control sequence on the large buttons with her gloved fingers. The boom extended out, unfolding and telescoping until it was a good nine meters from the rest of the *Sophie*, its heavy business end resting on the ice. Roberts gave it a quick visual check, then, satisfied, stepped back to the panel and keyed in another sequence. Around the head end of the boom jetted a brief cloud of steam, quickly freezing to ice crystals, as the head melted its way partially into the ice to ensure a good seal. The red light on its top started blinking, warning anyone nearby that the boom was now in operation.

Underneath that head end dome, a narrower pipe began extending from within the boom, a ring of steam jets around its edge melting a tunnel into the ice. The steam pressure forced the resulting liquid up into the pipe, where it was pumped back through a filter system and into the *Sophie*'s tanks. The process would create a great void under the ice, leaving enough surface thickness to maintain the seal with the head end. At least, that was usually the way it worked. Sometimes a crack or defect in the ice would cause a blowout, and the whole boom assembly would have to be moved to a new spot. It would have been much easier to refuel from a stream or lake, but those were hard to find outside of terraformed planets.

∞ ∞ ∞

Jackie sequenced herself back in through the airlock and entered the *Sophie*'s cabin, removing her helmet and shaking out her hair as she did so. "We're fueling." They could hear the pumps. "It will take a couple of hours to top off the tanks." She put the helmet down and sat to take the moon boots off. The gloves were already off. "So, Carson, any ideas?"

"Not really. I'm still of two minds about taking it back to Sawyer's World, but leaving it here is probably obvious. Anyone who backtracks us, or knows that we went to Chara and determines the obvious route back, will check here. And the last thing we need is a bloody great bull's-eye marking where we hid the thing."

"If you don't like a bull's-eye, I could do a couple of low passes with *Sophie*'s thrusters and make an X to mark the spot."

Carson looked at her, sighed, and said "you're not helping, you know."

"All right then, how about a detour?"

"What?"

"We don't go straight to Sawyer's World from here, we find another system, bury it in the dirt on a rocky moon somewhere, and then head back to Sawyers."

"Yes, that would work. Do you have a destination in mind?"

"No, I'll have to check the charts to see what makes sense. The systems *are* more likely to be inhabited though as we get closer to old space, even the non-terraform ones may have asteroid mining operations or research labs or something of the kind. No guarantees."

"Hmm. Well, it's still the best suggestion so far, Jackie. Can you take a look at your star data and see where we can get to and if it makes sense?"

"Okay. But I'll need to go back out and check on the fueling operation in a bit."

Chapter 36: Maynard

Dirty Snowball

RICKON MAYNARD paced the short length of his cabin, turned, and paced back again. At least there were on a planet now and had some slight gravity. The waiting in orbit had been getting ridiculous. Hopkins was a week overdue, what had gone wrong? He left his cabin and strode forward to the control deck. "Any word?"

"No sir," the pilot responded. "You know we'd have called you if there was."

"Damn. This is the right system, isn't it?" Maynard knew it was one of the very few stars within range as a stop on a return route from Chara, and the only one with a planet in a torch orbit. But then where was Hopkins?

"Uh, yes sir. Perhaps he's having radio problems."

"You think he might already be in-system? Could he be waiting somewhere else? This system has a couple of gas giants doesn't it?"

"It does, but they're not suitable for refueling. Their moons are small and rocky, except for one sulphur moon like Jupiter's Io. No, this is the best location in the system."

"Why wouldn't he find us in that case?"

"Perhaps he missed us, or thought he'd arrived before we did."

That seemed unlikely to Maynard, but the other possibilities were that Hopkins had double-crossed him, or that Carson had gotten the better of him. In which case . . . "Okay, take us up, put us in orbit and scan for a recent landing. Since he hasn't radioed, something is obviously wrong."

"Aye, aye, sir."

On their third orbit they spotted the bright aureole of exhaust-cleared ice that indicated a landing. And yes, there was a ship parked in the center of it. A squat delta. That was Roberts' ship, not the *Hawk*.

"How close can you land us without them noticing?"

The pilot examined the terrain below them. "It will be tricky, but if I approach low from the south I can put down behind those hills." He pointed to a large pressure ridge in the ice to *Sophie*'s southwest. "That's maybe a kilometer. If the thrusters don't kick up too much of a plume I might get closer." He paused and looked at the landing area again, then up at the position of the local sun. "In about a half-hour we can land up-sun from them; we'll be lost in the glare."

"Excellent. Do it."

∞ ∞ ∞

"You think this is our best option?" Maynard's man Taggart was pulling his suit on as he spoke.

"Are you questioning my judgment?" Maynard responded.

"No, Brother, but it seems complicated."

"I wish it were simpler. We don't want to destroy their ship until we have whatever they found, so we can't just blast them. And we don't know what weaponry they have, or what they did to Hopkins."

"But what if nobody comes out?" asked Rohm, the other man suiting up.

"They're still fueling, somebody will have to disengage and stow the boom when they're done. If you have to, damage it so someone has to come out to investigate."

"Right." Taggart pulled his helmet on and sealed the neck ring. "Comm to infrared," he said over the suit's speaker, and touched a control pad on his forearm. It was unlikely that the *Sophie* would pick up communications from their scrambled suit radios, but the radio signal alone might warn them. Using the line-of-sight IR system would keep their conversations private and their presence undetected.

Rohm touched a control on his own suit. "Got it."

Taggart and Rohm depressurized the *Star Wind*'s airlock and stepped out onto the ice. They were parked a hundred meters from the pressure ridge that had hidden their landing. The fastest way to the *Sophie* would be over the ridge. Even in one-tenth gee, climbing that would be a challenge. "Rohm, we'll use the climbers. Get the launcher."

Rohm unshouldered a piece of equipment that looked something like an underwater spear gun, with a spool of cable beneath its wide barrel and a barbed spear-point protruding from it. He aimed it just below the crest of the ridge, waited for the aiming system to lock, and fired. The spear launched itself up, trailing the rope behind it. As it hit the ice, a penetrator charge detonated to anchor it firmly. On the launcher a green light blinked on.

"Okay, it's secure." Rohm said.

"Right, I'll go first."

Taggart clamped a motorized pulley around the rope. He unreeled a short tether from the device and clipped the end of it into a D-ring at the waist of his suit. "I'm on. Climbing." He held on to the climber and slid its large thumbwheel forward. It began to pull itself up the rope, the tether taking most of Taggart's weight as he used his feet to maneuver around crags and protrusions on the ice. A minute later he was at the top. He looked back down at Rohm. "Piece of cake," he said, "come on up." Rohm soon joined him at the crest.

They made their way over the top of the ridge and looked down toward the *Sophie*. The fueling boom was still deployed, its warning light still blinking. Good.

"So, do we wait here for someone to come out, or what?" asked Rohm.

"No, we should get closer. Might give them too much warning if they see us coming." Taggart examined the approach to the other ship. There wasn't a lot of cover. A few low ridges, but they'd have to crawl. A large area around the ship was fresh snow and slick ice from their landing. About as many places to hide as a frikking skating rink, thought Taggart in disgust. Then he had an idea. "Okay," he said, tossing another rope down the pressure ridge and clamping on. "Let's get closer, I have a plan."

∞ ∞ ∞

Roberts checked a panel. The tanks were about three-quarters full, but it was time to check on the fueling boom. "I'm going out again," she said as she pulled her boots on. "We're almost done."

She airlocked out and walked back to where the ice boom protruded from the ice. She inspected the ice surface carefully, looking for cracks or telltale puffs of vapor that might indicate a potential problem. While she was bent over, she thought she saw a movement out of the corner of her eye. What was that? She turned her head, but then couldn't see anything but the edge of her helmet visor. She shifted up to turn her torso. What in the world? There was a cable or rope draped across the ice. She looked up at the *Sophie*. No, it wasn't anything from the ship—and she would have recognized it if it had been. She turned to look in the other direction.

There were two ropes, a couple of meters apart, and barreling toward her across the ice, holding onto motorized pulleys, were two figures in space suits. For a split second she wondered if Carson and Marten were playing some bizarre game, then realized the truth. She started to run for the airlock. "Carson, we've got compa—" Then one of the intruders slammed into her, the impact knocking her over. She regained her breath and shouted into the radio. "Mayday! Mayday! Mayday! Two intruders in suits on the ice!" She struggled with them now, trying to get loose, but she was tangled in some kind of net. "They've got me snared. Mayday!" She felt a hand grasp her wrist, and despite her struggles, watched as one of the men touched the control to turn off her suit radio. "God damn it, Carson!" she shouted, knowing he couldn't hear her, "Not again!" She tried to reach the tool pocket on her suit, maybe she had something to cut the netting with, but she was too tangled. She kept up a steady scream of curses as her captors grabbed the pulleys on the ropes and with her tangled in the net between them, began to reel themselves and her back toward the pressure ridge to the southwest.

∞ ∞ ∞

Carson turned at Jackie's first startled call. He had just reached the radio when her call of "Mayday!" triggered the ship's computer to sound an alarm, flashing an overhead light and sounding an urgent warble.

"Jackie, what's going on?" He switched on the windows as he said this, and what he saw to the southwest knotted his gut. "Jackie, do you read?" There was no answer; her radio must have been cut off.

He scrambled back to the airlock and pulled a suit from a locker.

"Carson, stop, what are you doing?" Marten grabbed his arm.

"They took Jackie," he tried to shake Marten's grip loose. "We have to go help her."

Marten held his arm tighter, and pulled Carson's face down to his. "Slow down. Think this through. What are you going to do? They're probably armed."

"So are we," Carson said, but he recognized the truth behind Marten's words and stopped struggling. "Right. You're right. And shut off that damn alarm."

"You won't go anywhere?"

"Not yet. Just shut off the damn noise and let me think."

Marten walked forward the few steps to the cockpit and cancelled the alarm, then turned back to Carson. "Okay. Now, who were those guys?"

Carson thought for a moment. "They couldn't be Hopkins' men. Perhaps the Velkaryans? I thought Hopkins was working for them."

"And maybe they didn't trust him, or he was supposed to meet them here. Jackie said there weren't many places to refuel. So why did they take her?"

"They want whatever we found. They'll probably call us soon to offer a trade."

"Are you going to do it?"

"Only as a last resort. We don't know what they'll do when they get it. We need more information." Carson looked meaningfully toward the traumapod.

"You want to thaw Rico out? But he's one of them." He also wasn't really frozen, just in a state of hibernation.

"No, he's one of Hopkins' men. As he said, it was just business. He might know something. And if he is one of them, all the better, he might know even more."

"Yes, and he'll be annoyed we kept him in the traumapod all this time." Marten shook his head. "We can't trust him."

"We don't have many choices, and even less time. Give me a better idea or I'm taking him out of the pod."

"All right, I hope you know what you are doing."

∞ ∞ ∞

Rico opened his eyes slowly, then snapped awake as memories came back. There'd been a crash. He'd been hurt. He tried to sit up, but was held down by straps across his arms and chest. He was in a traumapod. How? Then he saw Carson and the timoan and remembered. "How long?" He felt strange, too light. The gravity was wrong. "Where are we?"

"Take it easy," Carson said. "You've been out for a while. You had some bad skull damage, then it was just easier to keep you hibernated. This is a small ship."

"What's going on?" The traumapod had evidently done a good job on repairs, he felt fine.

"We're half way back to Alpha Centauri, a fueling stop. We've got trouble, and you might be able to help."

"Half way back? What the hell, you kept me in a can for two weeks?"

"Most of that was for your own good, Rico, you were bleeding into your brain. And as I said, this is a small ship."

"So you were going to keep me in a can all the way back? And what then, turn me over to the authorities?" *Wait, did they say something about a problem?* Rico was still processing a bit slowly.

"We hadn't figured out yet what we were going to do with you," Carson said. "Although the thought of turning you over had crossed my mind. That's irrelevant now. Who was Hopkins working for?"

"Hopkins? Why?" He must still be a little out of it from the hibernation. Wasn't Hopkins dead?

"Somebody just kidnapped my pilot, and they probably want to trade her for whatever we found at Chara. Can we trust them enough to do a deal?"

"So that's your problem." Rico thought for a moment. Hopkins had definitely seemed scared of whomever he was working for. "No, I don't think you can. I don't know exactly who they are but they made Hopkins nervous. He's not, wasn't, a guy to get nervous easily. How did they find you?"

"Us, Rico. You said you were on our side now—"

"Not if you're going to keep me in a can and turn me in."

"Okay. Help us out and we'll see what we can do."

"What's that supposed to mean?"

"You think Hopkins was the only one working for somebody else? I've got connections. I'll put in a good word." Carson paused as if thinking. Rico wondered how much influence he really had. "As far as I know," Carson continued, "you didn't actually hurt anybody, you were too out of it after the explosion. Anyway, none of us are going anywhere unless we deal with those guys."

"Okay, okay. So what's the situation? What assets do you, I mean we, have?"

"Their ship is parked somewhere on the other side of that ridge," Carson pointed out the window. "They're holding Roberts hostage. She was in a suit but they've probably got her helmet off at least."

Rico nodded. He would have done the same; it would complicate a rescue attempt. "What about us? Suits, weapons, explosives?"

"We have suits, but nothing that will fit Marten here. He'd have to go in a rescue ball if it came to that."

"Okay, suits and rescue balls. What about weapons?"

"We can't go in there blasting."

"Didn't say we were going to, but I need to know what we've got."

"Of course, you're right. Okay, rifles, sidearms, ammunition for that. No explosives, I wasn't planning on blasting anything. If it comes to that we can improvise. Melt off the propellant from the ammunition—"

Rico had thought of that too. He nodded. "Or pull one of the charcoal filters and mix it with liquid oxygen, yeah. Anything else?"

"Unfortunately a lot of our gear is still back on a mountainside on Chara, not that much of it would have helped."

"Yeah, sorry about that."

"What about the Maguffin?" The timoan, Marten, had been just observing the discussion until now.

Rico gave him a wild-eyed look. *Maguffin?* "You mean that gizmo from the pyramid? You saw what it did when we tested it, are you nuts?"

"Well, if nothing else, it is a potential bomb," Marten said.

"We're not going to blow anything up until we get Jackie back," said Carson, "but you may be on to something." He went to the locker where it had been carefully stowed and retrieved it. He placed it on the galley table. "Maybe we can figure out how to control it."

Rico eyed the device warily. "I think you're crazy, Carson."

"No, look." He pointed to the symbols and markings on the device near the handles, adjacent to the controls. "Marten, does any of this look familiar?"

Marten took a closer look. "That symbol," he pointed to a short line made of linked circles, "isn't that from the Feynman diagram?"

Rico looked back and forth from Marten to Carson. *Feynman diagram?* "What are you guys talking about? Can you read that?"

"Maybe," Carson said. "We found some interesting things in the pyramid after you, er, after Hopkins shut us in. I'll explain later, we don't have time now."

Marten had been examining the device. "Look here, Carson, these are numbers. Zero, one, two . . . up to eight."

Rico looked where Marten pointed. "Aren't you counting backward?" he asked.

Carson shook his head. "No, this script reads right to left, bottom to top."

"Shit. I must have had the thing turned up damn near full, then," Rico said, disgusted at the mistake.

Carson examined the controls carefully, noting the symbols beside each. "Look at this one, Marten. We decided this symbol meant 'matter', didn't we?"

"Yes, and the other end of the slider is that linked-circle symbol for energy or radiation. What about this little tornado shape?" Marten pointed to another control.

"Gravity or black hole, wasn't that what we decided?" The time they'd spent exploring the exhibits was paying off. Carson had worried that they had been wasting too much time on them. "Okay, assume this is a carving or excavating tool. Maybe they used it or something like it to dig out the base for the pyramid. What controls would it need?"

"We're getting rather speculative, Carson," Marten said.

"Like you've got a choice?" Rico said. "Anyway, you obviously want a power setting. I already know this is the on-off switch." He pointed to the big pushbutton. "You'd want a way to stop it blowing up in your face, which should be the friggin' default."

"Somebody left the safety off," said Marten.

"No kidding."

"It has to send the matter somewhere," Carson said. "If it converted it all to energy there'd be too much to deal with. And a shield of some kind so it doesn't suck air in from around it."

"No, look at these symbols. The gravity symbol combined with the radiation symbol."

"We know it creates a kind of event horizon, the radiation is either destroyed matter or Hawking radiation. I think." Carson frowned. "If Jackie were here, she would know."

"No, this means something different," Marten said. "In a starship, where does the energy go?"

"What energy?" asked Carson.

"The power from the fusion reactors that energizes the warp field, where does that energy go?"

Rico spoke up. "It radiates off as gravity waves. What did you think? Even I know that much."

Carson got Marten's point. "Right. And that gravity leaks into the hidden dimensions."

"Which is this symbol here, the parallel lines."

"Wait, you guys are saying this gadget can send matter into different dimensions?" Rico asked. "You got that from a few squiggles on the controls?"

"Plus what we learned in the pyramid. And no, we're archeologists, not physicists, but I *think* I understood what Jackie explained to us."

Marten nodded his agreement.

"Okay, okay. Say you're right. So what? How does that help us?"

"We use it to tunnel through that pressure ridge, through the ice under their ship, and even through the hull of their ship, and surprise them," said Carson, as though that ought to be perfectly obvious.

Rico just shook his head. "You are crazy. The thing's just going to blow up on you."

Marten looked at Rico, then at Carson. "I am inclined to agree, at least with the crazy part. Just because my prehistoric ancestors were tunnelers does not mean that I am, any more than you can swing through trees. Besides, as you said, we don't have a suit that will fit me. I cannot help you with that. What about Jackie? What if her suit is open?"

"We bring a rescue ball. We can stuff her in that and bring her back." A rescue ball was what it sounded like, a ball that could rescue someone in case of a ship depressurization. Essentially it was a spherical spacesuit; you climbed in and zipped up, it inflated, and you hoped someone came to rescue you.

"That might work," Rico said, "if you don't get blown up first.

"I have another idea, Carson," said Marten. "What if we use the fabber to make a copy of the device, and maybe some copies of the talisman too."

"That wouldn't fool them for more than a couple of minutes."

"That might be long enough for them to release Jackie."

Carson considered it. "Maybe if we just give them the talisman, and a few copies with different constellations. Tell them that's all we found. The fake copies should keep them guessing, at least for a little while."

Rico was shaking his head. "I don't know, that sounds like trying to pay off a ransom with counterfeit money. I gotta say I like the idea, it sounds like something I would try, but that can't end well."

It was then that the radio chimed.

∞ ∞ ∞

"Just set the stuff down outside your ship, away from the blast area, and take off," Maynard told Carson over the radio. "We'll check it out and if it looks good, leave Roberts there. Then you can come back and get her."

Jackie groaned inwardly. That wasn't going to work.

"No way. For one, I don't trust you." Carson's voice. "We need to make the exchange at the same time. But Roberts is our pilot, we can't move the ship without her."

"What about your co-pilot?"

"Not on this trip. And I still don't trust you."

Maynard looked over at Jackie. "He's telling the truth," she said. "I can't afford a co-pilot, and I didn't think I'd need one with Carson. Not that he knows how to fly."

Maynard checked the instrument she was wired to. It seemed to act like a kind of lie detector. She had tried to tell them that they hadn't found anything, but they had known otherwise. But what she'd just told Maynard was the truth.

"Okay, Carson. Neutral territory. We'll meet out on the ice. You leave the stuff, and after we check it we'll send Roberts to you."

"Tell you what. We meet on the ice. You can stay back with Jackie. Send one man over to check the artifacts. He signals you and you release her, and we walk away."

"You've got one hour."

"Make it two. I'll need to get over that ridge carrying the stuff, and I don't have the climbing gear your guys do."

"Very well. Two hours. Starting now." Maynard clicked the radio connection off.

Roberts sagged with relief. The last time something like this had happened, Carson had wanted to call her captors' bluff and refused to negotiate. She didn't think Maynard was the bluffing type.

∞ ∞ ∞

"Carson?" Marten said, back on the *Sophie*. "We still have climbing gear. What—"

"I know. I wanted to buy us more time. We'll have to move fast. We'll use the Maguffin—"

"I'm not touching that thing," said Rico.

"You won't have to. Here's my plan . . ."

Chapter 37: Exchange

The Icefield

RICO STOOD ALONE on the ice at the bottom of the pressure ridge. The nametag on the front of his spacesuit read "Carson," and he had one of the comm bracelets fastened inside his helmet, wired into the suit's radio. It would relay everything to Carson, and vice versa. Carson himself was busy elsewhere. Rico thought about that and suppressed a shudder. *Better him than me.*

The Velkaryan ship was about a hundred meters away. He checked that the suit radio transmitter was off, then spoke to Carson on the bracelet. "I'm in position, you set?"

"Close enough," came Carson's reply. "Go for it."

Rico switched his radio to the agreed frequency and hailed the ship. Then he shut up and let Carson talk.

"I'm here. I have the artifacts," Carson's voice said through Rico's suit radio. Rico hoisted the metallic cylinder and waved it. "Where's Jackie?"

"All right, Carson, we're coming out."

Rico saw a hatch slide open and three suited figures walked from it, one being held by the others. Was that Roberts?

"Jackie, is that you?" Carson's voice again.

The figure raised its free arm and waved. "Turn her radio on, I want to hear her."

"All right, just a moment."

One of the suits touched something on the forearm of the other. Rico heard Roberts' voice on the suit comm. "Don't trust them, Cars—" The first suit stabbed the radio button off.

"Can you still hear me, Jackie?" asked Carson.

"She can hear you, we just turned off her transmitter. We don't expect you to trust us, but this is a fair game."

Jackie raised her free arm again in acknowledgment.

"All right. No worries, Jackie, a clean trade, just like Raven."

"What the hell is Raven?" one of the captors demanded. Rico wondered the same thing.

"Similar situation," Carson said. "Tomb raiders grabbed Jackie and ransomed her for some artifacts I'd found. It all worked out."

"Is that right?" One of the figures put his helmet up to Jackie's, to get her response without turning her transmitter on again.

Rico held his breath. *Don't screw it up, Roberts, just nod or something.*

Her response appeared to satisfy her captors. "Okay, I'm sending a man over to check the goods. Put it down and step away."

Rico raised the device then slowly and deliberately placed it on the ice. He opened a pouch on his suit, pulled several objects from it, and put them on the surface too. Talismans. "Okay." Carson's voice. Rico stepped back a few paces, looking around to get his bearings, then casually reached behind him to loosen the pry-bar taped to his back.

A lone space-suited figure loped across the intervening space in an easy low-gravity bounce. Rico kept his eye on Roberts and the other back near the ship. He thought he saw a flicker of light under the ice. *Not yet.* He pulled the pry-bar loose, keeping it hidden.

The other figure reached the small pile and bent to pick the items up. "We've got four talismans," he said, "I don't recognize the patterns." He picked up the device and started to examine it. Rico edged closer to him.

The man turned it over in his hands. "What the?" He turned it over again. "This is a fake! Carson—"

"Now!" Rico yelled, and swung the pry-bar at the man, knocking him to the ice.

Near the ship, Jackie pushed away from her other captor just as the ice behind them erupted in a blue flash. She got away from him and started running toward Rico, turning her suit radio on as she did so. "What the hell, Carson? They've got guns, we won't get over that ridge in time."

"Taken care of," Rico said, and pushed a button strapped to his wrist. Behind him, part of the base of the ridge erupted in a spray of ice chunks and water vapor. He felt a thump as the shock wave traveled through the ice under his feet.

∞ ∞ ∞

Jackie saw the explosion and felt the ground shake. Was the ship firing at him? She slowed, that last voice hadn't sounded like Carson. She felt a push from behind. She turned, and recognized the face in the helmet.

"Come on, Jackie, let's go. Move it."

"Carson?" Where had *he* come from? She turned back to look at the other figure.

"That's Rico. Let's go. Go, go!" Carson was running, pulling her along.

Rico? Roberts moved, she could worry about the details later. Ahead of her, near Rico, the debris from the explosion had settled out and she could see that it had blasted open an entrance to a tunnel through the ridge. How? Never mind. "Carson, anyone still on the *Sophie*?" she said as she ran.

"Marten, why?"

"Marten! Control console. Punch in AE thirty-five, that's alpha echo three five, then execute. Emergency start sequence."

"Roger, Jackie." Marten's voice came back over the radio.

The man Rico had knocked down was back on his feet, the two of them wrestling for the pry-bar. The other man pulled it from Rico's grasp and swung at his helmet. Rico pulled back in time, falling to the ice, but swept a foot out and knocked the other's legs from under him. The other went down too. Jackie and Carson were almost there; maybe they could help.

It wasn't necessary. Rico wrestled the pry-bar away and slammed it across the other's helmet, starring the visor. A small plume of vapor jetted from the cracks. The man started to scramble back to the ship. Suddenly small fountains of ice erupted around them. Bullets!

"They're shooting at us!"

"I'll take care of it," Carson said. "Keep going, get to the tunnel."

Jackie ran.

∞ ∞ ∞

Carson had seen the bullet impacts too, and was already turning back to deal with it. He didn't have a gun. His suit gloves wouldn't fit through the trigger guards on what they'd had on the ship, and they'd run out of time to modify them. But he still had the alien disintegrator tool that he'd tunneled through the ice with. Pity it didn't have more range, ten meters would have to do.

The man at the ship was the one firing. He seemed to have trouble bracing himself on the ice in this low gravity. Carson aimed the disintegrator at him and pressed the control button. A small glowing spot appeared above the ground about halfway between Carson and the gunman. Too far. Carson lowered his aim, the glowing dot tracking the focus. As it touched the surface, it bloomed in a huge flash and chunks of ice flew everywhere. Carson released his thumb. *Oops, forgot to engage the safeties.* He grinned and started running back toward Jackie and Rico.

∞ ∞ ∞

Rico saw the gunman go down but he didn't stay down, he was scrambling to get back up. With no atmosphere to transmit the shock wave, explosions weren't quite so bad here. The gunman had regained his footing, and braced himself against the side of his ship.

"Keep going, Roberts. I'll help Carson." Rico called as he started running to do just that.

Rico still had the prybar in his hand. He threw it as he ran, its trajectory hard and flat in the low gravity. It hit the ship, soundless in the vacuum, and rebounded into the gunman. The gunman recovered and brought the gun to bear on Rico. *Guess I got his attention*, Rico thought.

Carson blasted out another chunk out of the ice, throwing the gunman's aim off. Rico caught up and pulled on Carson's arm. "Let's go!"

"This thing has no range," Carson said. "He'll shoot us in the back."

Rico cursed, and looked hastily around. Where was that tunnel Carson had dug? There, closer to the ship.

"Give it to me, I'll cover you."

"How will you get out?"

"Your tunnel." After his experience on Chara, Rico hadn't wanted to try digging the tunnel himself, but he'd seen Carson using the disintegrator, and it was their only chance.

Carson hesitated. "You go, I'll cover you."

Ice fountained around them again, the gunman was back in action.

"Damn it Carson, no time to argue." Rico moved quickly, snatching the disintegrator out of Carson's hands before he could object. "Now, you go." He fired the disintegrator at the ice to distract the shooter.

"Okay. Good luck." Carson ran.

Rico ran the other way, toward the tunnel, blasting the ice randomly between the gunman and himself. A bullet hit the ice near him. He blasted again and rolled away.

Carson's voice came over the radio. "Rico, we're in the tunnel under the ridge. Get clear and get out of there."

"I'm working on it. Keep going." It occurred to Rico that these guys would be happy if he just left the disintegrator for them. They might just let him go. *No.* They were batshit crazy. He couldn't let them have this and they probably wouldn't let him go anyway. But he might stall them.

"Ahoy the ship. I've got your alien device. If you keep shooting at me it's going to get broken."

"Rico, what the hell are you doing?" That was Carson's voice.

"Saving your ass, Carson. Keep going."

"Cease fire." That was Maynard's voice. "Rico, is it? Just lay the device down and we'll let you go back to your ship with Carson and Roberts."

"Right. And I know that how?"

"Taggart, walk away from the ship and put down your weapon."

"But—" That must have been Taggart.

"Do it. Rico, you do the same. Put down the device and walk away."

"Carson, what's your status?" asked Rico.

"We're nearly at the *Sophie*. Don't do it, Rico, don't let them have it."

"Keep out of this, Carson," said Maynard. "Come on, Rico, one device isn't going to make a difference. We could do more damage by bypassing the safeties on a warp engine."

Rico was smart enough to realize they wanted it too badly for that to be true. A movement on their ship caught his eye. A gun turret? Those sly bastards. He looked around again. Taggart was now a dozen meters off, his gun on the ground, his hands outspread. And there, there was the tunnel Carson had used to come up behind Roberts' captors.

"Okay, you've got a deal." Rico started walking toward the ship, making an adjustment to the device's controls as he did so. He noticed the gun turret tracking him. He angled his path between the ship and the tunnel entrance.

"Just stop and set it down, Rico, we don't need it delivered."

"Okay. I hear you." Rico crouched down and placed the device on the ice. The tunnel entrance was three meters away. "Here you go."

In one fluid motion, Rico thumbed the control switch, pushed the device across the ice toward the ship, and dived for the tunnel. As he entered the tunnel head-first, he could see bright light reflecting all around him, shining blue through the ice. He slid to the bottom of the tunnel and began to run for all he was worth. He was halfway to the ridge when the glow through the ice got even brighter and the ground jumped beneath him.

∞ ∞ ∞

Carson and Roberts were already aboard the *Sophie*. The emergency sequence had jettisoned the refueling boom head and retracted the rest, and brought the flight systems on line. Jackie pulled her helmet off and pushed forward to the cockpit. Before she reached it there was a squeal of radio noise from the speakers, and the ridge top to the southwest lit up a brilliant blue as light shone through the ice.

"What?" Jackie saw a broad wavefront rippling through the ground toward them at high speed. "*Brace—*"

Then the ground wave hit and the *Sophie* bounced, tossing them all to the deck and scattering anything that wasn't secured. Beyond the ridge a plume of vapor, ice, and debris was just starting to peak and settle out.

Jackie scrambled to her feet and to the control deck, quickly running damage checks. "Everyone all right back there?" she called as she scanned the displays.

She heard them pulling themselves to their feet. Somebody was groaning.

"I'm okay," Carson said, "Marten whacked his head on a locker. He'll be okay. How's the ship?"

There were yellow lights on the board but nothing critical. Objectively the shock probably had been no worse than a hard landing, it had just been unexpected. "She's fine, nothing serious. Let me guess, Rico blew up the Maguffin again. What the hell was he doing out there anyway?"

"That would be my guess too. And we were rescuing you. I told you this was just like the Raven."

"I almost lost it when you said that. You'd just walked away on Raven. I didn't know you'd set up the rescue. I didn't know how you'd pull it off here." She'd forgotten about Rico. In the traumapod he'd been more like cargo.

"So am I forgiven?"

"You've got to be kidding me, Carson. You got me kidnapped and almost killed *twice* now, and you want me to forgive you?" *On the other hand*, she thought, *he did get me rescued. Again.*

"Anyway," she said, changing the subject, "do you think anyone survived that? Do you think Rico got away?"

"Hard to imagine, but we worked out most of the controls on that thing, he might have figured something out. We owe it to him to look, anyway."

"We do. Okay, get things secured, I'll take *Sophie* up and we can check from above. If anyone else is around I want to be able to get out fast."

∞ ∞ ∞

As they flew over the ridge they were greeted by a dazzling plain of newly refrozen ice and fresh snow, fallout from the ice that had vaporized in the blast. Of Maynard's ship there was nothing but a crater and a few scattered hull fragments.

"That was a lot more powerful than back on Chara," Roberts said.

"Maybe Rico found a setting that went up to nine," said Marten.

Carson gave him an odd look. He turned back to Roberts. "Try the radio again."

"*Sophie* calling Rico, come in." She touched a control to try a different suit frequency. "Rico, this is the *Sophie*. Are you receiving?" There was no response. Jackie tried each suit frequency in succession. It was wasted effort. "Nothing. If he was out in the open . . ."

"I know. But I dug a tunnel. That's how I came up behind you."

"The radio should still penetrate the ice. Hang on, let me try something else." She brought up another display and touched several control pads. "Suit telemetry," she explained. There were three similar displays on the screen. "That's mine," she said, touching the window to close it. "And that's yours." She closed that one. "Which leaves this one, which must be Rico. I'm getting a faint signal, his suit is still functioning, anyway."

"Is he still alive?"

"I can't tell. He must be under the ice; this is a very noisy signal. Let me get a fix on it."

"How do we get him out?"

"Same way we refueled. The boom head's gone but we've still got the hoses, and plenty of steam."

∞ ∞ ∞

Two hours later a broken but breathing Rico was out of the ice and back in the traumapod. A half-hour after that they were headed back to Alpha Centauri.

Chapter 38: Home

UDT HQ at Sawyer City Spaceport

"WE'LL TAKE CARE of Rico," Ducayne said. "I can use someone with his talents, they just need to be focused."

They were all—Carson, Marten and Roberts as well as Ducayne—sitting in chairs squeezed around the desk in Ducayne's more public office.

"All right," said Carson. "And what about us?"

Ducayne took another look at file he had open on his computer screen, then looked up at them.

"Well, gentlemen, er gentle beings," he gave an apologetic nod to Marten, who nodded back. "First, congratulations. You found a significant cache of Spacefarer artifacts—from the sounds of it, some of them we have concerns about—and you also put Hopkins out of business, one of the more notorious artifact smugglers. Not that that's my department, exactly, but any operation that can smuggle things in and out of systems and raise large amounts of cash is a potential security risk, so I'm happy to see him gone. As for Maynard, I should thank you for settling a debt I owed him—"

"Your agent?"

"Exactly. But I would also have liked the opportunity to question him." Ducayne pushed a fist into the palm of his other hand until the knuckles cracked. "By the way, all of you," he said, looking at each of them in turn, "the Velkaryans are still out there, it wasn't just Maynard. They won't know what happened to him, and we'll certainly keep it quiet, but it's in your own best interests that they never find out. Understood?"

A chorus of agreement answered him.

"Right, then." He picked up the talisman from his desk. "So this is a key *and* a map, eh? Clever."

"There's one other thing, Ducayne," said Carson in a somber voice. Ducayne looked up at him, puzzled. Carson looked at Marten, and Roberts, making eye contact with each. Carson took a breath. "Something we left out of the report. We'll tell you about it once because you should know, and then never mention it again because we don't want people to think we're crazy."

That didn't seem to bother Ducayne. He looked almost as though he had been expecting something like this. "Does it involve a pyramid?"

The others started at this, then settled back. Perhaps he meant the archive pyramid. Carson looked at Ducayne suspiciously. "Yes, what about it?"

Ducayne paused. "How to put this? Let me hypothesize. You saw, you all saw, or experienced, something highly unusual, far more so than anything in your report. Unusual and yet related to something that people sometimes *claim* to have seen, and have their veracity if not their sanity doubted. Am I correct so far?"

They all nodded, wondering just what Ducayne knew and where he was going with it.

Ducayne paused, thinking. "Here, let me show you something." He pulled his computer screen over, took a small gadget out of his pocket and plugged it in, then placed his thumb on the scan pad for a moment. The computer beeped, and he keyed in a couple of commands to bring up an image. He turned the screen toward them.

The picture showed the surface of an asteroid or small moon. The surface was irregular, the ground uneven with hills and valleys, all of it overlain with a thick layer of regolith or dust and peppered with craters and small rocks. The sky beyond was black. The interesting thing in the picture, though, was a broad, fresh-looking crater with large pieces of very-regular looking debris scattered about it. The angles and flat sides on the debris—where it had not been broken or torn apart by the crash—could very easily have been fitted together to make a pyramid.

"We heard about some unusual wreckage on an asteroid in the Epsilon Eridani system—"

"That package I delivered?" asked Roberts.

"As a matter of fact, yes." Ducayne said. "The man who found it assumed it was just some unlucky explorer, but he took a couple of pictures and a piece of the debris and reported it. When we realized there was something funny about the wreckage we sent a team out. They took these pictures, and what equipment they could from the wreckage. That wasn't much I'm afraid. But look at this." Ducayne pulled up another image. Taken from the same vantage point as the first, it showed the same rough terrain of the asteroid, with the same fresh-looking crater. But the debris was gone.

"Somebody cleaned it up. You?" Roberts asked.

"No. These pictures are almost a month apart. After the discovery they brought back what they could—these pictures, some small artifacts and pieces of wreckage—and left a reconnaissance beacon. When we went back again recently, the only thing left was the beacon."

"And it recorded—what?"

"I'll show you mine if you show me yours." That got a grin. "What did you guys see that you don't want to talk about?"

"A large, flying pyramid."

"So did we. What else?"

"It landed."

Ducayne snapped his head up at that, and looked directly at Carson. "And?"

"Unfortunately we don't know. It was on the other side of the mountains from us, but it cleaned up the damage to the structure on the ground. What else did you record?"

"Not very much. The big pyramid landed and blocked the view of the recorder. When it took off again, the debris was gone."

"Apparently they like to keep things neat," Roberts said.

Ducayne shook his head. "They also seem to be avoiding contact or leaving evidence of themselves. I wish I knew why."

"So would I," said Carson. "They didn't seem to have this non-interference directive 15,000 years ago."

"If it was the same people."

Carson's gaze turned sharply to Ducayne. "You have some reason to think it wouldn't be? The pyramid shape of their ships seems a strong connection."

Ducayne shook his head. "No specific reason, just that 15,000 years is a long time." He touched another control on his computer. "There's one other thing. We let your search program run, and in fact we got it into a few private databases. It found a few things." Another image appeared on the screen.

It was the talisman, the passkey. Several of them, in fact, making an array of a half-dozen different images, most with different star patterns than the others.

"More talismans!" said Carson.

"Exactly. Apparently these things have been found all over known T-space, although we don't have provenances for all of them."

Carson thought back to his first encounter with Hopkins. "There's a chance some of them are faked. How many do you have in hand?"

"What makes you think we have any in hand, Carson? These are all in collections, some public, some private."

Carson just looked at him and raised an eyebrow. "I think I know you better than that."

Ducayne grinned, then pulled the screen back and checked a file. "Three, although one wasn't responsive—we checked for radiation and tried pinging them at different frequencies—that might be a fake, or it might just be dead. The patterns are all different." He turned the screen to face the others again and sequenced through the talisman images. "You know, if I had my way, as we could identify the locations we'd send a full Homeworld Security team out to each one of them. But we don't have the manpower or the budget, and won't anytime soon. It would also kick up an amazing ruckus." He paused for a moment, then came to a decision.

"So, Hannibal, do you feel like taking on a, what shall we call it, a broad archeological survey? I think we can find someone to back you."

"Well, I *still* don't have any incontestable evidence of my spacefarer hypothesis. This little expedition was hardly scientific. I suppose I could write something up on the terrace-builders of Chara III." He grinned at Ducayne. "Besides, if the spacefarers are still around, I imagine you'd rather I kept quiet about them."

Ducayne nodded. "You've got that right." He looked at Marten. "The offer covers you, too, if you're interested. I think we can work something out."

"Wait, what about my ship?" Jackie demanded. "The *Sophie* needs major repairs."

Ducayne turned to her. "Where's the ship now? On the field?"

Jackie nodded. "Yes."

"All right, I'll tell you what. Have it towed into the bay down there," he said, gesturing toward the hangar bay outside his office. "It will help our cover here anyway. We'll get it fixed up for you. In fact, if you're willing to come work for us—"

Jackie stiffened, her eyes narrowing as she gave a slight shake of her head.

"—or willing to take a retainer and contract work," Ducayne said, adjusting his offer at her reaction, "then we can even make certain, ah, improvements."

Jackie relaxed, one corner of her mouth turned up in a half smile.

"All right, but it's my ship, I get final say."

"Fair enough. Do we have a deal? That includes what I just mentioned to you, Carson."

Carson looked at Roberts and Marten. "What do you say, gentles?"

"Suits me," said Jackie.

"You know me, Carson," Marten said, "I left home for travel and adventure. I'm in."

Carson turned back to Ducayne. "All right, we'll do it, on one condition."

"Condition?" asked Ducayne.

"Yes. Can we avoid planets with any bloody mosquitoes?"

∞

Glossary

Alcubierre: Miguel Alcubierre derived a series of equations consistent with Relativity which describe warping of space in a way which permits Faster-Than-Light travel.

Chara: G0-type star 27.5 light-years from Earth, also called Beta Canorum Venaticum.

Finazzi instability: In 2009, Stefano Finazzi, Stefano Liberati, and Carlos Barceló applied a quantum analysis to the Alcubierre warp metric and deduced that quantum fluctuations could destabilize the warp.

Kakuloa: Alpha Centauri B II - terraformed planet orbiting the second largest star (B) in the Alpha Centauri system.

omni: Short for **omniphone** - compares to today's smartphones as smartphones compare to walky-talkies. (Search for "Nokia Morph" on YouTube for a nearly-there concept video.)

parsec: A distance of approximately 3.26 light-years.

Sapphire: A class of small interstellar scout ship, capable of sleeping about six if they're close friends, with a range of about 20 light-years on full tanks.

Sawyers World: Alpha Centauri A II - second planet orbiting the largest star (A) in the Alpha Centauri system, first extrasolar planet settled by humans.

supercircle: A special case of a superellipse, a geometric figure described in Cartesian coordinates by the formula:

$$(ax)^n + (by)^n = c$$

For $a=b$, if $n=1$, the shape is a diamond, if $n=2$, it is a circle., if $n > 2$, it looks like a square with rounded corners. In the mid-20th century, Piet Hein used a superellipse with $n=2.5$ (or 5/2), extensively in architectural and industrial design.

Taprobane: Epsilon Indi III - Third planet orbiting Epsilon Indi, ironically named for an old name for the island known as Sri Lanka or Ceylon, ironic because of its cooler climate.

technetium: Element 43 on the periodic table, it has no stable isotopes. With a geologically short half-life any that was present when the solar system formed has long since disappeared. Today, all technetium is made in reactors.

thruster: High-efficiency reaction drive, a kind of arc-jet.

timoan: (Analogous to "human") The sentient natives of Taprobane. Descended from the ancestral species of terrestrial mongoose and meerkats the way humans are descend from the ancestral species of apes, monkeys and lemurs. They independently achieved iron-age level civilization (*e.g.* Earth's Celts) before human contact.

T-space: Terraformed (or Terraform) space - Usual term for "known space," a spheroid of stars centered on Earth and about 20 parsecs in diameter. So called because many of the sun-like stars within it were found to have planets that were not merely Earth-like, but deliberately terraformed by people or aliens as-yet unknown.

Unholy War: A nuclear war which took place in the early part of the 21st century, involving primarily the smaller nuclear powers, purportedly for religious reasons.

Velkaryans: The bad guys. See chapter 9.

Verdigris: Delta Pavonis III - third planet orbiting the star Delta Pavonis, so named for the heavy jungle and greenish sky.

warp bubble: The thin shell of highly-curved space surrounding a ship in flight. Based on Van Den Broek's lower-energy configuration of an Alcubierre warp metric.

Acknowledgments

To thank everyone somehow involved at one remove or another would turn this into an autobiography; ultimately any novel is a product of all the influences in an author's life. But the more direct influences are worthy of direct thanks.

First, thanks to my (ex-) wife Jill, and my kids, Arthur, Robert and Selena, for their belief in my writing, for putting up with my long hours hidden away banging on the keyboard, and for early feedback on the drafts. And a particular thanks to Robert for his constant enthusiasm for the project, even to the point of persuading his teacher to let him use *The Chara Talisman* as the subject of a book review.

Thanks also to Dean Wesley Smith, Kristine Kathryn Rusch, and all the participants of their June, 2010 novel writers workshop, for the impetus to *finish* the novel, and for their feedback.

Stanley Schmidt, editor of *Analog Science Fiction and Fact*, thought enough of the short story "Stone Age," which I crafted from this book's first few chapters, to buy it and publish it in the June, 2011 issue of that magazine, making it my third SFWA-qualifying sale. Stan, I still enjoy writing the shorter stuff too -- there's one on its way as I type this.

My friend Lou Berger suffered through many iterations of parts of this novel, in particular the "Stone Age" chapters, and the opening of the book is much improved for his feedback.

And finally, but by no means minimally, my thanks to Toni Weisskopf of Baen Books, both for the very first personal rejection letter I ever received (years ago, for a short story) and for her early comments on the synopsis of this novel.

The story "Omnilingual" mentioned in chapter 26 is by H. Beam Piper, first published in the February 1957 issue of *Analog* (then named *Astounding*) and widely republished. If you haven't read it, you should.

The song Jackie sings to herself in that same chapter was inspired by Tom Lehrer's "The Elements," but I rewrote the verses to make the names fit a more regular pattern on the periodic table.

I try to get the details correct in my writing (hard SF authors do the math), but sometimes mistakes slip through. Like any experienced software engineer, I blame the computers.

-- *Alastair Mayer, Colorado, October 2011*

This novel, *The Chara Talisman*, was my first published novel. I would like to give a thank-you to the many readers gave me feedback on the earlier editions and printings of this novel, and especially to those who like it enough to keep reading the rest of the series, which as I write this has grown to three published Carson & Roberts novels with two more almost ready for publication, plus three *Alpha Centauri* novels and the first in the *Kakuloa* series.

This edition has many minor changes, mostly for consistency of style with the later volumes and to correct the typos that I swear must creep in by themselves no matter how many times a manuscript is reviewed and edited. While the temptation is always there to "retcon" an earlier work, I have avoided that as much as possible. If Han Solo were in this book (he's not), he'd still shoot first. ☺

-- *Alastair Mayer, Colorado, June 2019*

Preview: *The Reticuli Deception*

The following excerpt is from the book two, *The Reticuli Deception*, which follows the further adventures of Hannibal Carson, Jackie Roberts, and the rest.

Prelude

Approaching Earth, circa 100 CE

KUKUL DROPPED the ship out of warp high above the ocean which covered nearly half this world, on a trajectory that would take them over the south polar continent. That should keep them well away from the monitoring stations on the other side of the planet, where three continental masses converged around a large sea. The natives on the northern continents there had already developed a considerable, if still low-tech, civilization, and they were being watched.

The timing of their entry also ensured that they would be hidden from the monitoring base on the large moon; it couldn't look through the planet. The orbital radiation belts dipped lowest over the ocean and the other large southern continent, that would help mask their entry too.

The ship screamed into the atmosphere over Antarctica, skirting what would later become known as the South Atlantic Anomaly and hugging the western coast of the future South America. If he'd been given correct information on the monitoring satellites' orbits, the atmospheric entry flare would be lost in the glare of the setting sun.

Their trajectory took them north, following the mountain range.

"Kukul," Quetz, his passenger, said, "what is that glow ahead?"

Kukul checked the forward scanners and his crest feathers rippled in consternation. He zoomed the image and cut in other scanners, and realized with sudden dread what the towering clouds ahead were.

"It looks like the ash plume from an active volcano."

"Nobody said anything about volcanoes!"

Kukul banked the deltoid ship and cut in maneuvering thrusters. "We had limited data, geology was a secondary concern. I'll try to steer clear of the plume." Unfortunately this ship didn't have much crossrange.

"Can our hull take the scouring?"

"Perhaps, but we're still traveling at high speed, I can't be sure. There would be damage to the external sensors."

He'd managed to turn his trajectory away from the thickest plume when the glow suddenly brightened and he saw streaks of light rising from the base of the cloud. The volcano had just belched fire and magma. Kukul wondered how high and far the lava bombs could reach. If he cut in main thrusters to climb, the monitors would pick him up for sure. His crest feathers flattened back against his skull with anticipation.

A loud bang and an impact that shook the ship answered his question. High enough to reach them. He banked hard away from the volcano, trying to ignore a vibration which suggested the hull had lost its aerodynamic integrity. The ship dived lower into the thick air, shedding velocity. The volcano was behind them now; they would check out the ship when they reached the landing area. The ground below was all jungle; he'd crossed this planet's equator shortly before the volcano blew. They were now barely at twice the altitude of the mountains, and the ground quickly gave way to ocean as he passed beyond the southern continent and paralleled the narrow isthmus that joined it to the northern one. Their destination.

A sudden tearing sound, accompanied by a bucking, yawing vibration, told him things were not well with the ship. They had to set down *now*. But where? The jungle was out of the question. There were some cleared areas—fields cultivated by the natives, if they were that advanced on this continent—but too small for his purpose. If the hull were intact he could attempt a water landing, approaching from offshore and stopping at the beach if he planned it right.

He scanned the board. Damage showed on the port-side leading edge, but above the nominal waterline. He scanned the terrain beneath him. The irregular coastline was behind him and they were heading out to sea again, but to his left, near the horizon, the coast continued in a more-or-less northerly direction. He banked toward it, shedding air-speed to reduce the buffeting of their damaged airframe. There was no choice but to risk a brief radar burst to check the surface. *There*. To the north an offshore chain of islands showed.

"Stand by," he told Quetz. "We're going to ditch south of those islands."

"*Ditch?* As in water?" Quetz sounded not at all happy.

Kukul said nothing but his crest feathers flattened back in determination. He dropped lower, lining up for a water landing. The ocean surface ahead looked reasonably smooth.

Too late, Kukul saw the low line of surf at the edge of the calm water. A barrier reef. Perhaps he'd clear it before hitting the sea. He came in low, but left the surf behind him as he approached the surface. He pulled the nose of his ship up to let the trailing edge touch. Gently, gently. . .

The aft edge touched a wave and Kukul lurched forward as the ship suddenly slowed, the nose coming down and hitting the water with a *smack!* Kukul struggled desperately to keep the nose from going under; if he porpoised they would be done for. He had to keep it hydroplaning. Keep it up, up. Yes! The ship was slowing now; they were going to make it.

Bang! The ship shuddered again and pushed upward as though it had been hammered from beneath. Alarms screamed at him from his console, and Kukul realized with dismay that the hull had cracked. They hadn't cleared the whole reef after all.

"Get the life raft and whatever else you can grab quickly!" he called to Quetz. "I'll get the portable analyzers. Maybe we can salvage the mission." Water, thankfully warm, had begun flooding into the cabin, and they scrambled to pull emergency gear together.

It was time to abandon ship.

Chapter I: Insight

Sawyers World, Alpha Centauri A, 2122 CE

BUILT NEARLY forty-five years ago, the weather-beaten hangar in a remote corner of Sawyer Spaceport was one of the oldest structures on the planet, the second innermost circling Alpha Centauri A. Dr. Hannibal Carson, Professor of Exoarcheology, paused at a familiar door at one corner of the building. The "Office of Techno-Archeology" plaque was gone; the replacement, looking as aged as its predecessor had, read "QD Shipping."

This time the main hangar doors were open. An S-class starship filled the central bay. Carson recognized it as Jackie Roberts's *Sophie.* It had several panels removed and there was a tool cart next to one of the openings. A profusion of cables ran from connectors on the hull to some kind of diagnostic computer sitting on the cart with its lights blinking and graphs displaying on its screens.

He made his way to the back of the hangar and up the metal stairs to the mezzanine, meeting Ducayne at his office door.

"'QD Shipping'?" Carson said. "Isn't using your initials a bit of a giveaway?"

"Who said Quentin Ducayne was my real name? Anyway, we tell people it stands for quick 'n' dirty."

"That must discourage customers."

"That's the general idea, yes."

Carson shook his head. *Spooks.* "So what do we have? I take it Jackie came up with something?"

"I did." Jackie Roberts appeared from the office adjacent to Ducayne's.

Jackie looked as good as ever, from her dark-green hair in its characteristic page-boy cut—short enough to not be troublesome in zero-gee—to her Chelsea-style ship boots, although her coveralls didn't compliment the figure Carson remembered. He snapped himself out of it. "I didn't know you were here," he said.

"I wanted to be able to keep an eye on *Sophie* while she's undergoing repairs. Ducayne offered me quarters but this works."

"The offer's still open, Captain Roberts. It would be a lot more comfortable than that office or your ship while people are working on it."

"Let me guess," said Carson, turning to Ducayne. "These quarters are down in the same complex as the briefing rooms?" He remembered Jackie's aversion to enclosed, underground spaces.

"Of course."

"Then she's probably happier where she is. Unless," he turned back to Jackie, "you want something on campus? We've usually got dorm rooms available for visitors."

"No, thanks. I really do prefer to keep an eye on my ship."

Carson nodded in understanding. "So what do you have?"

Jackie looked over at Ducayne, who said: "We'll talk in the briefing room."

Carson sighed and nodded. "Very well."

Together they went back down the stairs to the hangar floor and across to a small office, which Carson knew served as a secret elevator to the lower levels. As they skirted the *Sophie*, Carson cast an appraising eye over the work. Much of the outer hull had been removed, and he could see that a warp module had already been removed. On Chara III they had spent days carefully moving that into position to compensate for attack damage. Now it sat on an equipment cradle toward the rear of the hangar.

"Your repair team has been busy," Carson said to Ducayne.

"It sure beats the duct-tape and wire we used to get back from Chara," said Jackie. "And not just repair, they're making a few modifications too."

Ducayne nodded. "A bit more range, and a few other tweaks. We want you to have more of an edge if you get jumped again. You got lucky with Hopkins and Maynard."

"Jackie's flying skills helped with Hopkins."

"Thanks, Hannibal, but Ducayne's right. We were lucky."

While they'd been talking, they'd entered the small office and the elevator had started down.

"Briefing Room Two" Ducayne said as they cleared the security post. The familiar briefing room was already occupied by a lone man. Carson recognized him as one of the two from his original briefing when he'd first met Ducayne.

"Mr. Brown, wasn't it?" he asked extending a hand, "Or was that Mr. Black?"

The man smiled and accepted the handshake. "To tell you the truth I don't recall. You can call me—" he cast a quick glance toward Ducayne, who returned the glance but with neither a nod or a shake of his head that Carson could see "—Brown."

"All right," said Carson. "I take it you know Captain Jackie Roberts?" he added, not sure if the introduction was needed.

"Yes, Jackie—Captain Roberts—and I have been working on your talisman star maps."

"Jackie is fine, Malcolm," she said, "We're not on my ship."

Malcolm? Carson wondered if that were also a cover name as he and the others seated themselves at the conference table. "So," he said, looking at Jackie and Brown, "what have you got?"

Jackie glanced at Ducayne, who nodded. "Locations," she said, "at least some." She touched a pad on the table and the main briefing screen lit up. It showed eight images of stone talismans, each in the shape of a rounded square or, more precisely, a supercircle. They all showed signs of wear, and all had line and gemstone decorations similar to that of the Chara talisman, a decoration which had proved to be a star map. And they were all different.

He let out a low whistle. "Eight!"

"That's right, your little net spider has been effective."

Carson had found a talisman fragment amidst stone-age ruins which turned out to contain a 15,000 year-old technetium battery.

He'd launched a net search to find images of similar-looking artifacts in private or museum collections. That search had called Ducayne's attention to him in the first place. It had turned up six by the time they returned from Chara.

"It turned up two more," Jackie continued. "Ducayne managed to pry some loose from their collections. We have three in hand," she touched a key, highlighting three of the talismans, "with one more on the way." She highlighted a fourth image.

"Fantastic! What locations?"

"This one," she singled out an image and filled the screen with it, "doesn't seem to point anywhere, at least, not so far."

"It looks different from the others somehow, the pattern feels different."

"Good call. That's the one that didn't seem to have any internal structure. It's probably a fake."

"I want to take a close look at it," Carson said. "If it's old, it could be an indigenous low-tech copy. For that matter, I want to look at all of them."

"You will," said Ducayne. "We want you to go over each in detail as we get hold of them. See if you can spot fakes or anything else unusual. We'll do a more detailed set of scans and take samples of—"

"Not before I examine them! The samples, I mean."

"No, of course not. Brown here has been giving us good advice on that."

Brown nodded agreement.

"All right. What about other locations?"

"We have tentative locations for three that we only have images of. We'll confirm them when we get our hands on them. At least one of those is much farther out than we've explored. Two of the images aren't clear enough to be sure of the gem colors, too much dirt on the artifacts, and our guesses haven't come up with matches yet." Jackie flipped up another image, show two talismans. "These two correspond, as best we can tell, to known locations in T-space."

"Where?"

"You're not going to like it."

"Just tell me, damn it."

"Okay, this one here," she gestured, "seems to indicate Delta Pavonis."

Carson turned to look sharply at her. "That's where I found that first fragment." He'd almost missed the talisman fragment, lying in the dirt in an ancient tomb. If it hadn't been broken, he wouldn't have detected the weak radiation from the technetium it contained, nor noticed its internal structure. The decay products of the technetium, an element with no naturally occurring isotopes, had let them date it at approximately 15,000 years old. That had been quite a surprise. "We know there were spacefarers there, but there's no sign of a pyramid, not like what we found on Chara III."

"But you did find a pyramid, didn't you Dr. Carson?" Brown's sudden question surprised him.

"Well, yes, but it was just a burial chamber, almost certainly built by the locals. I suppose we can go back to Delta Pavonis and look again, do a complete surface-scan. Anything could be hidden in that jungle." It didn't feel right though. The jungle in that region of Verdigris was recent. Up until a few hundred years ago it had been desert. Stone soft enough to be worked would be unlikely to last fifteen millenia covered in jungle growth; the material that the Chara pyramid had been made of might, but even it had shown slight signs of wear and deterioration. That pyramid had also been big enough to poke up above even the Verdigran jungle.

"Or it might be elsewhere on the planet, even under a glacier," Brown said. "That planet has gone through several climate shifts in the past ten or twenty thousand years."

"Yes, that's probably what wiped out the natives," Carson agreed. "What about the second talisman? Where does that point? Jackie?"

"Sol."

He couldn't have heard her correctly. "Say again?"

"Sol. It points to Sol, Hannibal. Earth's sun."

"I know where Sol is! There's no way there's anything connected with spacefarers on Earth."

"Are you sure about that? Pyramids, rumors of ancient astronauts—"

"Nothing that's old enough to fit the chronology. I spent years looking. The oldest Egyptian pyramids are nothing like what we found on Chara, and only a third as old. Half at most."

"Something that's been overlooked? Maybe still buried, or sunken, or under the ice?" asked Brown.

"Heck, maybe something buried on the Moon," put in Roberts.

Carson glared at her. She grinned back.

"All right," growled Ducayne, "that's enough. Carson, is it at all possible there's something on Earth?"

"We can't rule out an unproven negative. But I wouldn't know where to begin looking on Earth, nor am I sure I'd want to."

"Egypt?" asked Roberts. "I hear that's hardly radioactive at all anymore."

"That doesn't worry me. I've visited the pyramids. They have been so thoroughly explored, probed, investigated, neutrino-graphed, and probably dowsed that there can't be anything significant there we haven't found yet. No. Forget Earth for now."

Ducayne and Brown looked at each other but didn't say anything. Carson wondered if there was some agenda he was missing, but he was convinced the real answers would be out in, or more likely beyond, T-space. "What else do you have?" he asked.

"Several tentative locations," Ducayne said, "but we don't have the actual talismans to confirm them yet."

"What about commonalities?" Carson said. "Are these all the same size, same age, what? Or have you looked at that yet?"

Brown sat up. "From the information we have, these are all the same size to within a couple of millimeters. The two genuine talismans we have, and your Chara talisman, match to within a tenth millimeter, and that difference may be due to wear. As far as age—"

"Oh my gosh!" Roberts had been sitting staring at the images. Her sudden interruption caught everyone's attention.

"What is it?"

"I just realized something. Or maybe nothing. Wait one." Roberts' fingers hammered on a keypad as she retrieved data. "Ducayne, how do I access *Sophie* from here, or tie into an astrophysical database?"

"Are *Sophie*'s computers on?" Ducayne asked.

"It's running diagnostics, but she'll let me in."

Ducayne rose and stepped over to her console. He pressed his thumb against a scan-pad for a moment then tapped several keys. "Okay, you have a link to *Sophie*. You know her systems, that'll be faster. Does this have something to do with the patterns?"

"Yes." Roberts logged in to *Sophie*'s computers and kept working the console.

Carson was mystified. "What's going on, Jackie?"

"I don't know why it didn't hit me before, I've been working with these for a couple of weeks. Well, that and repairs." Jackie looked up at the wall screen and flipped an image onto it, the array of all eight talismans. "We have all these stellar locations represented in 2.5-D coordinates." The realization that the color of the gemstones encoded the distance, or "half" dimension beyond X and Y, had been the breakthrough in decoding the pattern on the original talisman.

"Except for the bogus ones, yes." Carson almost felt he knew where she was going this, but couldn't quite pin it down. Something about the coordinates.

"Right." She dropped those from the display. "But the thing about a 2.5-D display, just like a simple two dimensional representation, is that it assumes a point of view."

"But with the Chara talisman, you said we didn't know the point of view; that's why we needed the third dimension."

"To match the first one, yes, or any given one without any other context. But now they give each other context."

"So you can figure out a point of view?" Carson had it now. His heart thudded in his chest. If they all had the *same* point of view . . .

"More like a direction of view. But put several of these together—*if* they're all drawn as viewed from the same place—and the directions of view will intersect. Perhaps at the—"

"At the Spacefarer's home system," Carson cut her off.

"As of fifteen thousand years ago, yes. I'm working that out now."

"Carson, you're not suggesting we just go drop in on them, are you?" Ducayne asked. "That could be asking for more trouble than I care to imagine."

"How could we not go? If they're hostile they could have done us any time since the last ice age."

"Maybe they're only hostile to other spacefarers. Or maybe approaching their system will make them hostile. It'd sure make us nervous."

"Got it!" Jackie called out. "Near the edge of explored T-space, assuming fifteen thousand years. Looking for a current match . . . and we have it. Or rather, them."

"Them?"

"I don't know how precise those diagrams are, I'm allowing for a few parsecs of fudge."

"That's a lot of fudge," Carson said. "How many stars?"

"A dozen, but mostly red dwarfs or variable stars we can eliminate."

"On the other hand they might have picked an unlikely star as the origin just because we'd probably ignore it," pointed out Ducayne.

"What are the likeliest stars?" said Carson.

Roberts checked her screen. "The nearest to the center of the probable position is an orange-red dwarf, HD-40307. It's a bit over twelve parsecs from here. It does have planets, at least three big ones in tight orbits. Not habitable, but there may be others, or habitable moons."

"Huh, that'd be unusual. What else?"

"There are a couple of sun-like stars, type G, slightly smaller than Sol, about four parsecs each from the center—"

"That *is* a big ball of fudge," Carson objected. "That takes up about a third of T-space."

"Do you want to hear this or not?"

"Go ahead. G-type stars."

"One is Alpha Mensae, ten parsecs from here. I don't seem to have much data on it. The other is Zeta Reticuli, at just under twelve parsecs away. That's actually a double star, but it's a well-separated binary, over a light-month apart. Both stars are G-type."

"Excuse me, did you say Zeta Reticuli?" Brown, who'd been sitting so still and quiet that Carson had thought he'd dozed off, sat up and leaned forward. "That reminds me of something." He sat back and closed his eyes.

"What?" Carson and Roberts said simultaneously.

"Shush, give him a moment," Ducayne said.

Brown opened his eyes again and leaned forward. "Yes, Zeta Reticuli. About a hundred and fifty, no, a hundred and sixty years ago—1961, I think—an American couple named Betty and Barney Hill claimed to have encountered a UFO, an alien spacecraft, although the details didn't come out until later, under hypnosis. Bizarre details, and everyone but the UFO cultists discounted it. They claimed to have been taken aboard a spacecraft. One that came from Zeta Reticuli."

"What?"

∞ ∞ ∞

The story continues in The Reticuli Deception, *available in hardcover, trade paperback and ebook editions.*

About the Author

ALASTAIR MAYER was born in London, England, and moved to Canada with his family as a young boy. He describes his interest in space flight and science fiction as genetic: his father, Douglas W.F. Mayer, had been an early member of the British Interplanetary Society as well as a science fiction fan (who in fact published some of Arthur C. Clarke's first tales in *Amateur Science Stories*).

After attending school in Canada, Alastair became involved in both the L5 Society (now the National Space Society) and computers, publishing articles in *Byte*, *Final Frontier*, and other magazines, as well as becoming an accomplished scuba diver and a private pilot. In 1989 he moved to Colorado, where he still lives, and where he works for a satellite network company.

His short stories have been published in several anthologies and his work has appeared often enough in *Analog Science Fiction* magazine to gain him entry to the "Analog MAFIA" (Members Appear Frequently In *Analog*). Many of his short works can be found in e-book format on Amazon, Barnes & Noble, Smashwords, and other e-book vendor sites.

The Chara Talisman was his first novel, the prelude to *The Reticuli Deception* and the rest of the Carson & Roberts books. It takes place after the events of the *Alpha Centauri* and *Kakuloa* series.

Visit his web site at www.alastairmayer.org.

Other books by Alastair Mayer

Mabash Books trade paper editions are available from Amazon or order through your favorite bookseller. Some volumes are also available in hardcover.

The T-Space™ series comprises:

The Alpha Centauri Trilogy:	ISBN
◦ *Alpha Centauri: First Landing*	978-153-913229-5
◦ *Alpha Centauri: Sawyer's World*	978-154-691328-3
◦ *Alpha Centauri: The Return*	978-197-403548-9

The Kakuloa Series:	ISBN
◦ *Kakuloa: A Rising Tide*	978-1-948188-074
◦ *Kakuloa: The Downhill Slide*	*(forthcoming)*
◦ *Kakuloa: Crash and Burn*	*(forthcoming)*
◦ *Kakuloa: The Tide Turns*	*(forthcoming)*

The Carson & Roberts Series:	ISBN
◦ *The Chara Talisman*	978-1-948188-098
◦ *The Reticuli Deception*	978-1-948188-111
◦ *The Eridani Convergence*	978-1-948188-135
◦ *The Centauri Surprise*	978-1-948188-180
◦ *The Pavonis Insurgence*	*(forthcoming)*

Ebook editions are also available.

CPSIA information can be obtained
at www.ICGtesting.com
Printed in the USA
LVHW032035081019
633405LV00003B/756/P

9 781948 188098